the shadows we
know by heart

the shadows we know by heart

Jennifer Park

SIMON PULSE

New York London Toronto Sydney New Delhi

SIMON PULSE

An imprint of Simon & Schuster Children's Publishing Division

1230 Avenue of the Americas, New York, New York 10020

First Simon Pulse hardcover edition March 2017

Text copyright © 2017 by Jennifer Park

Jacket illustration copyright © 2017 by Neil Swaab

For information about special discounts for bulk purchases, please contact Simon & Schuster Special Sales at 1-866-506-1949 or business@simonandschuster.com.

The Simon & Schuster Speakers Bureau can bring authors to your live event. For more information or to book an event contact the Simon & Schuster Speakers Bureau at 1-866-248-3049 or visit our website at www.simonspeakers.com.

Jacket designed by Russell Gordon

Interior designed by Mike Rosamilia

The text of this book was set in Bembo Std.

Manufactured in the United States of America

2 4 6 8 10 9 7 5 3 1

Library of Congress Cataloging-in-Publication Data

Names: Park, Jennifer, 1981– author.

Title: The shadows we know by heart / by Jennifer Park.

Description: Simon Pulse hardcover edition. | New York : Simon Pulse, 2017. | Summary: Leah Roberts has been secretly watching Sasquatches in the woods behind her house for years, but when she notices an enigmatic teenage boy living among them, her complicated family life starts to unravel.

Identifiers: LCCN 2016015503 | ISBN 9781481463515 (hc)

Subjects: | CYAC: Sasquatch—Fiction. | Secrets—Fiction. | Family problems—Fiction. | Love—Fiction. | Animals, Mythical—Fiction. | BISAC: JUVENILE FICTION / Fairy Tales & Folklore / General. | JUVENILE FICTION / Animals / Mythical. | JUVENILE FICTION / Family / General (see also headings under Social Issues).

Classification: LCC PZ7.1.P359 Sh 2017 | DDC [Fic]—dc23

LC record available at https://lccn.loc.gov/2016015503

ISBN 9781481463539 (eBook)

for the believers

And for Mom,
who made me believe
this story should be written

chapter one

The first traces of indigo line the sky when I hear the creatures call through my open bedroom window. Distant whoops echo through the forest, growing closer by the minute.

Eyeing the glowing "4:30" on my clock radio, I slip out of bed and slide my socked feet down the faded wooden floor of our old farmhouse, knowing from experience which creaky boards to avoid. Dad's voice enters my head, as if in anticipation of my actions.

Cardinal Rule One: Don't lie. God will know and I will, too.

Cardinal Rule Two: Don't go into the woods. Ever.

There's no excuse for what I'm about to do, and breaking several house rules will be the least of my problems if I get caught.

Down the stairs and into the kitchen, I grab a plastic grocery sack from the pantry and fill it up with apples from the bowl on the counter. As I reach for a flashlight, someone clears their throat. The burst of adrenaline that floods my body sends spots across my vision. Turning, I see my father sitting at the dining table, just on the other side of the closed glass doors that separate it from the kitchen. In the dim lamplight, I didn't notice him sitting there peering down at paperwork spread in front of him, both hands threaded through his sandy blond hair.

He hasn't seen me. Not yet.

Dad reaches for his white coffee mug. One glance up is all it will take. My hand could reach for the flashlight drawer or the doorknob, but there's no time for both.

In one smooth motion I open the door and move through. As the door clicks shut my mind is screaming at me to go, that I just dodged a holy bullet and should be running instead of standing here waiting to be caught.

But I have to be sure. There's no room for mistakes in this house.

Silence envelops me on the back porch, punctuated by the occasional call of one of Mr. Watson's cows. After a whispered count of twenty, I step into my pink rubber boots, tiptoe down the steps, and trek through the yard. A quick climb over the fence and then I'm treading through the wet pasture, the threat of a sticky, humid day only hours away. A pair of doves flies up from the high grass in front of me and I swallow a shriek. Once again I remind myself that I shouldn't be doing this.

Technically I'm not really lying. I have never uttered a word about what I've found or what I do. But Dad would call it a lie, regardless.

The old stump sits at the edge of the forest where I deposit most of the apples from my sack. Darkness fades from indigo to violet, and high above, wisps of cloud begin to burn. I enter the trees, moving like a wraith, and tuck myself into my secret spot to wait. A blue jay lands in the branches overhead, invoking the ceaseless chatter of a disturbed squirrel. Wings flutter and claws scratch bark as each defends their space, and the

jennifer park

cooing of doves is hushed by the cry of a hawk heralding in the morning.

This is the moment when I can forget about my life. The second I enter the trees, everything that is Leah Roberts stays behind. It used to puzzle me why my parents would move us from our familiar neighborhood home to an old farmhouse on the edge of the forest, and then establish the rule that we do not, for any reason, go into those woods. The first time I did, it was both terrifying and exhilarating. Bad things happened in the woods. That's what I grew up believing. But standing in the silence of a winter forest, watching darts of red fly among pine branches, I knew where I belonged. The forest called to me, offering solace and peace from a family torn apart by the death of a child.

It didn't take long until I figured out the storage shed in the backyard could cover my escape all the way to the trees. And there I would run along the game trails, free to be whoever I wanted, or nothing at all. I'd run until the joy faded, until the walls fell and I saw Sam's face, until fear and pain threatened to strangle me like the vines hanging around me, until the tears finally came and brought me back to earth.

It was cathartic then, and still is today. The forest is the only place where I can see my brother, where I *let* myself see him, where I can take down the barricades I place around my heart for the rest of the world, and just *feel*.

The girl who steps into the woods is not the same one who steps out. There are two of me, and they fight to stay hidden from each other, because one cannot live in the world of the other. Instead of sharing their grief with my brother and me, our parents closed themselves off. So I did the same. I don't know that they would recognize the part of me that exists in the woods, the one that cries at memories and lost futures, and climbs trees until I can see the entire world beyond my own. I laugh at scurrying squirrels and scream at spiders and snakes so loudly that it's a wonder the trees don't fall down around me.

But I'm real. I'm *me*. There are no lies there beneath the trees, only the person I want to be. And I don't know if anyone will ever see that girl for who she is, or if she'll simply live and die alone within the protection of the forest shadows.

I wait in breathless silence as the forest comes alive. My fingers twist into the soft ground beneath me, and I imagine I can feel the rotation of the earth as the sun slowly comes into view. Everything is in motion but me. In the faint light of an East Texas dawn, I try to become nothing but a shadow.

A soft breeze blows through the pines, rustling the plastic bag beside me. I tuck the loose ends beneath my legs, knowing they are near. A branch snaps in the distance and my body goes stiller than death. Except that a dead person's heart doesn't tend to beat out of their chest in terrified anticipation. My eyes strain through the mist that's creeping in from the field, carrying the warm scent of fresh-cut hay. The urge to flee invades my mind, and I press my back against the tree in mute defiance.

I can do this. I won't run. They will use the same trail they always have. There is no reason for them to see me.

That's what I tell myself to stall the fear, likely just another lie to add to my collection.

jennifer park

The truth is that they are fast, strong, and fully capable of sensing my presence if I screw up. Though what they would do if they found me is still uncertain. I'd like to think the part of them that resembles a human would show mercy.

Heavy steps echo through the trees, the surefooted sound of creatures that have nothing to fear in this world. Off to my left, I can see the old stump where the apples wait. It took me months find this spot, one that has the perfect view of both forest and field while still keeping me hidden.

Their smell comes first, ranking somewhere between skunk and wet dog, though it's not as harsh on my senses as it used to be. Just as three massive shadows emerge from the foliage, a rusty truck door slams in the distance and a reluctant motor sputters to life. I bite back a frustrated hiss as the shadows pause. *Dammit, Mr. Watson, do you really have to leave at the crack of dawn?*

It's not as if the feed store isn't open all day. But he's got to stop at Carla's Café first, where every retired male over the age of sixty-five meets on Friday mornings for coffee and heart-attack-inducing breakfast platters. That's all there is to do in this tiny speck of a town besides Friday-night football and Saturday-morning livestock auctions.

I don't breathe again until the aged truck fades into the distance and the shadows merge with the light.

The result is a family of Bigfoot.

The immense male is the first to enter the field. He sniffs the air, his head turning slowly as he determines the safety of his surroundings. He's got to be every bit of eight, maybe nine, feet tall, covered in thick, dark brown hair all over his body, and with long arms swinging down to his knees as he walks. He grunts softly and the others follow, an eight-foot female and a six-and-a-half-foot baby. Yes, baby. When I first saw them years ago, she was half my size, bouncing around like a chimpanzee on chocolate.

Now she's just as still and silent as the others, as careful as deer nearing a feeder.

I'm captivated as they gather around the apples, eating just as many as they gather into their arms to take. As long as I live, this will be the most amazing thing I've ever seen, though it's still tainted with memories of why I'm here to begin with.

They never let their guard down. One of them is always watching their surroundings. Last year Old Man Watson fired up his John Deere too early and they took off like a shot. They didn't come back for a month.

I've thought about bringing a camera, but the light's rarely good this early and I'm way too far. They could probably hear the camera click. Every little sound catches their attention. Besides, the proof is before me. I don't need anything else, especially something that could be found. This is mine alone, my secret that I don't have to share with anyone. It's not like they would believe me anyway.

The apples are disappearing quickly. The wind picks up and I crouch down lower, afraid they can smell me. The big one lets out a short, grunting bark, loud enough that my heart trips. It's almost like he's calling someone. It's not until I see another shadow appear through the trees that I realize he is.

jennifer park

Adrenaline floods my body as I lean forward, cringing when the apple sack crinkles. I've never seen four of them.

The sun is shining through the tree line now, laying bright patches of light across the trail. I watch in awe as the new one slowly, carefully emerges from the trees. He's small compared to the others, a little taller than me. They encourage him with gestures and soft noises, but he refuses to leave the protective shade of the forest.

There is something different about him.

The male grunts again, impatiently, while the other two retreat back into the trees. The new one slowly slides a foot out, painstakingly making his way toward the stump. He waits for a minute, his head turning every direction like it's on a swivel, before he hurries out of the shadows.

It takes everything I've got not to gasp out loud.

He's not like the others. I can see his skin, pulled tight over muscle and bone, but I can see it. Not hair or fur. *Skin.*

The hair on his head falls well past his shoulders, and a dusting of light brown covers his arms and legs. The hands that reach out desperately for the apples are just like mine.

After a few minutes more, the big male walks back into the forest after the others, leaving the new one on his own. In moments the Bigfoot have disappeared.

Without a second thought for my safety, I start walking. I watch as he shoves the apples into his mouth with a desperation I've never known. His ribs are showing; his stomach is flat but not emaciated. Before I realize it, I am standing out in the open for anyone, or *anything*, to see, and I don't care.

When I'm close enough to throw something at him, he looks up.

I know without a doubt I will remember this moment forever. The smell of hay and apples, the feel of wet grass on my skin, the warmth of a new sun, and the way the light falls across his face and makes his green eyes glow. *Beautiful* is the first thought that enters my mind.

We stare at each other, me in my pink unicorn pajamas and he in his almost nothingness. The boy's got some sort of animal hide wrapped around his waist, but that's it. He looks like he could be my brother's age, eighteen, give or take, not really a boy but closer to a man.

He's breathing fast just like me, and I'm close enough to see the surprise in his eyes. A thousand different emotions pass through them, leaving his gaze haunted. He watches me warily, his fists clenched, but doesn't run.

I should, but I'm too entranced.

And when the bellowing roar from the forest breaks the silence, I do. I've never known terror until that moment, and it reaches down into my core, like arctic water shooting through my veins. The boy doesn't speak, but his eyes are screaming at me to run.

I tear through the field, toss myself over the fence, and stumble through the grass to the back door. I almost forget to see if the kitchen is empty but manage to stop long enough to press my face to the window, leaving smudges and fog on the clear glass. Dad is gone, and my feet don't stop until I hit my bedroom. As I lie under the covers, waiting to have

jennifer park

a heart attack, breathing so loud I'm sure everyone in the house will hear me, I tell myself that I will never go back. I will never cross the field again. Never leave my gift of apples on the stump. Never, never, never.

But it's just another lie I will add to my collection, another secret I will keep.

Because I will never forget the haunted eyes of the human boy in the midst of the Sasquatch.

chapter two

The sounds of breakfast drift upstairs after a while. My stomach growls, but I ignore it. I'm too busy trying to find a way to process what I've experienced. A sane, normal person might go down and alert their parents as to what they've seen, but I'm pretty sure they would stop listening at *Bigfoot*, if they even listened at all.

I've watched something that technically doesn't exist come and go in the forest behind our home for years like it's nothing. And yet one human boy has me freaking out like I've seen a monster. It's bad enough I know about them and haven't said anything to anyone, but now there's this. A boy. A human boy who obviously lives with them and how in the world did that happen and I don't know but *what am I supposed to do?*

Deep breath. Just keep breathing. Just. Keep. Breathing.

That's great. I'm on the verge of a meltdown and the words play in my head to the tune of Dory's swimming song.

This day is not going as planned, because in approximately thirty minutes, I have to appear downstairs, dressed for a youth retreat to the Angelina River. I say "dressed" because I will be the only girl there wearing a tank top and shorts over her bathing suit, which is also a one-piece. It's dark blue and very unsexy. About as boring as a bathing suit can get. Not that anyone's going to see it because I'll be wearing *clothes*.

Some days I'm surprised Dad even lets me leave the house.

A heavy fist bangs on my door. Matt's voice drifts in as he passes by. "We're leaving in twenty minutes."

"Thirty minutes." I throw a pillow at the door, regardless of the fact that he can't see it. "And I'm not going."

Those words are way more effective than a pillow. The footsteps that were heading down the hall stop and backtrack, and my door opens. "Sorry, what?" Shaggy blond hair enters the room followed by my brother's face. "You know this isn't optional, right?" He grins, chewing a mouthful of bacon, the hand on my door holding at least half a dozen more pieces.

"I don't care. I'm not in the mood."

Matt snorts, truly amused now. "Oh. Okay, so you want me to just go downstairs and tell Pastor Roberts that his daughter is not participating today in the event that she helped plan?"

I throw another pillow.

Matt knocks it harmlessly out of the way.

"I didn't plan it. All I did was suggest we have it at the river."

"Same thing to him. From the look on his face, he thought you'd grown a freaking halo." Matt shrugs with a wide grin. "Come on, it's Friday, a school holiday, plus we've won enough games to earn a bye week, so it's a win-win for everyone." His eyes drop to the floor, locking on my wet, grassy rubber boots, which should never be inside the house. "You've already been up." There's no question in his voice.

"Nope."

the shadows we know by heart

"Seriously? Your filthy boots are sitting right there. What were you doing?"

I cross my arms and sink into the pillows around me, feeling mutinous. "I went for a walk."

Matt's eyes narrow on the boots again. Before I can move, he's in my room and tossing back my covers. His eyes widen when he sees the grass and mud stains covering my pajamas. "What the hell happened?"

"I tripped."

He shakes his head. "Nope. Give me something else."

"I tripped over a stick."

"Uh-uh."

"Please go away."

"Like that will ever happen."

"Leah," Mom calls from downstairs. "Breakfast." I catch Matt's eye. He nods, confirming my fears. She has that tone, the one that precedes a Bad Day. It means she's been thinking about things I don't think about outside the forest and sneaking sips from her silver flask, which always leads to a fight if Dad can't get out of the house soon enough.

It's silent downstairs, so maybe he's already left.

"Leah?" I cringe. Nope. Dad's still here. Every time my name comes out of his mouth, I am reminded of its origins. I am back in church, years ago, on the day I first heard the story of Jacob and Leah, of how she was unwanted, the second choice.

I never know whether to sympathize with her or hate her, because Dad says my name the same way he said hers.

I drag myself out of bed with a groan. Suddenly a blur passes

jennifer park

behind me as Matt lands on my bed, pieces of bacon falling into the sheets.

"Matt!"

He glances down with a shrug at the mud and grass left in my indention. "What? You're going to wash them anyway. You weren't in the woods, were you?"

"No." I look away.

"You're crazy, you know that, right? What are you going to say when he catches you out there? I mean, eventually he's going to have a sane moment and realize he has two kids and that one of them consistently breaks his Cardinal Rules beneath his nose."

"So do you."

"Yeah, but I don't do it here, and I make sure he'll never catch me." Matt glances out the window at the distant trees. "I don't know why you go out there anyway." His tone suggests he's thinking of the reason we're forbidden from the forest, why Mom is probably already semisober this early, and why Dad is so concerned with fixing everything else but what's really broken.

I do it because I'm making up for something that can never be atoned, no matter how much I acknowledge the truth of what is in the woods.

Matt stuffs most of the bacon in his mouth, his cheeks stretching like a chipmunk's.

"Why is Mom mad now?" I say, changing the subject.

I stare, waiting for him to finish chewing so he can speak. He takes too long, and I can feel the corners of my eyes tightening up into a glare.

Matt gives me a knowing smile. I growl as I throw open my closet door. The last thing I feel like doing is hauling myself off to a youth group retreat. What I want is to pull my filthy boots on and walk out the back door to discover if I'm losing my mind or I really saw what I think I saw. Forget the "never again." Now that the fear has faded, rationale has returned. Or maybe just an influx of crazy. Either way.

"What time do you think we'll be home today?" My mind is already working out the logistics of my poorly thought-out plan.

"I don't know, maybe midafternoon."

"Did you have plans tonight?"

Matt shrugs, tracing a pattern on my comforter. "Not really. I was thinking about going out."

"With who?" Matt doesn't have a girlfriend. He's too busy dating.

"Maybe Kelsey."

"Wright? She's pretty nice." At least compared to Kelsee Connor, the girl who used to chunk dodge balls at me in fifth grade.

"Yeah," he says noncommittally. "But it's no big deal."

"Don't you like her? You two have been off and on for a while," I say carefully as I peer out my window.

"Sure, she's great. Long legs, nice tan . . ." He flashes me a smile. Then he goes back to plucking listlessly at my comforter. He pulls one of my sandy blond hairs off and makes a show of dropping it to the floor.

"Who would you rather go out with?" I look away and out

the window just as something flickers at the edge of the forest, near the tree stump.

"No one. Not right now, anyway."

My gaze is so focused it takes me a minute to realize he answered. "But you don't *like her* like her."

"It doesn't matter. It gets me out of the house. You should try it sometime." He leans over and thumps me on the arm.

"I don't think so. That would require me to actually *like* someone." I strain my neck to peer around Matt's head. I swear I see *something*. "And it doesn't matter anyway since I can't date." One shadow suddenly detaches itself and drifts slowly along the edge of the trees. My heart jumps into my throat.

"I know, but still." Matt tosses a stuffed bear into the air and catches it.

A fox darts out of the trees and into the hay field, disappearing from view. So not the wild boy, then. The crushing surge of disappointment actually surprises me. I turn around to find Matt staring at me. "What are you looking at?"

"I just thought I saw something in the woods."

"Like?"

I shake my head. "Nothing."

"Keeping secrets?"

"I wouldn't dare," I say lightly as Mom yells for us again.

"Are you going to get ready or not?"

"Are you going to tell?" I answer, glancing down at my boots.

"I'll think about it." He shoves the final piece of bacon in his mouth and rolls off my bed. As Matt turns to leave, I lift a stuffed unicorn off the rainbow pile of animals at my feet. He senses me and bolts for the open doorway just as the unicorn leaves my hand, his laughter echoing down the hallway. The stuffed animal slams into the door and falls uselessly to the ground. That's exactly how I feel right now. Useless. I'm trapped by circumstances, so any plans I want to make will have to wait.

I change clothes and head downstairs. Dad is sipping coffee with his Bible lying on the table, wearing the usual dress shirt and tie that I don't think will look appropriate on the river today. Mom's stirring her scrambled eggs around on her plate, staring at the table in tense silence, her blond hair pulled up and makeup put on a little heavier today to hide the shadows under her eyes. Neither of them looks like they've slept in a week.

Slowly I pull my chair out and sit, trying not to draw attention. Mom's smile is less than sparkling this morning, and she eyes me like she knows I'm hiding something. Dad flips a page before looking at me from over the rim of his glasses. "Matthew says you're not feeling well?" It's never Matt, always Matthew, said with the same formality of mine.

I glance at Matt, sitting across from me, realizing I actually need an excuse for sleeping so late. "I'm just tired, couldn't sleep well last night." I shrug, thinking I should have come downstairs earlier to avoid all of this now. I'm good at lying about the things I want to cover up, like lip gloss at school and contraband copies of *Cosmo* that Ashley sneaks me, but I'm not sure I can lie about this. It's too important. It feels . . . urgent.

"Well, I've got to go to the hospital this morning, so I won't be at the retreat today," Dad says with a sigh, already moving on. "Mrs. Ellis had a fall last night. They think it's a broken hip."

"That's terrible," Mom says absently as she stabs a bit of egg.

Dad stares at her, the frown line between his brows getting deeper. "I'm sure she would appreciate seeing you, Nora."

"And I'm sure she's so full of painkillers that she won't notice if I'm not there."

Dad clears his throat, like he's about to start preaching. Knowing what kind of a day it is, and what's likely to happen, I wish he'd just leave her alone.

"Nora—"

Mom doesn't even give him a chance. Her hand slaps the table, and glasses rattle as she meets Dad's gaze. "Don't preach to me, Michael. Not today." Her eyes burn with fire, but she still can't stop the quiver of her bottom lip. Dad sighs, shaking his head as he looks down at his Bible again. Mom tears herself from the table, snatching up dishes of half-eaten food from everyone. Matt grabs the last of the bacon from his plate as it's being carried away.

It's definitely a Bad Day.

Dread coils in my stomach like a living thing. I hate this feeling. The fighting never gets easier. I used to think it would, or that they would eventually stop, but I'm still waiting.

I can still remember my first youth retreat down at the river. I was five, and Mom had packed our picnic basket with enough food to feed an army. Dad sang silly songs with us in the car, even when he was tired and we kept insisting. When the youth minister began playing a guitar, Dad twirled Mom around in the sand, and then they danced with each of us until we all fell down in the water laughing, a completely happy family.

But that was another lifetime ago.

Dishes rattle and threaten to shatter as Mom flips down the dishwasher door and turns on the sink water as fast as it will go. It's only going to get worse from here. The anniversary of the end of our perfect lives is weeks away, and like it or not, preparations have to be made.

Dad's tired voice breaks the tense silence. "Matthew, don't make plans for tomorrow. We need to get the deer blind ready." Matt gives me a resigned glance. Our father, the mighty hunter on Saturday and convicting preacher on Sunday. One of these days he's going to realize that Matt hates hunting and killing things—basically anything to do with the woods. Or maybe Dad knows, maybe he sees the truth and this is his way of trying to smother it. Dad refuses to let either of us be less than what he expects.

Dad gets to his feet, grabs his Bible, and sips from his white coffee cup one more time. "I know I don't have to remind both of you to conduct yourselves properly today at the youth retreat. I know this is a . . . casual event, but it is still a church activity. Remember you are Robertses."

"Hard to forget," I mutter into my juice glass.

"We know, Dad," Matt says loudly, kicking me under the table. "Tell Mrs. Ellis she's in our prayers." Dad nods absently, his focus already miles away. Matt shakes his head at me and I roll my eyes.

More dishes crash into the sink and Dad's fist tightens on his cup. Just when I think he's going to slam it down, he stops, the cup's bottom hovering just above the linen tablecloth. His lips are pale and pressed flat. A muscle in his jaw ticks.

With a shaking hand, he sets the cup down and walks away.

Our family is anything but the perfect one everyone believes us to be, even with our tragic history. To the community, it makes us even more picture-perfect. To have survived something like we did and still appear normal and sane.

But I know the truth. Mom walks around with a Kleenex to hide the fact that her red eyes aren't from tears. Dad hides his bitterness so well it's become second nature. I'm still amazed at the way it melts away the second we leave this house, how he replaces it with a reverent smile as he takes the steps to the pulpit on Sunday morning, raising his hands in welcome as if all is well in the world.

We're all liars. We have to be. It's not like we can try to forget and move on with our lives in a town like this. You can see it sometimes, in a too-long glance or subtle whisper. Small towns make time slow, as if the tragic, horrible events happened only yesterday. I think it's the collective memory of an insular, backwoods community. It's all they can think or gossip about until the next big incident comes along. All I've ever thought about is getting out of here after graduation and never coming back.

But that's a lie as well. I know I can't stay here forever, living in and out of the forest, though the thought of leaving for good frightens me more than staying in this broken home. I feel that if I take that step, it will break some unspoken trust I share with the forest and with these creatures. My refuge will disappear, and them along with it.

I don't know if I can let go of that, if my freedom is worth the cost of losing myself. I think I would rather maintain the precarious balance between my two worlds than fall one way or the other and risk ruining everything.

And now a giant complication in the form of a wild boy has appeared, threatening that balance I've worked so hard to protect.

A car starts outside, and the sound of crunching gravel echoes over the soft rumble of the dishwasher. As soon as Dad's gone, I hear the utensil drawer open, the one where Mom keeps her secret, and then her ragged sigh of relief as she presses the silver flask to her lips.

chapter three

The murky river swirls far below as I slide my carnation-pink toes to the edge of the diving platform, polish remover waiting in the car to hide the fact that I painted them on the way over here. It's taken me hours to get the nerve to come up here and jump, but unlike the other girls before me who have questioned the depth of the water or the likelihood of alligators or gar, my thoughts go a little deeper today.

A log floats by, and it brings a vision of the past so strong that I forget, for just a moment, that it's not real. Matt, Sam, and Reed sprint to the water, already boasting about who will be the first to reach the tree trunk coming around the bend. Ashley and I stay on the sandbar with our parents, knowing we can't outswim the boys with their head start. Matt's and Sam's matching blond curls make them almost impossible to tell apart in the spray, and then Reed's dark head splits them, pulling ahead as the log begins to spin in the current as it draws closer.

I don't know what they're going to do when they catch it. It's twice as long as they are. Sam and Reed are neck and neck, but at the last second Matt kicks, and all three boys slap their hands on the wood simultaneously, whooping with success.

My parents laugh. I slow the memory, just to watch their faces, to remember what that looked like. When the boys swim back to shore, Matt and Sam tackle Dad in the sand, but the combined strength of their eight-year-old bodies is no match for him, and within moments Dad grabs each of them under an arm and leaps into the water, splashing half the river out onto its banks.

Reed hands me an empty clamshell as he sits beside me, the pink and aqua swirls catching the sunlight. "You should make a necklace with it."

"I don't know how." I place it on top of the sandcastle at my feet, admiring it.

"Here." He holds out his hand. "I'll make one for you."

"Can I help?"

"Can't make it without you." He reaches down with a smile and pulls me to my feet.

I blink, and they're gone, the memory fading into the currents below, until it's just another murky swirl.

"Come on, Leah, just do it," Ashley, my best friend from birth, yells from the shore, her impatient tone making my stomach churn. Of course she can be cocky about it. She's jumped three times already. As if she's trying to tempt death. Or maybe just shove her middle finger in its face because that's the kind of girl she is. Her bright green belly-button ring, which was quite the scandal when she got it done in the sixth grade, blinks in the sunlight.

In the tiny East Texas town of Zavalla, anything new is a big deal, and anything tragic, even bigger.

jennifer park

Sometimes I think this town doesn't see me but the tragedy I represent. If I faded into the trees behind me, would anyone notice? How long before the straitlaced preacher's daughter's absence would cause concern? If Matt and Ashley weren't here, I might try it, if only to push the boundaries of my imaginary cage once more.

But now I wouldn't be alone. Another soul has claimed my woods, made it his home, and now shares my sanctuary. And he is more a mystery than the darkest shadows of the deepest part of the forest. He's the towering tree I'm too intimidated to climb, the cave I'm too afraid to enter, or the strange noise I'm too wary to explore.

And the lure is overwhelming. I can't walk away from it this time, no matter my fear. The boy's face haunts me. Without warning it appears in my mind, those wide eyes full of surprise. The more I picture him, the more I want to see him again. I *need* to see him again. Every time I close my eyes he's standing in front of me, like I've found a puzzle piece but don't yet have the puzzle he fits in.

Had he not been shaped so differently from the others, I wouldn't have marked him as anything else. His movements and actions reflected their own. He *was* one of them. Up until the moment I realized he wasn't.

And it's slowly driving me to do something reckless.

The platform vibrates as someone starts moving up the ladder below. "Let's go, preacher's daughter." Ben Hanson climbs the last step and joins me.

"You have got to find a new label, Ben. You've been calling

the shadows we know by heart

me that for years." I don't turn around. There's no way I'll be able to *not* stare at his perfect body in those black board shorts. I've seen it too many times at my house, sitting next to Matt on the couch watching football. It's a shame his personality doesn't always match, but it hasn't stopped my epic crush on him.

"Don't want you to forget it, little Leah. You need someone to show you how this is done?" He elbows me jokingly, moving to stand beside me at the edge. His skin brushes mine, and he doesn't move away.

"I'm not little." Heat creeps up my skin when I feel his eyes on me. "And I know how to jump," I grumble, always feeling out of my league when I'm near him.

"It's not the jump that counts, Leah." Ben places a hand on my bare stomach. My brain shorts out as he pushes me away from the edge before swinging his arms back and forth. "It's the fall."

In one swift motion Ben propels himself off the platform, dark hair and wet skin flashing in the sunlight. After he rolls into a tight ball, his body straightens out like a board the second before he hits the water. He slides under the surface like a pro. Flawless, just like the rest of him.

I should have shoved him off the platform. Of course, if he hurt his arm or something and couldn't catch my brother's passes on Friday nights, the entire town would blame me. Coach Banks is standing by the grill, shaking his head grimly as he waits for Ben to break the surface. Even if he drowned because of his own foolishness, it would probably still be my fault.

On the other hand, I'm a Roberts, and that tends to come

jennifer park

with a Get Out of Jail Free card in this part of the world. People would probably just give me a sympathetic stare like they usually do and leave it alone.

Ben is already laughing when he finally comes up for air, breaking into a muscle-flaunting breaststroke as he swims for the bank and a shore lined with semi-bare bodies. I'm probably not the only one who releases a heavy breath. Ashley shrugs with a smirk, giving me a look that says *you can't deny that was awesome*.

I shuffle back to the edge, a little less excited about the jump than I was, now that I know how clumsy I'm going to appear after that perfect dive. Country music from another decade drifts through the air from one of the trucks, mild enough to be acceptable for a church function. Besides, we're all wearing shorts and bikinis, so it's not like the music we're listening to is going to change what some of us are thinking about.

A shrill whistle echoes down below. Coach Banks is waving a silver spatula in the air as smoke from the grill streams across the shoreline. The aroma of roasted hot dogs permeates the air along with the lingering scent of muddy river water. The younger kids in our youth group run to line up, grabbing Styrofoam plates with wet, sandy hands and shoving each other to be first. I can remember when stuff like that mattered, when life was something called "fun."

Strands of hair cling to damp skin as I drag my sticky ponytail off my neck. The air is heavy with humidity that never really goes away, even in early October. We don't have that buffer zone known as "fall." We have an oppressively hot summer that one day slips into winter. And then the temperature just fluctuates until January, when we get a hard freeze that kills everything that's been trying to bloom, and then it gets warm again and starts over.

Ashley peels herself off her bright pink towel, dusting the dried sand off her legs. "Now or never," she calls up, shading her eyes. The muddy water swirls lazily as stories of what lies beneath zip through my mind. I don't know for sure what monsters live below, but I've seen what lives above.

A deep breath, one step, and suddenly nothing is below me but air. I break the glassy surface, arms crossed and nose pinched. Darkness closes in like a heavy blanket as I push for the light above. Bubbles swirl around me, and I'm caught in a tornado of diamonds. My foot brushes against something that I'd rather not think about, and I kick violently just to make sure my legs stay attached to my body.

I'm shamefully relieved when my feet touch bottom. They slide deep within the slick mud that coats the river floor, and it's an effort to pull them out. I try not to look like I'm in a hurry, but fear of the unknown has me moving fast.

Ashley stands there smiling at me, green eyes glowing. "See? Not so bad."

"Thanks, Ash." I catch the towel she tosses me.

"Stop worrying. You look killer in that bikini, and your dad won't find out since he's not here." She rolls her eyes as she slides her feet into flip-flops. "I don't know why he worries in the first place. It's a freaking youth retreat. It's not like people are going to go hook up behind the trees or anything."

"I know, but I'd rather avoid another talk about modesty and propriety. Did you know that *I* got a lecture when *you* got that piercing?" I point to her stomach, where the jewel flashes. "Not my decision, not my body, but I get the speech. How is that fair?"

"Ben's hot," Ashley says, tossing her half-dry brown hair over her shoulder and completely ignoring my rant. "Did you totally die when he touched your stomach like that?"

I glance around quickly to see if anyone heard her. "Be a little louder next time."

"Oh, come on. It's not like he doesn't know he's drop-dead gorgeous. I'm just stating the obvious." We walk toward the line, passing up slower groups of girls. "You probably see him half-naked all the time."

That comment draws some attention. Conversations taper off around us. "Ashley," I warn. Yes, I have seen Ben shirtless at my house on occasion, usually when he and Matt have been throwing passes in the backyard and he strips off his shirt when he gets too hot. But that's beside the point.

"Please, Leah, you've got the reputation of a saint. You could be caught completely naked—"

I slap my hand over Ashley's mouth, the rest of her words smothered behind my palm. "I swear, if you finish that sentence."

Her emerald eyes sparkle as she peels my hand away. "You're so easy. I love you." She swings her arm over my shoulders. "Did you know your face matches that towel? It's like the perfect shade of pink. Pure and innocent."

"Shhh!" I elbow her in the ribs, but she keeps her arm around me. "I really don't like you sometimes."

"I know, but we're stuck with each other, tossed upon our

the shadows we know by heart   *27* lofty pedestals of tragedy this tiny hick town will never let us down from." When my body stiffens, Ashley sighs. "Sorry, forget I said that."

Forcing my shoulders to relax, I reply lightly, "Already forgotten."

Ashley stares at my fake smile long enough for me to know that I haven't fooled her, but she lets it go. "I think I'm going to have two hot dogs since I don't plan on throwing them up afterward," she says loudly as we walk by a glowering Carlie and Brittany, both of whom have been rumored to visit the girls' bathroom every day at the end of lunch. I don't know if it's actually true, but they made the mistake of telling Ash she gets away with everything because half her family's dead. Needless to say, she's made sure their reputation has suffered ever since freshman year.

"And then we're going to follow Ben Hanson up that ladder and shove his perfect, sinful body into the river." We laugh, falling back into familiar patterns, and for a moment I forget the shadows of our past.

"Causing trouble again?" Matt comes up behind us and slings his arms around both of us. Ashley's smirk leaves her face immediately. Matt doesn't notice. I swear he never does, for someone so observant.

"Just taking advantage of our status. It helps to be the best friend of the preacher's daughter."

Matt snorts. "It also helps to be *you*, Ashley. You don't care what anyone thinks."

"Why should I? It's a waste of time," she says lightly, but her body is wound tight with Matt's arm around her.

jennifer park

"That was a nice jump, Leah. Maybe next time you could try to *not* splash half the river onto the bank."

"Very funny, Matt. I haven't seen you jump yet."

"That's because if I did, everyone would realize they'll never look as good as me and give up."

"Except for Ben." Ashley smirks.

Matt frowns. "What? No way. I'm the king of the river. Officially."

"Well," Ashley says. "*Officially*, I'm going to have to see it to believe it."

Matt stops, his hands tightening on our arms. "Is that a challenge?"

"It's whatever you want it to be. There's no way you can beat Ben." She lifts his hand off her arm and drops it. "Come on, Leah, I'm hungry."

Ashley walks away to stand in line. Matt shakes his head. "I'm going to have to make Ben look bad, aren't I?"

"I guess so," I say flatly. Boys are so dumb sometimes. I slap Matt on the shoulder and follow Ashley.

"Is he going to jump?" she asks, staring straight ahead when I join her.

"Yep. Mission accomplished."

The corner of her mouth lifts into a wicked grin. "Perfect."

By the time Matt and I drag ourselves home, it's too late to make it back to the woods. All I can manage is to sit and stare out the window all through supper, waiting for the barest glimpse of movement.

Dad relates his day with the sick and elderly, skipping over the parts where Mom was missed or asked after, and Mom nods and does her best at conversation. Before everything changed, we would make up games at dinner, play tic-tac-toe on our paper napkins, or Mom would call out our spelling words and see who could spell the fastest. The winner got to clean dishes with Dad, because it always led to soap bubble Santa beards.

Now, when supper is over everyone goes their separate ways: Dad to his office, Mom to her room, and Matt to the couch. But I linger. For a tempting moment I'm alone. The back door is within a few feet and no one is here to watch me leave.

"Leah, we need to talk." Dad appears in the doorway, staring at his phone.

"Okay," I say warily, sliding back into my chair.

"How was the retreat today?" His gaze never leaves his phone.

I stare at him in silent confusion. He already asked us this question over dinner. Why is he asking me now? "It was fine. Fun. Everyone had a good time."

Finally he breaks his gaze from his cell to look at me. "It certainly looks like you had a good time." Dad places his phone on the table and slides it across to me. As soon as my hand grabs it I freeze. There on the bright screen is a distant shot of me, standing on top of the diving platform, wearing Ashley's borrowed bikini, with Ben Hanson standing next to me. I can't see his eyes clearly, but from the tilt of his head, it's obvious where his attention is.

If I could melt into the floor, I would. I know what's coming.

"You know the rules, Leah."

jennifer park

"Yes."

"Then why did you feel the need to break them? And in such a shameful way?"

I glance down at the phone again, weighing my options. It could have been worse. The picture could have shown the exact moment Ben's hand was on my bare stomach. My initial reaction is to tell him that it doesn't matter because I looked the same as every other girl, and maybe he should be lecturing them instead of me. But the last thing I need is to have Dad paying extra attention to me for breaking a minor rule when my goal is to continue breaking his most valued ones, because they are the ones that make me feel alive. Seeing the forest at dawn, waiting for the Bigfoot—and now the wild, nameless boy who dominates my thoughts—I do it all to prove, if only to myself, that there's more to me than this seemingly passive girl.

"I'm sorry, Dad. A bunch of other girls were there, and they dared me to wear it, and it just happened." I shift in my seat, trying my best to look uncomfortable. "Peer pressure is hard to get away from sometimes." I glance down, sniffing. Would it be too much to wipe at my eyes? I can't tell if he bought that ridiculous, cheesy line because I'm afraid to look up and have him see the truth. I twist my fingers together, hoping I look repentant enough to forgo one of his infamous lectures.

Dad sighs, reaching for his phone. He hits a few buttons, and I wonder if he's deleting the picture or saving it. I prepare myself as he takes a deep breath. "Leah." There it is again. That tone. "You're going to—" His phone dings with a text message. Dad's face slides into a frown as he stares down at the screen.

His lips move silently as he turns and walks away.

"Dad?"

He stops. The look he gives me says he completely forgot I am still here, waiting for my sentence. Dad shakes his head, distracted. "You should spend the evening contemplating your actions and asking forgiveness." Without another glance, he leaves. A few seconds later the door to his office closes.

That's it? No lecture? No long-winded discussion of why I continue to disappoint him with my poor choices or why I have to try harder to be a good example because of my place in the community?

I tramp upstairs, having no intention of thinking on my actions or asking forgiveness.

I've done nothing wrong.

Not yet.

jennifer park

chapter four

I sleep too late.

The engine of the Ranger cranks loudly outside my open window, sending me flying out of the bed. I shove the wooden pane the rest of the way up and stick my head out. "Matt!" I wave wildly, trying to get his attention. But the bright red Ranger, with Matt and Dad in it, turns quickly out of the yard, running parallel along the fence line until it enters the forest.

So much for my plan. Going with Matt and Dad to help with the deer blind would have gotten me into the woods. Dad agreeing to let me go would have been another story. Cardinal Rule Three: Matt and Dad are the only ones who go into the woods, because we live in East Texas and we have to kill at least one unsuspecting, innocent deer every November just because.

Whatever. On to plan B.

The rattle of dishes downstairs means Mom is still here. I dig my nails into the soft, faded wood of the windowpane and stare at the trees, deciding how to maneuver this. White flakes of paint fall to the shingles below. I know what she's going to want, but at this point, what's one more lie?

After a few moments a soft knock raps on my door and Mom peers in. "How do you feel?"

"Fine," I say after a moment's hesitation, remembering the lie Matt concocted for me yesterday. My opportunity has presented itself.

Mom eyes me up and down, like she's trying to convince herself I'm telling the truth. "Your father and Matt have already left. I thought you might like to go into town with me. I've got some errands to run."

The question in her voice is there, and oh, it's tempting. Even as badly as I want to go into the woods, I still want to go with Mom. She'll take me places, buy me little things, and for just a while, all will be normal. This is how she makes it up to me, for the fights, for her bad moods, and I guess it's not much.

But it's something.

I grab my arms and shiver. "Is it cold to you?" She moves into my room and places a warm hand on my forehead.

A line forms between her brows. "You don't feel too warm." She holds her hand there for a moment longer, and I try not to press into it. "I'll get you some aspirin."

I glance out the window again, restless, as Mom walks down the hall. Through the badly insulated wall comes the sound of her moving around the bathroom and sifting through the crowded medicine cabinet. I close the window and hop onto my bed moments before Mom walks in, aspirin in one hand and a glass of water in the other. "Here." She hands them to me. "If you don't feel like going, it's fine."

I swallow quickly, cringing at the sour, bitter taste of the pills. "Are you sure you don't care?"

She sits on the bed beside me, touching my face again. This

jennifer park

time I lean into it, knowing it won't last. "Not at all. You try to rest, okay?"

I nod, knowing it's another lie.

"You'll be fine by yourself?"

"Of course, Mom."

"Just checking," Mom says, her walk reluctant as she heads toward the door. "I'll be back in a little bit." She waves good-bye and leaves the door cracked.

I squeeze a stuffed animal to my chest, listening to every sound in the house until I hear the one I've been waiting for. The front door shuts and I'm on my feet, tearing through my closet. Clothes aren't complicated for me. Jeans, boots, T-shirt, and ponytail. I don't even glance in the mirror.

The crackle of rocks echoes through the window as Mom pulls down the drive. I pause at the back door as a wave of uncertainty rushes through me. It's not like we planned anything today, so I don't know why I should feel so guilty. Maybe it's the lies, or maybe my subconscious is warning me against what I'm about to do.

I have to see him again. It's as if I've finally gotten the answer I didn't really know I've been waiting for. *Here,* Leah. *This* is why you've been drawn to the forest, even knowing it's wrong, why you've been watching the Bigfoot in secret all these years, yet never said a word. It's all so you could be the one to find this boy.

But now that I have this knowledge, what should I do with it? Fear twists its way into my mind as I remember the anger from the male Bigfoot and the same I could encounter from my father. Am I so eager to return to where I shouldn't go?

Yes. I twist the cold handle of the door and leave without a backward glance.

I jog along the fence line, following the path the red Ranger took. White egrets swoop through the air and stalk the freshly mowed field beside me; their slender, sinuous heads dip and bob for whatever prey managed to escape the tractor's blades. In the hazy distance, the tractor sputters to a stop, leaving the world in sudden silence.

I've never been to the deer blind. For all I know, I could walk up on Matt and Dad in five minutes or five hours. But the idea of getting caught doesn't stop me.

Part of me wants to be found. Just not by them.

When I step into the cool shadows, it's like shedding a second skin. My body relaxes, and tension fades from my shoulders as my feet ease into familiar paths worn down by creatures other than me. I feel myself coming back to life as I lose the other me in the shadows I know by heart. This forest is my religion, the towering cathedral of trees my church, and I'm reborn every time I leave.

The trees are tall and thick enough that little grows on the ground but lush ferns. Deeper in, scorch marks cover the bottoms of the trunks, evidence of controlled burns in years past. The wind picks up and the shadows become cold. I stand in a patch of sun until the chill goes away, soaking in as much warmth as I can.

Somewhere ahead of me a chain saw cranks up, the whine as it cuts through wood as faint as a buzzing gnat. It's got to be Matt and Dad. I jog for a little ways until the sound

jennifer park

grows louder and voices become clear. There is a flash of red about fifty yards up the trail and the snapping and thrashing of branches from a tree being pushed out of the way, likely blocking the path. Soon the Ranger starts up and continues on, and I follow.

After a while I get the distinct feeling of being watched. I glance around, seeing nothing but shadows and light in erratic patterns across the trees and ground. I slow my pace and silence my steps, but the sensation doesn't leave. In fact, the farther I go, the stronger it gets. I look over my shoulder frequently, fully expecting to see the boy standing there, or a Bigfoot. Yet there's nothing.

A half hour has gone by when I hear the crank of the chain saw again. I veer off the game trail toward the sound, until I can see the green deer blind peeking through the trees with the Ranger sitting below. Even from here it looks like a giant vermin nest, with vines and tree branches crawling through the windows.

Off to the left sits a clearing, part of it in view of the blind, the other part hidden by a thick stand of brush that follows a narrow creek, cutting through the center of the meadow like a ribbon. I navigate my way toward the side obscured by trees, fingers trailing against rough bark as I move from pine to pine, completely at ease. The sky is a deep blue overhead, the kind of color you see only when the heat of summer is gone. A squirrel chatters in the trees high above me, and cardinals dart from branch to branch, their red bodies stark against the deep shadows of the trees. A dove calls from the field, and I walk toward the sound, keeping my steps light and silent. Matt's and Dad's voices echo through the silence, too far to understand, but close enough to offer security.

The dove calls again, closer this time as I step around the thick stand of brush, trying to keep out of sight from the blind. Something about the sound is different, and alarm bells blare through my head.

I'm not alone.

Instinct takes over. *Run. Run now,* it screams. I spin around and freeze.

The boy is five feet from me. My running-away option just ran out the door.

He's a statue, standing in a single patch of sunlit forest, the bright rays casting him in gold and shadow. His bronze skin is stretched tight over sinewy muscle, and he hovers on one foot, as if I caught him following me.

But I feel like the one who's been trapped.

Struggling to breathe, I tuck my violently shaking hands under my arms. Green eyes leave mine long enough to track their movement with the alacrity of a predator. He slowly lowers his foot to the ground but still seems frozen in motion.

I press my hands to my sides, clenching them into fists, steeling myself not to panic. He watches me, and his own fists clench momentarily. I uncoil them and place flat palms against my thighs. He mimics me again. I bite my lip against the flood of emotion threatening to burst forth. I'm not sure if I'm going to laugh, cry, or scream.

The boy watches me like a dying man might view a glass

of water. It's unnerving, like he's seeing every inch of me. Scorching heat creeps up my face. I can see almost every inch of him, all except what is covered by a piece of deer hide, tied roughly around his narrow waist. I'm staring, and my face burns with the knowledge.

I should speak, say something, but I'm afraid he'll run. He wears wildness like a cloak, and every movement is animal-like, from the way he tilts his head at a distant noise to the way his nostrils flare when the breeze blows.

I tell myself this is what I wanted. I wanted to see the boy again, wanted him to find me.

But when he takes a step toward me, I forget everything I wanted and run.

For a moment the only sound is the crashing of my body through the brush, when only seconds ago there was silence. Heart racing, lungs heaving, I try to get my bearings and listen for sounds of hammering or sawing from Matt and Dad. But even if they are there, the pounding and rushing of blood in my ears has drowned them out.

A familiar whoop echoes in front of me, and I slide to a stop.

Before I can pull myself out of my frozen state to run again, a hand comes over my mouth, an arm around my waist, and I'm dragged down into the brush behind me. The boy doesn't move, just keeps me pressed hard against his chest, his head next to mine. I try to yell past his hand, but he makes a shushing sound near my ear and points into the trees.

A massive dark shape moves in the distance, slow and purposeful.

It's the big one, the male. Fear, sharp and metallic, coats my mouth like sand. I can't help it, I shrink back against the boy, pushing both of us farther back into the shadows.

The shape stills, not more than twenty yards away.

The boy tightens his arm around my waist and his hand leaves my mouth, sliding down to wrap around my shoulder. His heart is racing, but not nearly as fast as mine. I'm the one who shouldn't be here.

It's killing me to sit like this. The urge to run is overwhelming, overshadowed only by the desire not to be seen. My body shudders as my hands wrap around my stomach and over the boy's arm. He flinches at the contact but doesn't loosen his iron grip on me.

It feels like years since I've blinked, waiting for the dark shadow to move. An ache pulses behind my eyes, and the only thing I have to distract me is the faint, rhythmic brushing of the boy's thumb over my collarbone. I guess he's trying to calm me, or maybe it's just a nervous tic, but it's almost as distracting as the realization that the Bigfoot are watching us. Spying on them safely within view of my house is one thing. Being miles into the forest and knowing they are watching you in their territory is another thing entirely.

Finally the Sasquatch moves, his gaze directed beyond us.

"Where is he going?" I whisper.

The boy is silent, his features focused. The shadow drifts silently through the trees, and when I hear the telltale sound of a hammer, my skin grows cold.

"He's going to them, isn't he? Matt and Dad?" Once again

jennifer park

the boy doesn't speak. His gaze has shifted to me, though, and he stares hard at my mouth, his own lips moving softly, speaking words with no sound.

For the first time I wonder if he can even talk. What if he can't? But then, who would he talk to if he lives with creatures that technically don't exist?

When the Bigfoot disappears, I stand, and the boy's arms slide off like water. I duck down, moving out of the brush, but he grabs my arm and pushes himself in front of me. He opens his mouth to speak but nothing comes.

Sympathy, along with something sharp and nameless, surges through me. We're so close now, I can see how green his eyes are, just as rich as the forest around us. His eyes drop from mine, and strands of sun-bleached hair drift across his face, at odds with the deeper browns that hang across his shoulders.

He reaches out a hand to my face. Air freezes in my lungs. He doesn't touch my skin but slides his fingers through the hair behind my ear, tugging a stray leaf from the tangles. His hand drops, the leaf tucked into his fist. His eyes never leave mine.

My chest burns with the lack of oxygen, reminding me to breathe. I wish he would look away so it wouldn't be so hard.

The loud bang of metal makes us both jump. Then a procession of bangs follows. Moments later a gunshot rings out. I push past the boy and start to run. I know where I'm going only because I can hear Matt yelling. The deer blind comes into view, and just as I see the Ranger, the boy jerks me behind a tree, but not before I see a rock come flying out of the trees to land on the metal hood. There are several littering the ground around the Ranger, and just as many dents in the shiny red metal.

A fierce roar echoes through the forest. I flinch, and the boy moves me around the tree, away from view of the blind. When he moves closer, I stop breathing again. He glances at me curiously before he leans away to peer around the trunk.

Another gunshot echoes through the silence, and this time I'm the one jerking him back. I switch places with him so fast I can see the surprise pass across his features when it's his back up against the tree. Placing my hands on his chest, I press hard. "Stay. Here." Maybe he understands, maybe not, but I have to find Matt and Dad. I don't want them shooting the boy by accident. "Stay. I mean it." I dart around the tree as his fingers grasp for my arm. I yell for Dad before I change my mind and let the boy pull me back, just to avoid the coming confrontation.

"Leah?" The shock in Dad's voice is evident. I will pay for this. "Where are you?"

"Here." I run through the trees to where they stand beneath the base of the deer blind.

"What are you doing here?" Dad whispers harshly, jerking me behind him. Matt eyes me like I've sprouted horns or something until another rock hits the Ranger. Dad hasn't let go of my arm, and his grip is only tightening. "We're leaving."

"What?" Matt says. "We're just going to let this guy get away with this? Come on, Dad, we can't just leave. Look at the damn Ranger!" Another rock comes flying out of the trees, leaving a softball-size dent in the hood.

"Now. Get in." Dad drags me along, basically propelling me into the backseat face-first. He doesn't even wait for Matt, just cranks the motor and swings around, letting Matt jump in as the Ranger slows.

"What about our tools? You're just going to leave it all here?"

"We'll come back later," Dad says, pressing the gas and slamming me against the backseat. I scramble for a handhold, finally sitting up against the faded leather. When Dad catches my eye in the rearview mirror, I wish I'd stayed down. Or maybe stayed in the woods to begin with. My sanctuary has been ripped apart and stained with violence, and I can't help but feel it's my fault.

The list of things I've done wrong today seems to be growing.

I spin around, grasping desperately for a secure grip so I can look back as we careen down the trail.

The boy is standing there, right where I stood only moments ago, his eyes hooded and fists clenched.

And just before we turn a sharp corner, a dark, massive shape joins him, and then they are both gone from sight.

chapter five

This time I've done more than simply break a Cardinal Rule.

"Have you lost your mind?" Dad jerks me from the backseat after the Ranger slides to a haphazard stop in the backyard. "What were you—why—you've crossed a line, young lady!"

Here we go, I tell myself as I fall into repentant daughter mode. "Dad, I'm—"

"I don't want to hear it. There is nothing in this world you could say to justify your presence in those woods. Do you have any idea what could have happened to you?" I stumble as he yanks on my sleeve, but Dad never slows in our stampede to the kitchen. Somewhere in my mind I register the fact that Mom is pulling into the driveway.

"We have these rules for a reason, Leah. They're not there for you to test, but to protect you." The fact that Dad personally escorts me up to my room is the first clue that this is more than simply breaking a house rule. "Don't come out of this room. I don't want to see you right now."

The second clue is when Mom tromps up the stairs minutes later, grocery bags and car keys still in hand, and stares at me through the open door. "I thought you were sick."

"I . . . the aspirin helped. I just went for a walk."

"You went into the woods by yourself? What if you'd gotten hurt? Run across hogs or got bitten by a snake?"

"I stayed on the trail, Mom. I was careful."

She sighs. "But you know the rules. They're there for a reason. What else happened? Your father seems excessively upset and neither of them will stop arguing long enough to answer my question."

"Something—someone was trying to mess with us, throwing rocks, being stupid. Probably some kids or something."

Mom's eyes widen, and then she abruptly shuts my door and hurries down the stairs.

Matt's raised voice echoes up through the floorboards, answered by Dad. Their words are muffled, angry, and minutes later my brother's in my room. "What the hell were you doing out there?" Matt slams the door behind him.

"Just walking. I was coming to find you, so I don't know why it's such a big deal." I'm sure not going to explain what I was doing out there. I can't even imagine Dad's reaction to that.

"Between you showing up and that guy throwing rocks, Dad's about to lose it, and he'll probably start with you if Mom doesn't start with him first. You picked a hell of a day to get caught breaking the rules, Leah."

"He's overreacting."

"Yeah, tell that to our parents. You'll be lucky if you leave this room again before Monday morning."

"It can't be that bad."

Matt shakes his head like it is. "I'm going to see if Dad has called the sheriff yet. The damage is ridiculous. I mean, who does that? Who throws rocks at people in the freaking woods?" He swings the door open again, closing it just as loud as he did the first time.

His voice echoes up through the floorboards, but this time Dad doesn't argue with him. Finally Matt stomps up the stairs and slams the door of his room, leaving the house in silence.

It's barely midday and it looks like I'm stuck in this room for the rest of it. It's probably too much to hope that I'm staying in here tomorrow. Dad may be furious, but there's no way in hell he'd let me skip church. I'm sure the sermon will be related directly to me and my actions, worded so that no one else realizes I'm getting a thirty-minute lecture in front of half the community.

After a while Dad's voice drones downstairs, his business-like tone suggesting a phone conversation; high-pitched at times, and then so low I think he's not speaking at all. I could go down and try to explain myself, but he's right, there's no possible reason to justify my presence that far in the woods, or in the forest at all. Plus, Mom knows I lied about being sick, so I'd have to see that look of disappointment on her face again.

I drop to the bed, resigned. It's been ten years since the incident that led to the rule about the woods, although why we would move here afterward, literally next to a massive forest, is still a mystery to me. I stop my thoughts before they go too far. If I'm not in the solace of the trees, I can't think about it. Those are my rules, the only ones I truly obey.

∽∾∽

jennifer park

It's only when I open my eyes that I realize I fell asleep. The shadows are long on the walls of my room, painting patches of bright orange and deep blue across the faded wallpaper. The house is so silent my ears start to ring. Then the door opens suddenly, revealing Matt, hair damp, wearing fresh clothes and a look that makes me slightly nervous.

"Come on, get dressed."

"What are you talking about? I am dressed."

"Something else." He eyes my dusty boots and grass-stained jean knees.

"Last time I checked, it doesn't matter what I'm wearing because I'm not leaving this room."

"Mom and Dad are gone. They said they'd be back late, and I'm not staying here. Come with me, it's better than staying here with your nose stuck in a book."

"They left? Why? Did Dad call the sheriff?"

"Yes, don't know, and yes."

"Dad will kill me if I leave this room."

"Do you think it can get any worse? You're not freaking five years old. He's not going to throw your toys away because you broke the rules. You don't have a car or a phone, so worse would just be longer in this room than you already stay anyway. What's the difference?"

"Are you going to yell at me the whole time? Because if you're still mad at me, I'd rather just stay here."

"I'm not, I'm just pissed at Dad for letting that guy go, I think he's too hard on you, and I don't want to stay in this boring house on a Saturday night."

"Where are we going?" I ask warily.

Matt glances down at his watch. "People are usually in the parking lot by now. I'm sure we'll find something to do."

"At the high school?"

Matt nods, checking his watch again. "I'm leaving in ten. If you're coming, meet me downstairs." He gives me half a smile and closes the door.

Against my questionable better judgment, I change clothes and find Matt in the kitchen. I feel like I'm about to break a Commandment or something. "I don't guess it'd do any good to tell them you made me leave if we get caught."

"Dad said late. That means way past dark, and I doubt he checks to see if you're in your room. It's not like you'd be crazy enough to disobey him a second time."

"Obviously you think I am."

"Obviously." Matt grins and grabs the keys to Mom's car off the hook. "Off to the dark side we go."

"They're going to see the car is gone."

"Yes. But I'm not grounded."

"How will I get back in the house if they're here waiting?"

"That magnolia tree is pretty close to your window. It'd be a jump, but you could make it."

"You're joking, right?"

"Do you want to get caught?"

"So you're making me break more rules *because* you're on my side? It's like you *want* me to be grounded until I'm eighteen."

"Exactly." He winks as he slides into the driver's seat, cranking it back to accommodate his long legs. "Besides, I think you've been the good preacher's daughter long enough."

I almost tell him he's got no idea how long I've been breaking Dad's rules, but explaining that is the last thing that's going to happen.

We tear down the dirt road, my white knuckles gripping the seat when Matt slings us onto the two-lane highway. Pine trees line the road, full of shadows that tease my eyes. Shapes zip by, more than I can count, and every one could be something or nothing. Ten minutes later Matt swerves into the parking lot of the high school, where a dozen cars and trucks are parked randomly around a group of students, all of whom I recognize. It's impossible not to know everyone in a school this small.

Matt rolls down the window on my side as the car grinds to a stop on loose gravel. "What's up?" He nods at a group of boys.

"Hey, Matt," Kelsey Wright calls, waving from across the parking lot. Matt waves back casually, his most winning smile pasted on his face.

Ben Hanson saunters over and leans on the door. His dark-eyed gaze drags across my legs before he meets Matt's eyes. "What are you two doing? No church tonight?" he says with a smirk.

"Dude, it's Saturday," Matt jokes back.

"What are you doing out of the house, preacher's kid?" Ben turns his attention back to me.

"Nothing," I say too quickly, ignoring the comment. But Ben wouldn't know I'm not supposed to be here, so why am I sweating this? "Just, you know, out."

the shadows we know by heart

Ben blinks. "You? Out? Does your daddy know what you're doing?"

"Lay off her, dude." Matt rolls his eyes. "Hey, where are we going?"

"Well, let's see. Shelly Johns's parents are out of town, so there's that. Rob Kelly's brother is getting us . . . libations." Ben eyes me cautiously, as if I might call my dad immediately and tell him they're all about to get drunk. Anger flushes my body, sending heat prickling along my skin.

"Wow, Ben. That's a big word. Are you old enough to use that?"

Matt laughs loudly, causing Ben's face to darken, then grin. Something flashes in his eyes, and for a moment Ben looks at me like I'm someone other than Matt's little sister and Pastor Roberts's daughter. I would be lying if I said it didn't make me nervous in a butterfly-fluttering way.

"I'm sure you'll get the chance to prove yourself before the night's over, little Leah." Ben slaps the roof of the car. With a whoop he signals the rest of the group to load up.

"Is this usually what you do on a Saturday night when you tell Dad you are over at Ben's house or out on a date?" I say when Ben walks away, gritting my teeth over the way he continuously calls me something other than simply *Leah*.

"Yep." Matt puts the car in reverse, swinging around to follow the caravan out of the parking lot. "Small-town Saturday night."

"Isn't that a song?"

"Isn't everything?"

"Probably. Is this going to be one of those pasture parties where everyone just stands around talking, listens to music, and drinks? Is that really fun to you?"

"Just call it a party, okay? You make it sound cheesy."

"Um, it's in a pasture. 'Pasture party' makes sense. You don't want me to call it that, have it somewhere else."

"Well, Shelly Johns lives in the woods, so technically it's not exactly a 'pasture party,'" he says, emphasizing the words with his fingers.

"But drinking and explicit music and generally everything Dad would disapprove of?"

"Um . . ." Matt bite his lips and nods. "Well, it's not Sodom and Gomorra kind of stuff, but yeah, he'd have a minor cardiac arrest if he knew what we were doing."

"I heard some of the football boys got extra inebriated and decided to jump naked over a bonfire a few weeks ago after the win. You know anything about that?"

"I can neither confirm nor deny it."

"How do you get away with this?"

"I make sure I know everyone's deepest, darkest secrets and threaten to reveal them to the world if they tell Dad what I do."

I stare, silent.

"Just kidding. You punch a few people, they quit trying to rat you out." Matt laughs at my wide eyes. "Come on, Leah, no one is going to tell on us. If one person talks, then it's over for everyone, you know? Lighten up, it's going to be fun, and Dad will never know you're there."

chapter six

There is no way my dad is *not* going to hear about this. I swear
if one more person gapes at seeing me here, I'll go home and
tell him myself. Bonus points for honesty, maybe.

Yeah, right.

I've got these sick, dizzy butterflies I haven't felt since I
was young, dreading school and leaving the known for the
unknown. Memories rise from the darkness where I always
fight to keep them, pushing through the cracks, striving for the
surface of consciousness. It's always the last ones that appear
first, the strongest, the ones that are still bound within my
heart, still capable of wounding after all this time.

Before we moved to the woods, we used to live on the same
street as Ashley and Reed, only a few blocks from the elemen-
tary campus. It's the first day of school, and Mom and Dad are
waiting with us for the bus. Mom offered to drive, but the boys
have already been riding the bus for a year now, and since we
do everything together, Ashley and I are riding the bus too.

But it doesn't keep the tears from rolling down my cheeks.
It's hard to be brave, even for something so silly as riding the
bus. But it means the end of summer, the end of Mom getting us out of our beds and snuggling in hers until Dad leaves
for the church. No more surprise afternoon visits from Dad

bearing snow cones or ice cream and watching us run through the sprinklers or down the Slip'N Slide.

Now we're up before the sun and down before it sets, and the whole thing makes me sad.

The bus squeals to a stop at the corner of the street. Sam and Matt charge up the steps to claim the last row seat, and Ashley follows behind them. I rub a fist across my eyes, and Mom squeezes my hand. "You want me to take you, sweetheart? We can still drive to school."

"No, I'm fine," I whisper.

Someone nudges me, and there's Reed, still standing next to me, dark brown hair now cut short for the new school year, and vibrant green eyes meeting mine. He holds out his hand, and all I can do is stare at it. Mom loosens her grip, my hand slips into Reed's, and I let him lead me onto the bus. Ashley has managed to squish herself between Matt and Sam, and she waves and points to the empty seat across the aisle.

I slide in first, pressing my face to the window while Mom and Dad wave and the bus jerks to a crawl, then turns the corner. More tears come when they disappear from sight, but Reed holds my hand until I'm ready to let go.

The memory takes my breath away, twisting my heart into something that feels like it's going to burst from my chest, and the tears that fall are far too real. No. I can't do this. Not here, in the open, in the real world. The walls are breaking too easily lately; memories are finding me more and more outside of the forest, the only place it's safe to relive them.

And then I realize ... It started with the appearance of the boy.

It takes a while to pull it together, and I'm still sitting in the car when Ben pulls up next to me. Kelsey dragged Matt out of the car the second he put it in park, and I haven't seen them since. Ben stares at me for a long moment, like he's chewing something over in his mind. It took him long enough to get here; I've been suffering for nearly thirty minutes. I'd ask him where he's been, but I don't want to look like I care.

He slides out of the cab of his truck, his muscles flexing under the tight black T-shirt he's wearing. I stare too long and the corner of his mouth lifts. My face is hot by the time he opens my door. "Nervous?"

"Bored." I shrug.

Ben grins like the Cheshire cat, seeing my lie immediately. "Don't be scared, little Leah. I could entertain you."

"Somehow I don't see that happening."

"What? C'mon, it's not like I'm going to make a move on my best friend's sister."

"Isn't that what you're doing now?"

"Please. You'd know if I was, and trust me, I'm not." He holds his hand out with a grin so cocky I'd like to slap it off his face. "I just want you out of this car."

"Why?" I take his hand and let him pull, but I imagine it's a much darker hand that holds mine and wild green eyes that stare back instead of dark.

With a chuckle, Ben spins me around. "So I can see your ass in those jeans."

"Ben!"

I swat and he dodges, slamming the door and jogging off

jennifer park

into the trees with a deep laugh. "Come on, preacher's daughter. Come slum with the rest of us sinners."

That's the second time he's called me that in the past hour. His nicknames are getting under my skin, and not in a good way. I'd like to throw something at him, but before I can reach for one of the pinecones littering the ground, he's gone, warm laughter drifting back to me. Thumping bass vibrates in the distance, so I follow the trail of bodies merging with the trees and shadows ahead of me.

The sun hasn't set, but as I walk through the field of young pines, it's as dark as night. They're lined perfectly and so close together I have to duck to get through the narrow path, but it's soothing to be so hidden, even for a short time. The clearing at the end of the pines is littered with stumps from freshly cut trees, creating plenty of natural seating and makeshift tables. A four-by-four made the trek around the trees, its tailgate providing the platform for both keg and stereo. The number of kids has doubled from what was in the parking lot, and even more are filing through the trees behind me. So basically the whole school should be here soon.

"Leah!" A familiar squeal rises above the blaring music, and Ashley comes tearing out of the trees. "Kelsey texted me that you were here. How did you manage that?" She slams into me, wrapping her arms around me in a tight hug.

"Oh, you know, Matt invited me to come, so . . ."

"Wow! You never get to come to these things. I thought . . ." Ashley pulls away suddenly, holding me at arm's length, eyes narrowing. "Does your dad know you're here?"

the shadows we know by heart

"Um . . ." I bite my lip and she gasps.

"Leah Roberts, did you sneak out?"

"Ash, please, could you be quiet? I'd like to live to see Monday morning."

"Oh. My. God. You snuck out." Ashley's eyes are wide. "What was the straw that broke the proverbial camel's back?"

"Unreasonable punishment."

"You were already in trouble? Why? What did you do?"

"I went into the woods."

Ashley's hands drop from my shoulders. She stares at me for a long moment, her face growing pale. "Why would you do that?"

"Because I wanted to." Ashley is the queen of rebelling, so I don't know why I feel so defensive. "I mean, we're standing in the woods right now, so it's not like it's a big deal."

"It is when you go by yourself. We don't know if . . ." She stops, shaking her head. "You're right. You should do what you want. And now you're here." Her smile fades from forced to easy. "Let's go have a good time, because after tonight you might never leave the house again."

"Tell me about it." I link my arm with hers, glad she dropped the taboo subject. Maybe I am stupid for going into the woods, but my reasons for doing so far outweigh everyone's reasons I shouldn't. At least that's what I tell myself.

It's been ten years; it's not like the guy has come back and is waiting in the woods just for me.

I follow Ashley to the keg, grateful for anything to take my thoughts away, take a swig from a red cup, and choke down the

jennifer park

beer. It's awful, but it pushes the darkness back. I take another drink, swallowing faster, and the memories go back into the locked box at the darkest corner of my mind. I won't let them out again.

We move away, making room for others eager to fill their cups. There are people everywhere, some dancing, but most talking in small circles. I follow Ashley through the fray, hearing more than a few surprised voices say my name. We stop at a couple of stumps near the outer edges of the field, where Ashley sits and I do the same. The sun is impaled on the treetops, and I try not to stare as it slides down through the pines, casting shifting rays on the moving bodies.

"Cheers." Ashley holds out her cup. "To your first official party."

"Cheers." I clink my cup to hers with a smile. "First and likely last."

"Where are your parents?"

"Don't know. They just left and Matt said they'd be back late tonight."

"Well, that's interesting, I guess. Makes the whole sneaking-out thing easier."

I nod. I don't want to tell Ashley about what happened at the deer blind. It would only freak her out and I'd have to omit half of it. The rational part of my brain says maybe I could have avoided all of this if I had been honest from the beginning about the boy. But to do that I'd have to confess my sins and secrets. I mean, who's going to believe that I've seen Bigfoot? Seriously, it sounds crazy even to me.

I glance up to see Ben staring at me from across the way. He's standing next to Matt, who has an arm slung around a giggling Kelsey's shoulders.

I frown.

"What?" Ashley follows my gaze. "Oh. Mr. Greek God. You know one of these days he's going to finally notice you, right? I mean, he's over at your house all the time anyway."

"So?"

"*So*, I'm saying it makes sense. I know he picks on you, but that's the thing that leads to flirting and he looks like he'd like to be over here flirting with you."

"He said he wasn't."

"You asked him?" Her voice rises.

"I thought he was earlier. He said I'd know it if he was."

"Yikes."

"Yeah."

"Well, it wouldn't be a bad thing, would it? I mean, look at him, Leah. I'm drooling here, and show me someone who doesn't when they look at him. He's freaking perfect."

"He's kind of a jerk. And he's almost too pretty."

"No such thing. I'll never get tired of looking at him."

"So why don't you go for him?"

Ashley gives me a look, and I wince. She could have Ben if she tried. Ashley's pretty enough to get anyone, in my opinion. Just not the one she wants. *He* never looks twice at her.

Matt glances at me for a moment, nodding in acknowledgment before talking to Kelsey again. Ashley tenses when he leans in to whisper in her ear. Deep down, I think Matt knows

jennifer park

about Ashley. How could he not? But it's not something I'd ever want to get involved in. Matt goes from girl to girl and I don't want my best friend to be one of them.

"Let's go over there." Ashley nudges me.

"Why?"

"I want to see what Ben does when you're five feet from him."

"Ashley," I warn.

"Oh, c'mon. I'm bored and you should be having more fun than this."

"I am having fun."

"No, have another beer and you will be, though."

"That doesn't sound like fun, Ash."

"It will be, until tomorrow." She waves me along, and I follow her once again through the maze of bodies. Ben watches me until it's obvious where we are headed, and then he doesn't look at me again.

"Did you hear about the break-in at the Millers' place?" Joel Rodriguez says.

"Yeah, I heard they saw the guy too," Matt chimes in.

"What?" Ashley says. "Who was it?"

"Don't know," Joel says. "But there were two of them. Broke into the barn, took some of their deer meat out of the freezer."

"Luke said he saw something, but he won't talk about it," Ben says.

"That's the youngest Miller brother, right?" Ashley interjects.

"Yeah, Jake said Luke was the first one out of the house when the dogs started howling. Said he saw something big and black walking around the barn, carrying a couple of chickens."

"How big?"

"The kid swore it was seven or eight feet tall, but you know he's only nine years old. Everything's gonna be huge to him in the dark. Said the other one was smaller, maybe six feet or so."

I should have known I would hear that description, but I still gasp. Unfortunately, I also choke on beer and proceed to cough my head off. Ashley slaps me on the back and takes my drink away, like I went too far. Matt just shakes his head with a knowing grin.

"You okay?" Ben says, placing a hand on my shoulder. I'm too distracted to brush him off, so I nod helplessly in between ragged gasps.

"She's fine." Ashley continues to pound my spine until it hurts worse than my throat.

"I think you've got it, Ash." Ben pulls me away until I'm standing next to him. One second I think she might claw his eyes out, the next she looks between us, grins, and takes a sip of my beer before handing it back to me.

"You okay?" Ben asks again, this time barely above a whisper, like his concern should be a secret.

"I'm fine. Not used to this, I guess." I hold up my red Solo cup.

"Well, it's poison anyway."

I glance down at the nearly empty interior of his. "You drink it easily enough."

Ben shrugs, glancing around to make sure no one is listening. "Out here it's a prerequisite."

jennifer park

"Ben Hanson. Are you telling me you drink because of *peer pressure*?" I stopped whispering somewhere in the middle of that sentence, and Ben looks like he'd like to disappear.

"What are you two talking about?" Ashley asks.

"Nothing," Ben and I say, then smile at our jinx.

"Anyway," Joel continues. "By the time Mr. Miller went back for his gun, they were gone."

"Deer meat and live chickens? Can two men carry that much?" Kelsey asks.

The boys exchange glances, and Ben shrugs. "I mean, it's possible, I guess. They'd have to have something to carry it in. But just to run in and out like that, and then disappear? That's odd for sure."

Chills run down my neck, lifting the hairs along my spine. It *is* odd, just not to me. And the Millers live only about five miles from us, and their land sits along the edge of the national forest just like ours.

Ben is staring at me again, only this time there is a light in his eyes, as if he knows exactly what I'm thinking. Since that's not possible, I glance down at my cup, now barely half-empty, and excuse myself to refill it.

I can't shake his gaze off. I know it follows me across the field and I wonder why now, of all times, does Ben Hanson choose to give me attention? The only face in my head is that of a boy who can't even speak to me, with eyes as green as the deep forest that have the ability to erase the world when they meet mine.

And I have no explanation for it.

Ben is what I've wanted for a while, because he makes perfect sense. He's likely the only guy Dad wouldn't run off, because Sheriff Hanson is Dad's BFF and a deacon at our church. Ben spends half his life at my house because of Matt. He fits into my life so easily because he's already in it.

I take a long swallow of whatever just came out of the keg, blink away the burn, and lock eyes with Ben across the field.

Maybe I should take a page from Ashley's book and say, *what the hell have I got to lose?*

Maybe it's long past time I thought that way.

chapter seven

I can't stop giggling when Matt pulls into the driveway.

"Shh . . . Leah, you've got to be quiet." But he can't stop smiling either.

"We're going to get caught."

"Then why are you laughing?"

"I have no idea. I only had two cups."

"Hell, you had at least three. Every time your cup got low Ashley was dragging you back to the keg."

"She wanted me to have fun."

"No, your best friend wanted to get you drunk." He leans forward, peering through the darkness toward the house. The porch light is on, but nothing else. "How are they not back yet?"

"What?" I lean forward, the motion making me dizzy. "They're not back?"

"I can't believe we lucked out." He glances in the rear-view mirror as if Mom and Dad might turn down the drive behind us at any second. "You should probably hurry and take a shower, just in case."

"Do I smell that bad?"

"No, I mean, you smell like beer. Is that the right answer?"

"Your girlfriend spilled it on me."

"Yeah." He smiles. "Now that girl can drink."

"Is that why you like her?"

Matt frowns, like I might not be making sense. "Get in the house before we get caught. I can't sneak you out again if Dad puts bars on the doors and windows." We laugh all the way to the porch.

It's well after midnight when I roll into bed. Light is streaming in through the bedroom window from the nearly full moon, and I'm not sure if I can sleep. The funny feeling is gone now, fuzzy memories are becoming clearer, and I'm left feeling restless and exhausted at the same time.

The reflection of headlights passes by the window. I slide out of bed and watch as the car creeps slowly beneath the carport, just within view of my window. Someone must have been in the hospital or having a crisis for them to be out this late.

Mom walks around to the back of the car, and Dad meets her there. When he reaches out and pulls her into an embrace, I press my face to the glass in disbelief. Our parents never hug, yet there they are, arms tight, heads pressed together like they . . . *like* each other. Dad's lips graze her forehead, and then they part as he opens the trunk.

I must still be drunk. There's no explanation for this.

They pull out black duffel bags and camo backpacks from the back of the car, nothing I've ever seen before in this house. Mom slings the packs over her shoulders, knocks her shoes against the tire, and disappears around the side of the house.

It's much too late to process any of what I just saw, and I decide I'll deal with it in the morning. I ease into bed, tension leaving as I hear the familiar sounds downstairs. I close my eyes,

jennifer park

remembering the party and how Ben's eyes would meet mine, how his smile would linger when it reached his eyes. But then I drift, and my thoughts turn to green eyes and dark forests, to cold shadows and warm hands on my skin.

The loud crack in the forest gets me to my feet.

I fly out of bed and stare at the trees, but there is only darkness where the moon doesn't reach. Slowly, registering each shape before moving on, my eyes make their way from the apple tree to the distant stump bathed in moonlight. And there someone, or something, is sitting.

The figure is so still, perched on the flat wood like a statue. I think it's the boy, only because he looks so small from this distance. I mean, at one o'clock in the morning, it sure isn't going to be Old Man Watson.

Adrenaline surges, even as a voice screams inside my head, telling me this is the most stupid thing I've done yet. Ignoring it, I grab my boots and tiptoe down the stairs. I'm halfway through the kitchen when I realize I'm not alone.

A quiet sniff halts me in my tracks. Mom is sitting at the table, her head propped up on her hands, palms pressed to her eyelids. I feel like a deer in headlights. My head swivels, wondering if I can get back up the stairs without her knowing.

The silver flask is lying on its side next to a pile of crumpled Kleenex.

And a photograph.

It's surrounded by the tissues, but nothing touches it, as if she was at least careful enough to protect it in her sorrow. I recognize the photo. I have the same one, tucked within a book on my shelf.

A sob escapes her. I've stood here too long. As I back up, I sneak a glance through the back door window. The boy's still there, waiting, but I have no choice. I tiptoe up the stairs to my room.

I don't know how long Mom will stay down there. I should have said something to her, but then we would both have to acknowledge her secret lying there empty on the kitchen table.

Not even close to tired now, I stand in front of the window. Something tickles my foot and I flip on the bedside lamp, afraid it was a spider. Seeing nothing, I turn it off, too late realizing what I've done. He's seen me, and likely took that flash of light as a signal. Sure enough, when my eyes adjust back to the darkness, I find him running across the field, straight for the house.

Crap. Mom's going to see him, I know it. Or maybe she's too wrapped up to notice anything but her pain. One can only hope. God, sometimes I'm heartless. I push off the bed and shove my lack of compassion out of my mind, because a wild boy, raised by monsters, is running through the field to my house.

So instead of closing my window, I'm raising it.

There are so many reasons why I should lock it and hide. Or tell Dad. Or tell anyone.

But I won't. Because that's the thing about having a secret like this. It's yours. Totally and completely. Because if I slide out this window, no one on earth will know about it. Just me. And him.

jennifer park

And something about that just feels . . . inevitable.

Leaving my boots behind, I crawl through onto the roof of the back porch. Perched on the shingles, I watch as he slows to a stop near the apple tree, waiting in the shadows. Inching toward the edge, I peer down at the ground below. If this goes badly, I won't be able to explain why I was on the roof. Certainly not why I was trying to jump off of it. The magnolia tree sits just within reach, but I don't dare try to reach for the closest limb. It's a risk, and Mom would likely hear.

The boy leaves the shadows of the tree and stands in full moonlight. His bronze skin is now pale, his messy brown hair flecked with strands of silver. Though his eyes are dark, I know their shade. A deep emerald green, the color of the forest after a summer rain. I wonder if he's ever smiled. If he's ever had a reason to.

The next thing I know I'm falling forward. The shingles slip out of my fingers as I scramble for a hold. My heel hits the edge of the gutter. I jerk it away with a gasp, both out of pain and fear that someone heard me, but all that accomplishes is sending me over the edge of the roof.

For a split second I hear my dad's sermon voice, telling me I'm being punished for my deceitful actions, that this is what I deserve. And then all thought is wiped away when I land in a pair of steel-like arms.

"*Ohthankgod,*" I mumble, eyes closed, prepared for the impact of hard ground that didn't come. The boy goes down on one knee, his breath whooshing across my face as he stops my descent inches from the grass. I can't believe I'm alive, and he looks completely surprised that he caught me, which will probably freak me out if I dwell on it too long. His heart is racing against my skin, making me embarrassingly aware that I'm in thin cotton pajamas, little more than shorts and a tank top.

Suddenly he rises to his feet, lifting me like I'm nothing, and moves into the shadows of the magnolia. I'm hoping he'll let me go, but if anything, I think his arms tighten around me more. The wind picks up, sending wild strands of his hair blowing across his face and mine.

"Can you . . . put me down?" I clear my throat nervously. He's staring at my neon-painted toenails glowing in the moonlight. His head jerks around, his eyes staring intently at me, at my mouth. A faint line forms between his brows.

"Down?" I point to the ground. He tosses his head in an effort to move his hair, and something seems familiar about the motion. Probably because Matt does the same thing.

Slowly he puts me on my feet. As his arms fall away, leaving me chilled, a light flickers in the kitchen, like someone moved in front of a night-light.

I don't think, just react.

I grab his hand and pull until we're running around the corner of the house toward the storage shed. His hand is warm, and it grips mine like we've done this before, another thing that rings familiar. The moon is bright and unhindered on the far side of the shed, but we are completely hidden from the house now. I gaze fleetingly across the pasture, wondering if he came alone to find me, wondering what he risked if he did.

Our hands are still linked, and, blushing, I try to disentangle

jennifer park

mine from his. He doesn't seem to want to let go. He stares like he can't get enough of watching me, like looking at a human isn't something he's done in a while. Maybe he hasn't.

There are a million questions I want to ask him. But they all fade away when he takes a step closer. I can't meet his concentrated gaze for long, so I let my eyes drop.

Obviously a mistake.

His body is cut in shadow and light, nothing but angles and sharp lines that tell me any part of him would likely be hard as stone if I were brave enough to touch it. The boy tilts his head. His eyes become swathed in darkness while his hair glows with moonlight.

Guilt stabs at me, as if I'm committing a sin just by letting him stand here and stare at me. It's just that I've never felt so *seen* before. The forest has come to me, not the other way around.

I'm not Leah, the preacher's daughter; not Leah, Matt's sister; not Leah Roberts, whose family went through that terrible *incident*.

I'm just me. A girl, nameless, standing with a nameless boy who might need rescuing more than her.

chapter eight

This time, when his gaze meets mine, I don't look away.

But when the solid crack of wood echoes through the forest, he scans the tree line. Fists clench, his chest heaves, and I can't tell if he's scared, worried, or angry. When he takes a step away, I find myself reaching out to him.

"Wait. Stay." I don't even know if he understands me. I don't even understand me. Standing here in the moonlight with a wild boy from the woods, I'm pretty sure "sane" isn't in my vocabulary anymore.

But all I want is for him not to run.

He pauses, his gaze darting between me and the forest. When I feel him pulling away again, I blurt out the first stupid thing I can think of. "Thank you. For, you know, saving me." I point toward the house. "I've never tried to climb down the roof before."

He tilts his head, frowning as his eyes search mine. We stand in silence, until the tension eases from his body. There are no more signals from the forest. I've read about the wood knocks, one of the Sasquatch ways of communicating, far less conspicuous than the bone-chilling howls and whoops that I hear late at night.

"Can you talk?" I whisper.

He releases a heavy breath, pursing his lips as a frown appears, drawing his straight eyebrows together. The boy looks at me through long, lowered lashes, giving a slight shrug.

I bite my lip, only to release it quickly when his gaze narrows in on it.

"My . . . my name is Leah." I point to myself, then him. "Do you have a name?"

His lips are moving again, whispering soundless words that I can't make out. He visibly steels himself, and then he takes a breath. "L—lee . . . yah." His voice is rough, straining with the effort of use. "Leeahh."

I reach a hand up to cover my smile. This time the word is just a whisper but clear as day. "Leah."

"Yes!" *Too loud.* I wrap my arms around myself, unable to contain my excitement. "You said my name." I point again to him. "What's yours?" Disappointment settles over me when he remains silent. "You don't have a name?"

He shakes his head.

It occurs to me he knows enough of communication to realize that motion means "no."

Another crack echoes in the distance. I nearly come out of my skin, but he barely flinches. "You have to go, don't you?"

His eyes are pleading with me to understand. I glance down and tuck my hair over my ear when it falls across my face. It won't stay. When I look up, his hand is already moving.

I freeze, waiting, breathless.

Light fingers touch my hair, hesitant and wary. He tilts his head again in that very animal-like way of his. His fingers slide down

the shadows we know by heart

the strands as he leans forward to inhale the citrus shampoo scent I'm sure it smells like. He's so close I stop breathing. Again. That habit has really got to stop. When he moves the hair along my face and behind my ear, my heart stumbles. Rough fingertips trail feather-soft down my skin, leaving my jawline burning.

My eyes close because it's easier than enduring the intensity of his gaze. Fingertips graze my eyelids, lightly brushing my lashes before sliding down my nose. The breath I finally release is shaky and loud.

And when the primal roar echoes from the forest with angry impatience, I open my eyes to find him gone, fleeing across the field like a wraith. Once again I run back to the safety of my dark house, make sure the kitchen is empty, slip the spare key from beneath the doormat, and add one more secret to the arsenal within its walls.

But this secret burns bright and fierce, unlike the others that smolder in the ash of long-dead fires.

I wonder how long I will last before it consumes me.

Dad has cleared his throat three times in the last five minutes. Matt shifts beside me as I pry my eyes open and glance up, catching Dad's stare as my gaze drags across the choir and my eyes roll back in my head again.

"He's going to say something," Ashley hisses with an accompanying elbow to my ribs.

"No, he won't," I murmur, enjoying seeing the backs of my eyelids. "Then he'd have to publicly acknowledge I'm not perfect."

jennifer park

"I'm never taking you out again," Matt whispers, but I just smile.

It's so warm in here from the heaters, turned on for the first time this season, resulting in the entire sanctuary smelling like burned dust, and the urge to sleep is overwhelming. Dad will be so pissed. I'm sure his eyes are doing that tight glare thing, and the muscle in his jaw is ticking. But I don't care enough to open my eyes to see.

"First sneaking out and drinking, now sleeping in church? What are you thinking, preacher's daughter?" Ben whispers over my shoulder from the pew behind us. It jolts me awake like ice water, and the obvious grin in his voice makes me blush.

"Apparently one night of hanging out with you has ruined her," Ashley answers.

"Well then, we need a do-over. How about today?"

Ashley raises an eyebrow at me, but I don't dare answer because Dad is looking over here. Again. As if he's determined to catch us not listening or, worse, talking. Ben is perfectly hidden behind my head, so he's out of sight at least. My luck, Dad's going to ask me trivia questions about the sermon on the way home and then corner me over why I didn't pay attention.

I shrug in answer to Ben. It's safe. Noncommittal. But he whispers, "Awesome," and sits back against his own pew. Ashley pats me on the leg, though in consolation or congratulations, I have no idea.

We wait in the car nearly twenty minutes for Dad to finally exit the church to join us. I don't understand why we can't take separate cars, but he insists. Matt's stomach is rumbling, and Mom is picking at her nails with a slight frown when the driver's side door opens. "Sorry I'm late. We had to reschedule the finance meeting for later this afternoon. Sheriff can't make it until four."

"Oh?" Mom says distractedly, still picking at her chipped polish. Dad stares at her until she glances up at him. She sits up suddenly, alert, staring back. I have no idea what passes between them, but after a moment Dad cranks the car, and Mom looks away, fists tight in her lap.

Sometimes I wish they'd just get a divorce. I'd rather them be separate and pleasant than together and unhappy. But then I think they'll never be happy wherever they are or whoever they're with.

"Leah, what did you think of the sermon?"

Here we go. "I think it had too many metaphors." Let him think on that for a moment.

"It's Revelation, Leah," Matt says. "It's one big, gigantic, cataclysmic metaphor."

"Well, it's really—" Dad begins.

"I mean, come on. Do you really think a dragon with ten horns and seven heads is going to come out of the sea? It's not even symmetrical. Where are the extra three horns? Why are there even three extra horns to begin with? Right, Dad?"

Dad tears his gaze from the rearview mirror when he nearly rear-ends the car in front of us.

"And explain to me how a beast is going to have two horns like a lamb. Lambs don't have horns. They're baby sheep. That's

jennifer park

the point. Don't you think that would hurt the momma sheep to give birth to a baby with horns? That's brutal."

Dad's mouth snaps shut. He flexes his hands on the steering wheel and slowly shakes his head. "Well, I'm glad it made you think about it. I guess," he murmurs.

"Yeah, because it doesn't make sense." Matt pops his earbuds out of his pocket and plugs them into his iPod. "We were just talking about how you can already get a chip with your credit card number or something like that implanted in your hand. Did you know that? I mean, that's mark-of-the-beast stuff. Why would you want something like that in your hand? You could never hide from anything. I'd totally chew it out like the dinosaur in *Jurassic World*. Just leave a big hunk of skin lying around with a beeping tracker thing."

There is dead silence in the car until Mom turns around. "The dinosaur chewed its skin off?"

"Well, I mean, if you're asking *specifically*, the velociraptor DNA mixed with the base genome of the T. rex gave it a higher intelligence level, allowing Indominus rex to remember where they placed her tracking implant when she was a baby. But it's due to the addition of both cuttlefish and tree frog DNA that allowed her to camouflage herself and remove her own thermal signature, enabling her to escape in the first place."

For a moment Mom tries really hard not to smile. Matt caught her by surprise, and I can tell the exact moment she remembers why he usually hides his dinosaur obsession, because her eyes darken and shoulders sag. "I'm sorry I asked," she says softly, turning around.

the shadows we know by heart

Matt frowns but shakes it off. He winks at me, knowing his diversion was a success, and stares out the window with his earbuds blaring.

The memory surges through my defenses, laid bare in the expanse of my mind. It was the last week of summer, and Mom and Dad took all of us to the Museum of Natural Science in Houston. Dad had to borrow the church van just to fit all of us kids. Ashley and I had the middle row, and the boys were in the back. And they tugged on our ponytails the entire three hours it took to get there. Dad even stopped at one point just to let us get out and run around an empty parking lot, screaming and chasing until we were breathless with laughter and could get back in the van like the civilized humans he expected us to be. Of course, back then he said everything with a smile that reached his eyes. And I adored him for it. Things were better when he was around, not worse. And Mom was exactly what she was supposed to be. Love and hugs and happiness, her attention on us whenever we asked for it and especially when we didn't.

The dinosaur exhibit literally changed the boys' lives. From the towering skeletons to the tiniest detail behind glass, they soaked it up like water in sand. They lived and breathed anything and everything dinosaur from that moment on, both Matt and Sam. The dinosaur birthday party they had that year was over-the-top, and Dad even showed up dressed in a T. rex costume that sent all the children screaming across the yard in fake terror. The piñata was a stegosaurus, the cake was a three-foot brontosaurus that Ashley and Reed's mom made from scratch, with tiny toy dinosaurs placed along its body, and the punch was green. It was the best party the twins had ever had.

And it was the last.

We spend the rest of the car ride in silence, until Dad asks Mom what's for lunch as we pull into the driveway. "You're welcome," Matt whispers as we get out of the car.

"I owe you."

"I know. Your price is playing video games this afternoon."

"Why? You know I don't like the stress of all that stuff."

"Because Ben is coming over and he wants to hang out."

"With who? Me?"

"I believe you're the one who agreed to it."

"I didn't. I shrugged. That wasn't a yes."

"Well, he wants to talk to you. I told him it's fine as long as I'm there."

"Why does that make it sound like a date and you're the chaperone?"

"It's not a date. But if my best friend wants to hang with my little sister I'm sure as hell going to sit in on it. Got it?"

"I didn't say yes."

"Well, then you should have said no. But it's too late now. He'll be here in an hour."

"Please don't make me play Halo."

"Shhhh . . ." Matt says, shooting a glance at Dad as he opens the back door into the kitchen. "He doesn't know Mom bought it for me. You know he said no violent games."

"Then I'd hate for him to find out you have it."

Matt glares. "Let's not forget I just saved you from a long lecture and likely more jail time."

"Let's not forget you forced me to go to a party and drink. I go down, we're going down together. You did drive home buzzed."

Matt chews his lip, eyes narrowed. "Fine. No Halo."

"Agreed." I hold out my hand.

Before I can jerk it back, Matt spits in his hand and slaps it to mine. "Agreed."

"Ugh! I hate you sometimes. Do you know how disgusting that is?" I wipe my hand on my blue-jean skirt. "Sick person."

"Well, would you have rather used blood?"

"I don't understand you. Like at all."

"You don't have to understand me. You just have to keep my secrets. You're good at that."

I meet his gaze with wide eyes, but he just smiles and walks through the doorway. The day Matt realizes how good I really am at keeping secrets will be the day I can no longer keep them.

chapter nine

I'm wedged between Matt and Ben on the couch that sits beneath Matt's bunk bed. It's been ten years since there was a bottom bunk. Laughter rings up from the kitchen from the meeting of deacons' wives that I also didn't know about. Ben's mom is one of them, which explains a lot about my current circumstances. Had I said no, he would have just come anyway.

"Why aren't we playing Halo?" Ben says flatly, focused on the black McLaren speeding across the screen. Every time he jerks the control to move his car, his knee and elbow touch mine. I'm not even sure he notices it, but since there are only two controls, neither of which I have, it's all I can focus on.

"She didn't want to," Matt answers as his yellow Lamborghini Diablo speeds past.

"It's not that bad, Leah."

"I don't like getting killed."

"It's not real."

"It feels like it. It makes me want to go outside and run or something. I don't like all the tension and anxiety."

"So we're going to race cars all afternoon?"

"You can leave."

Ben grabs his chest. "Ouch, little Leah. I think you're trying to hurt me." He nudges me with a grin, leaving his arm against mine. My heart picks up speed, but I can't tell if it's because of butterflies or the fact that Matt is sitting next to me while his best friend is flirting. He leans across me, obviously in my personal space, and whispers loudly to Matt, "I brought Fallout."

"Aaaand we're done here." Matt hops up and turns off the car game. "Where?"

"Here." Ben pulls it out of the pocket of his jacket and tosses it across the room to Matt.

"Let me guess, lots of shooting?"

"Is there any other kind?" Ben says, leaning back against the couch. It feels strange to sit this close to him with Matt's space empty. I don't know whether to move over or stay, because I'll just have to move back when Matt returns. Ben stretches his arm across the back of the couch, and the movement causes me to slide closer, until I'm pressed against his side. He pretends not to notice, or he actually doesn't notice. I'm not sure which one I'm hoping for.

This is Ben. Matt's best friend, the son of Dad's best friend, although I'd call Sheriff Hanson more of a professional best friend, because they don't exactly do friend things. More like run the church business meetings, deacon meetings, and other meetings that I don't know about and that happen behind closed doors. Regardless, I'm not sure how to make the leap from *friend* Ben to *more than friend* Ben, or if he even wants to.

I remember when he became friend Ben. Before I can stop it, another off-limits memory crowds into my mind. We sit in Ashley and Reed's tree house, a pile of first and second graders, on a Saturday in October. "I don't like Ben Hanson," Ashley says, throwing acorns across the deck, watching as they bounce and fly off the edge.

"Me neither," I say, taking one from the pile in my fist. But mine doesn't bounce, just sails straight over the edge to hit the tree trunk below.

"Ben's in my class," Sam says. "Why don't you like him?"

"He pulls my hair in music."

"Well, he pulls mine in art," Ashley says.

"Just tell him to stop," Matt replies, sharpening a stick with a deer antler knife Dad gave him.

"We do, he just doesn't listen."

Matt shrugs, but Reed answers. "I'll make him stop." He picks up the acorns that have slipped out of my hand and holds them out to me. I take them, one by one, and throw them. Our backs are pressed against the wall of the tree house, Reed, me, Ashley, Sam, and Matt, and our dirty bare feet lined up in a row could be on a greeting card.

"You know he lives down the street," Sam taunts. "Why don't you just do it now?"

Four pairs of eyes swivel to stare at Reed.

"I'll do it."

"No, you won't." Sam shrugs, fashioning a slingshot from a stick and a piece of rubber band he found in Dad's shop.

"Yes, I will." Reed leans across me, staring my brother down.

"I dare you."

"Fine."

"Well, I double-dog dare you." Matt grins. "'Cause I don't think you'll do it."

Reed jumps to his feet and slides down the rope ladder, and the twins follow him. Ashley and I scurry after them, acorns scattering, because there's no way we would miss this.

Five minutes later, our bikes lie carelessly in the ditch outside Ben's house. Reed knocks on the door, which is answered by Ben's mom. We're all speechless for a moment, and I'm probably not the only one wondering what exactly Reed is going to say. I take a step back, ready to rush for the bikes. "Is Ben home?" Reed asks, like it doesn't really matter to him.

"Yes, he is. Ben!" Mrs. Hanson calls over her shoulder. "Your friends are here."

Ben comes to the door. "Hey, guys, what's up?"

"My sister said—" Reed begins.

"*Our* sisters said," Sam cuts in, "that you've been pulling their hair."

Ben looks past the wall of brothers at Ashley and me. "Yeah. So?"

"Well, quit. They don't like it," Matt says.

Ben shrugs. "Okay."

"Want to play baseball?" Reed asks.

"Yeah, I'll get my glove."

And just like that, it's over. Ashley rolls her eyes as we get our bikes, the boys already arguing over who's on what team, like nothing even happened.

The memory slides away, leaving bitterness in its wake. So when Ben's hand slips down to rest lightly on my shoulder, I do the most obvious thing I can think of and shoot up off the

jennifer park

couch like a coward. "I'm thirsty. Anyone want a drink?" I ask, not looking back and not stopping.

"Um, Cokes?" Matt yells as I hurry down the stairs and into the kitchen full of women. No one notices me for a moment as they all study a sheet of paper on the kitchen table. Mom has her ever-ready fake smile pasted on her face, almost on the verge of a grimace. She hates this kind of stuff, but it's expected of her. Today it's a discussion of the food for the church wide Christmas party. They're planning it now, so they'll have a couple of months to squabble over who is cooking what. Some of them have been cooking the same thing for decades. Heaven forbid someone shows up with the same cherry pie as Mrs. Lewis, or a sheet cake that has the same color and texture as Mrs. Brennan's.

So they sit over coffee and discuss the sign-up, each claiming her own dish before the sheet is tacked up to the events wall for the rest of the congregation to add their names.

I slip around the corner and into the hallway, shoulders hunched until I make it to the front door and freedom.

Why is this so hard? Ben Hanson literally had his arm around me and all I could do was freak out and run. He'll probably never look at me again. My next thought is that Ashley is going to kill me. The one boy I've been hung up on and he makes the first move and I can't handle it. Yep, she'll likely have a heart attack right in the hallway at school. I'd call her and ask for a pep talk, but I don't have a phone, and the two landlines are in the kitchen and Dad's office, so that's not happening.

The distant wood knock is familiar now, even though it

sets my heart racing like nothing else. But instead of coming from across the pasture in the distant forest, it's coming from the woods running along our driveway. I weigh my options. Dad said nothing about going outside, just not back to the woods. The driveway runs through the trees, but it's technically not in the forest. He can't yell at me for just walking down the road a bit. No one else lives down here except Mr. Watson, and his mailbox is nearly a quarter of a mile up the road.

Mind made up, I walk down the steps and hurry toward the trees before anyone thinks I've been gone too long. Just as I'm starting to worry that Ben will think I'm hiding from him, another knock sounds closer, and my mind goes blank.

It's hard walking through the fear. Instinct tells me to run, and it feels foolish to be out in the open like this and not surrounded by brush. I go as far as I can stand, and then stop, still within view of the house.

Silence falls. Even the birds have stopped calling, leaving only the wind to whistle softly through the trees. I close my eyes, listening for the slightest sound, but nothing comes. It's like the forest is holding its breath, waiting. Suddenly the feeling of being watched sweeps over me like water, leaving me shivering. It crawls over my skin and under, into my core, until my stomach twists with nausea. I can't shake this. I can't even stand here any longer.

I feel like prey.

Turning slowly, I walk back to the house. It takes every ounce of self-control not to run because I can feel eyes watching me,

jennifer park

and they don't feel like the boy's. I've never felt that sick fear before without seeing its source. Not once. Terror rips through me to think I might have been walking toward the Sasquatch instead of the boy.

Too numb to care about what I'll say to Matt and Ben, I walk back into the house and up the stairs past the gaggle of women and close my bedroom door. I'm chilled. It's warm as summer in the house, but I feel like I've been left out in the cold for too long. I wrap up in a blanket and huddle down on my bed until the anxieties subside and the feeling of being stripped bare goes away.

It takes a long time, long enough to make me think I just avoided a trap.

"So." Ashley walks up to our side-by-side lockers, dragging me out of my thoughts. "I guess if you're still alive your dad hasn't found out about Saturday night?" Today the only bit of color she's wearing is the pink strip of hair that's hanging down from her ponytail. Everything else is black. Clearly the result of being in the company of Matt and Kelsey too long on Saturday night.

"For now, I guess. I really can't believe we lucked out and made it home without them finding out. I'm surprised I didn't just disappear in a pillar of flames the second I sat down in the pew yesterday. And speaking of flames, you know you look like a vampire, right?"

"I know, and you know whose blood I would like to drain right now?"

"I can imagine." I grin, spinning the combination on the locker with the precise ease of a junior but without the casual mastery of a senior. Matt can almost find the numbers without looking, but that's because he's requested the same locker every year of high school. I don't care where mine is, so long as it's not next to Coach Banks's room. It's too much trouble to go to the girls' bathroom every time I need to refresh my lip gloss or use some of Ashley's cover-up. No makeup is another of Dad's rules, and Coach Banks is in Dad's little flock of deacons, and therefore not to be trusted.

"Here." Ashley pops open a package of Reese's cups and hands me one. "I think it's good that you got out of the house. Even if it was unauthorized."

"You make it sound like I did something illegal."

"No, just to your dad. I mean, you can't spend your entire high school life locked inside your room reading books. Look at my mom; she's fine if I go out on a Saturday night."

"Yeah, but your mom's normal."

"I wouldn't go that far, but she's not a complete control freak like your dad. She knows she can either let me go or I'll just leave."

"I can't do that. Dad would never let me."

"Have you tried? Have you ever said, 'Hey, Dad, I'm nearly seventeen, and I'm going out with some friends'?"

"Easier said than done."

"Come on, Leah. There is a finite number of nights that I have left in me to spend sitting in your room on a weekend pretending we're *not* painting our nails. Pastor Roberts is going

86   *jennifer park*

to have to get a grip. I mean, we graduate in two years. What do you think will happen then?"

I don't give Ash an answer because I don't have one. But leaving is the last thing on my mind.

Ashley changes the subject. "Did Ben ever talk to you after church? Or maybe just stare intensely at you like he did at the party?"

"He came over yesterday so we could . . . hang out."

"Now see." Ashley slaps her hand on the locker door. "That would have been useful to say five minutes ago. 'Hey, Ashley, guess what? Ben came over to see me yesterday, which is kind of like a date with the boy I've been drooling over for years.' See? Easy. Now spill. Everything, right this second, and no, I don't care if we're going to be late." Ashley's stare pins me to the wall, but her eyes flash to the side. "Dammit. Speak of the devil and he shall appear."

"Please don't tell me he's walking over here." I slink down against the lockers.

"Why? What happened?" She grabs my arm.

"He sort of put his arm over my shoulder on the couch."

"And what did you do?"

"I went downstairs."

"And?"

"I didn't go back up."

Her eyes close in sympathy. "You should have called me."

"No privacy. Deacons' wives' meeting in the kitchen."

"Well, it's about time he noticed you. I mean, he's basically seen you grow up, you know? Maybe it's one of those romantic things where he suddenly looked up and saw you in a pool of light and rainbows and realized you've been here all along."

"Please."

"Or maybe he can't forget how good you looked in my bikini." We laugh as the warning bell rings. "And you're welcome for that, by the way."

"For what, the bikini? Not sure you did me any favors there, at least not with Dad."

"Yeah, heaven forbid you look like a normal teenager." She hands me her water bottle and rolls her eyes when I check for floaties. "You know it was probably Coach Banks that sent your dad that picture. No one else would have cared."

"I know, I've got that sparkling reputation to uphold."

Ashley pulls a book out of her locker. "I know, but if I was going to ruin my rep, it would almost be worth it to let Ben do it."

"Really?" I stare at her. "I thought you wanted my bro—"

"I will kill you. Right now. Lit-er-al-ly." Her hand stretches across my face but can't even begin to cover my grin.

"Payback for the bikini. Oh, and that mild headache I had yesterday. One would think you were almost trying to get me drunk."

"Oh, I was. I don't deny that at all. I just wish I would have succeeded." She closes her locker with a grin. "Imagine the fun we would've had. Hell, imagine the fun we could've had with Ben."

"Ashley!"

"Leaving, see you at lunch," she calls over her shoulder.

jennifer park

"See you." I shake my head, trying to find my math spiral.

"Leah," a deep voice says next to my ear.

Crap. I slam my locker door a little too loudly before turning around. "Ben."

He's wearing an eighties metal band T-shirt that is super faded and super tight. It is taking every freaking ounce of self-control I have not to stare at any part of him except his eyes. I am so glad Ashley left because I know she wouldn't be able to keep herself from making the most of this moment.

"Hey," he says slowly, like a question. And we both know what that question is.

Might as well get this over with. "So, I'm sorry I disappeared yesterday." My gaze drops to his neck, a fairly safe place to stare, since his dark eyes are making me nervous.

"No, don't worry about it. I get it."

"Get what?"

"It was stupid to just hang out and play games all day."

"But wasn't that why you were there?"

"No." He grins just a little bit, and I swear the hallway just heated up to ninety degrees. "I wanted to talk to you."

I find anywhere else to stare besides Ben.

"Look, I knew I was pushing it yesterday and it freaked you out, but you're Matt's little sister, and that kind of freaks me out too."

"It does? Then why even bother—"

"I like you," Ben admits, almost reluctantly, as he shuffles his feet and runs a hand through his hair. "And I know it's going to be weird for a while, but I want to get to know you as more than my best friend's sister." He rolls his eyes. "If your brother doesn't kill me first."

"What happened?"

"He jumped all over me after you left, asked what I did."

"What did you say?"

"That I think I scared you off."

"What did *he* say?" Because Matt hasn't said a word to me about any of this.

"He said not to even look at you again."

"You're kidding."

"Sort of. And he did leave a pretty good bruise." Ben laughs as he lifts up his shirt to reveal a fist-size purple mark on his chest. A perfect, chiseled chest above abs so cut that I could wash clothes on them.

And now I have to look away so I can speak. "That looks like it hurt."

"Nah, it was nothing. I take worse at practice. But did you at least have fun Saturday night?"

"Um, yes, I guess. It was a little different than what I expected."

He grins. "Too wild, or not enough?"

"Not enough, actually. I was told there would be chanting and bonfires and nudity, so I'm a little disappointed."

For a single moment, he's surprised, then his laughter fills the hallway. "Well, next time I'll make sure it meets your expectations." His eyes crinkle around the edges, and his tan skin is stretched tight to reveal a straight white smile, the kind that lights up his entire face. God, I wish he wasn't so pretty. "I guess we've got to get to class," he says.

jennifer park

"Yeah, I can't be late."

"I know, preacher's daughter."

"Don't." I pull away from him.

"Don't what?" Ben's smile falters.

"Is that all you think I am? A preacher's daughter?"

"I . . . I don't mean it like that."

"I know how you mean it, Ben. It's almost an insult, the way you say it. It's all anyone can see, Leah Roberts, the preacher's daughter, like that's all there is to me, all I'll ever be."

Ben stares, wide-eyed, and I know I've completely taken him by surprise again. I kind of feel guilty, jumping on him like that, but I can't take it anymore. It's not cute and flirty the way it used to be, when I basked in whatever attention he gave me.

"I'm sorry, Leah." Ben pulls himself together. "I didn't know it bothered you. I won't do it again. Promise." He smiles, and before I know it, he's taken my books and moved his hand to my back to guide me down the hall.

"Ben, what are you doing?"

"Nothing," he says lightly.

"Then why do you have my books?"

"Can't I be nice and hold your stuff?"

Words that would send me straight to hell cross my mind. The whole school will think we're dating by lunchtime. "No. No, I don't think so."

"You don't sound sure."

"I'm not, but I think I need my books back."

"Well, if you insist," he teases. "I don't need a matching set of bruises."

the shadows we know by heart

I hold my books up like a shield so I can't stare at his chest again, but Ben only laughs. "I'll see you around, Leah." He stands in the hallway, watching me leave, along with half the student body.

"Can't wait," I say numbly, walking into precalculus with a distinct feeling that I won't be paying attention to a single thing the teacher says. I take my seat, thinking of Ben, this sudden change in him and what it means. But it doesn't take long for Ben's face to change, for his dark eyes to fade as another takes his place, warm light and cool shadows surrounding eyes so green that every other color seems to pale in comparison. That is the image that stains my sight, like a watermark covering everything I see, refusing to let me go.

jennifer park

chapter ten

"How was your day?" Mom asks as I slide into the front seat after school.

"Fine."

Mom eyes me with vague suspicion. I should have practiced saying "fine" without the tone. "Want to talk about it?"

"Not really."

"Is it something your father is going to hear about?"

"No. It's just . . . Ben is, I don't know, talking to me. Like, more than usual."

She's quiet for a moment. "I thought you liked Ben?"

"I did. I do. It's just . . ."

"Complicated because he's Ben?" She smiles.

"Something like that." I smile back, grateful she's in a good mood. It's surprising, given the weekend we've had.

"But he is a nice boy. I wouldn't be against you having a boyfriend, you know."

"Like Dad's going to let me."

"Honestly? I think he'd be okay with Ben Hanson, if that's what you wanted."

"Only because Sheriff Hanson is his BFF."

"Is there another boy?"

Just a wild one who lives in the woods and won't leave my thoughts.
"No, there isn't."

"Then maybe you should think about it. You know Ben, probably better than most, as much as he's over here. I'll talk to your father if you want."

"I didn't know you two were talking." It slips out before I can get it back.

"Leah," she says, her voice heavy. "Your father and I do the best we can, but it's hard some days."

"Apparently it's hard all days, because I don't remember the last time the two of you smiled at each other." And down the rabbit hole we go.

"We smile," she argues. "We just . . ."

"Don't do it around us, I guess? The kids who would like to see you act like you can stand to be in the same room as each other."

"Leah, you don't understand—"

"What do I not understand? I've been here the past ten years just like you, so I'm pretty sure I understand."

Mom is silent, her narrowed eyes trained on the road. I stare out the window, wishing I could disappear, until she speaks again, saying something about an apple.

"What?" I must have misunderstood her. Surely she didn't say that.

"Why did you put an apple on your windowsill?"

I stare at her, uncomprehending, because my mind is trying to accept what she is saying. "Um, in my room?"

She frowns. "Outside of it. Sitting on the edge of the sill. I almost knocked it off the roof trying to get it."

jennifer park

My heart races as I try to logistically reason why an apple would be on my windowsill. There's only one, because the apple tree is too far from the house for it to have fallen there.

"Oh. I had my window open this morning and I guess I forgot about it when I closed it."

"Hmm, well, that's fine. I just thought I would ask since I didn't think you liked them."

"I eat them all the time," I say without hesitation.

She blinks. "Oh."

It was an easy lie, but my hands are shaking by the time we pull up into the driveway. I force myself to do all the normal things I do when we get home; grab a drink, get a snack, and put my backpack on the kitchen table.

"You have much work to do?" Mom asks, pulling out ingredients from the pantry.

"Not too much, just a short essay for English and some math. I'll be right back."

I swing open the door to my room, hoping to see the apple, but it's gone. I know she said it was there, but if I can't see it, I don't really believe it. Would the boy be so reckless as to leave an apple on my window in the middle of the day? Mom could have seen him, and then what?

But knowing him, even for so short a time, I know the last thing he would do is be seen.

I press my face to the glass, looking all around the roof. I'm not sure how he could have gotten up here, unless he climbed the magnolia and jumped. Which I'm sure he did, being raised by giant apes and all.

"I moved the apple."

I nearly jump out of my skin and pray she doesn't notice. "Yeah, I figured you did. Just checking." Acting casual about it is so hard. I grab a thesaurus from the stack on my desk. "Got it."

I sit on the edge of my chair in the kitchen, forcing myself to pick up a pencil and begin my essay. It's killing me. What if he's waiting for me? Did he see Mom take the apple instead of me? Mom pulls out pots and pans for supper, and judging from the amount of ingredients sitting on the counter, she's going to be here just as long as I will.

Her hand moves to the drawer with the flask, then stops. I watch as she closes it into a fist before reaching for a spoon instead.

It's going to be a long afternoon for both of us, then.

The sun is sinking into the treetops when I sprint across the backyard. Matt's in his room, Dad in his office, and Mom in her room.

I'm not where anyone thinks I am.

Mr. Watson has moved his cattle into the hay pasture for the winter, and they lift their heads, jaws working and ears flickering as I fly by. It feels reckless to be running out in the open like this, knowing what could be waiting in the woods, but I have to see if the boy's here. Smoke from Mr. Watson's burn pile drifts across the pasture, creating a thin layer of cloud above the grass. When I stop at the edge of the trees and look back, I can't see the house anymore.

jennifer park

A branch snaps.

Fear trickles in.

The sun has gone past the trees, casting the forest in deep shadow, and what light breaks through is blinding, so basically I have no idea what's standing ten feet from me.

One of the shadows moves. My eyes strain to see past the shadows, until red eyes peer back at me from the hazy forest.

I'm too terrified to turn my back for the second it would take to spin and run, and the harder I stare, the clearer the features become. It's the smaller one, the one I think of as Baby Bigfoot. It watches me from behind a tree, as still as a statue. It's so close I could toss an apple if I had one.

I've never been this close to one before, and I can't help but study it just as much as it's studying me. The face is a mixture of human and ape, with a protruding forehead, large eyes, and a flat, wide nose. It stands well over six feet tall, while the body is covered in coarse black hair, with a barrel-shaped chest and long limbs. I've seen silverback gorillas at the zoo, and they've got nothing on these creatures.

The light is fading around us. I test the waters, taking a small step backward. The creature tilts its head. I take another breath, another step, and it mirrors me, closing the space between us as it steps forward. This time, one breath, two steps.

It does the same.

We can't do this across the entire pasture. I'll die of a heart attack first. Or a cow stampede.

I take another step and my heel catches on the edge of the stump. I go down hard and something cracks in the general region of my tailbone. Air leaves my lungs in a whoosh as I scramble backward, desperate for oxygen just as much as escape.

The Sasquatch advances. Its steps are hesitant and wary, sliding forward with careful grace.

Suddenly it stops. The red sheen fades from its eyes as it steps out of the darkness. I blink enough tears away to realize it's not watching me anymore, but something behind me.

It's the boy, standing so close I could touch him.

Baby Bigfoot watches him as he moves in front of me, its wide, black eyes drifting from me to him and back. Then, as suddenly as it appeared, the creature backs away. Neither of us moves until it completely disappears into the shadows.

The boy spins around, and I feel like an idiot, as he must think I am. His eyes burn, the fury and panic in them speaking clearly. I took a dangerous chance.

"I wanted to see you." I hope I sound unapologetic, because I'm not sorry.

Whether he understands me or not, his eyes soften. He steps forward and holds out his hand.

I take it and lose my breath once again.

My fingers burn as sparks run across my skin. The boy flinches, but he doesn't let go as he pulls me up. An impatient huff echoes from the woods, but he pulls me closer, until our shoulders brush. Breathing is getting next to impossible.

A door slams in the distance. Mom calls my name, but neither of us moves.

"I have to go." The words sound hollow even as I speak

them. Leaving is the last thing I want to do, because the pull of this mystery overshadows the fear of what I'm risking.

His eyes are unreadable as his hand slides from mine, his fingers slowly brushing across my skin as he pushes me away from the trees. It's hard not to walk away backward. I trip twice because I can't stop turning around to see if he's still watching me.

He never moves.

Once I'm through the fading smoke that covers the pasture and out of his sight, I run to the house. Mom is standing in the doorway, a cup of tea in hand.

"I was worried about you."

"Oh, I went out to see the cows. Mr. Watson moved them over here today."

"You didn't go into the woods?" she asks doubtfully.

"Nope. Just cows." No eye contact. I walk right by her and up to my room. Inside, I flip on the light and hurry to the window. With my face against the glass, I strain my eyes until I can just make out the boy in the distance, barely visible through the smoke and fading light.

I wave, thinking he probably can't see me, then realize he's not alone as a shadow leaves the trees and joins him.

For a moment nothing happens. And then the two figures wave back.

I have a terrible feeling that "complicated" doesn't even begin to explain what I've gotten myself into.

chapter eleven

The sun is warm on our faces as Ashley and I jog around the track. Wind whips across the football field, promising a hint of cold soon to come.

Coach Perry blows the whistle and we slide into a walk along with the rest of the class. Kelsey is ahead of us, gasping with laughter as she protests whatever Lauren Ellis is teasing her about. "No, you're just making that up."

"I am not!" Lauren giggles. "Tell her, Abby."

"She's right," Abby Munroe says. "You have to keep all your trash and food locked away in your car, or hang it from a tree, because the animals will come get it. Do you really want a bear in your tent in the middle of the night?"

"Stop it. You two are just scaring me on purpose." Kelsey laughs.

"Oh, come on, Kelsey, it's just camping. It's not like some monster is going to come out of the woods and kill you," Lauren teases.

Gasps rise from those closest to them, and we all come to a collective halt. Every eye bounces between us and Lauren. Ashley bristles, her hands clenching into fists. I cross my arms and stare at my feet, wishing I was anywhere but here. It's been so long since anyone slipped up around us.

Lauren looks over her shoulder, eyes wide as saucers. "Oh God . . ."

Kelsey pales immediately. "Oh no. We didn't mean . . . I'm sorry, Leah, Ashley . . ." She turns away, embarrassed, as the rest of the girls stare like vultures waiting for the kill. I reach for Ashley's arm, wanting her not to make this into a thing.

She jerks away from my hand. "Why should you be sorry?" Ashley spits. "Your father, brother, and best friend's brother weren't killed by a psychopath in the woods. But don't worry, Kelsey, I'm sure the guy's long gone by now. Have fun camping this weekend." Ashley breaks into a run, shoving her way past them and sprinting ahead to where the coaches wait by the gate.

The shuffling of nervous feet echoes the pounding of my heart. Kelsey shakes her head, pleading with me, her eyes luminous and wet. "Leah, I am so sorry. We didn't realize what we were saying."

"I didn't mean anything, I swear," Lauren whispers. "I wasn't even thinking about that."

"Don't worry about it." I can't look at them anymore, can't stand the pity and the memories it's unearthing. "I've got to check on Ash." I navigate out of the group, jogging slowly down the track, as Ashley walks past the coaches toward the gym, kicking a garbage can by the bleacher stairs.

Knowing it won't do any good, I'm going after her. This is what I do. It doesn't matter that she'll be inconsolable and full of rage and not want anyone near her. I'm the only one who understands. By this time tomorrow, she'll be back to normal like nothing happened. Except that her hair might be green, or she'll get another piercing. Worst-case scenario, Lauren has a broken nose and Ashley spends the rest of the week at home.

I lock the feelings away before they carry me with them, like it's someone else whose seven-year-old brother was murdered. Someone else's best friend who lost her brother and father. Someone else's family was ripped apart and never put back together.

Just like that, I flip the switch.

The pain is gone, the memories banished, and my best friend is just having a bad day that I need to help her through.

By the time I get to the locker room, Ashley's already changed clothes. "Hey, Ash."

"I'm going home."

"What? Come on, Ash, they didn't mean anything. It was just an accident."

"It doesn't matter. The whole school will hear about it and I'll have to suffer through the looks. It's only two classes anyway." She shoulders her backpack and brushes past me to the door. "You seem to be fine with it, so you can stay and have the attention all to yourself."

"What? What does that mean?"

"You never react, Leah, not where others can see. It's like you don't want to let them see it get to you, and sometimes I wonder if you even feel it at all."

Her words are like a slap in the face. "Of course I feel it," I snap. "Just because I don't get angry and scream and cry and go home doesn't mean I don't feel anything. Samuel was my

jennifer park

brother. Matt's twin." The image of small white caskets in a church overrun with flowers pushes at the corner of my mind. I shove it back with the rest.

"I know who he was!" Ashley shrieks, tears pooling in her eyes. "But I can't shut it off like you. The first thing I think of every day is Reed, Dad, and Sam. *Every day.* For God's sake, Leah, do you know how many drawings I have saved of you putting Reed's name in little red crayon hearts?" Black tears streak down her face. I reach for a paper towel by the locker room sinks and hand it to her. "It was supposed to be us. We were supposed to be together forever," she whispers, staring through me.

I'm too busy fighting the memories to answer her. I can't break. Not here.

"Whatever. I'm going to the office. I'll see you later." She storms out, and I know I should follow her. I should apologize for being the way I am, the way I've made myself, but I can't. Instead I walk over to the bench and change clothes as the rest of the girls file into the locker room, hushed whispers echoing off the walls. I lean back against the wall, letting the voices wash over me as a single memory slips through.

Our dads are taking us camping. And because we do everything in fives, Ashley and I agreed to go, because we'd rather be scared out of our minds than ever admit that's why we wouldn't.

Boykin Springs is deep within the national forest and within walking distance to the abandoned town of Aldridge. They promised to take us, even though a town in the middle of the woods abandoned for nearly a century sounds about as scary as it gets. Dad brought a bottle of spray paint so we could write our names on the walls, said he and Mom did it years ago too. Sometimes I think he might not really be a preacher. But he's fun, and he's my dad, so it doesn't really matter to me.

We tumble out of the car in a flying mess of legs and arms and run across the clearing where the campsites have been marked by previous tenants, looking for the perfect spot. Dad and Mr. Hutton pop open the back of the Huttons' SUV and begin hauling out supplies to reach the tents packed beneath.

"We get this spot!" Sam yells, bouncing up and down on a flat area beneath a towering pine.

"Well, we get the spot next to Dad!" Ashley yells back, hovering by her father as he carries the tents out to the clearing.

I kick at the tall grass, head down, following a faint trail that goes around the perimeter and ends near a stack of firewood someone left behind. Reed is standing there, staring down at the pile. "Stop, Leah."

"What?" I ask, when I run into his outstretched hand.

"Do you see it?"

"See what?" Something in his voice sends fear scuttling across my nerves.

"There's a snake lying on the wood." He points to something small and brown curled among the haphazard logs, something I wouldn't have seen until it was too late. "Go get Dad."

He doesn't have to tell me twice. I sprint across the field, waiting until I'm far enough away before screaming, "Snake!"

Both of our dads come running, one with a shovel, the other

jennifer park

with a pistol. Ashley grabs my hand and we run after them. Mr. Hutton grabs Reed and pulls him out of the way before Dad points the pistol and fires. The gunshot echoes loudly; we flinch and cover our ears as another round goes off.

"Got it," Dad says, and the boys cheer. Mr. Hutton scoops the limp body of the copperhead up and carries it out into the woods before tossing it among the trees. "You kids need to watch where you're walking and playing, okay? We're a long way from the hospital out here."

Mr. Hutton walks back and claps Reed on the shoulder. "Good eye, son."

"Yeah, or Dad'll have to cut your arm and suck the poison out, right, Dad?" Matt says with a grin.

"That's gross, Matt," Ashley says.

"But that's how they did it in the old days."

"In the old days, you probably just died," Sam answers.

"All right, guys. If you want to see the ghost town today, we need to get set up. Come on." Dad waves us forward.

I catch up to Reed, just as he grabs one end of a cooler. "Thanks."

"For what?"

"I didn't see the snake."

"Oh, you're welcome." He smiles.

"You two are going to get married someday," Ashley says, swinging her skinny arms around the both of us.

"No, we're not," I say, embarrassed. Reed looks down at his feet, cheeks as red as mine.

"Yes, you are. That way you can always be my sister."

"Then you have to marry one of my brothers. It's only fair. Which one do you want?"

Ashley looks thoughtfully at Matt and Sam, arguing over the tent they're trying to put up. "I don't know. How about both?"

"Okay." I giggle and turn around to grab the other end of the cooler to help Reed.

"See?" Ashley says. "We'll be together forever."

There's an apple sitting on my windowsill when I get home. I lift the window and grab it just to make sure it's real.

My heart tumbles as my feet fly down the stairs. "Mom, I'll be outside. I need leaves for art class."

I don't elaborate and I don't stop to wait for her answer as I breeze through the kitchen. "Supper's in two hours," she calls out as the door closes behind me.

Amazingly enough, this time I'm not lying.

I comb the backyard in five minutes, ending up with a handful of leaves. I purposefully walk them to the back porch, placing them on the table where Mom can see me. I lay them out, studying them, or at least pretending to. Then I look over my shoulder at the woods.

Mom is watching me when I turn around. I point to my leaves, then at the forest, mouthing the words "I'll be back."

She lifts the kitchen window. "I need ten different leaves, Mom. It's for art tomorrow. Can I go to the woods? I'll stay at the edge, just until I can get what I need."

After a moment's hesitation she nods. "Your father will be here soon. I wouldn't be out there when he gets home."

"Okay, thanks." I wave and head for the forest. I just hope I remember to actually bring back leaves.

I rub my sweaty hands across my jeans and step quietly through the trees, the thick layers of pine needles softening my footsteps. Birds call above me, easing the apprehension that courses through my body. I'm not used to feeling this way in my woods.

Maybe it's because he's been raised by top-of-the-food-chain predators, because once again the boy appears behind me, only a whisper of movement announcing his presence. His gaze travels up and down, studying everything from the toes of my boots to the orange ponytail holder in my hair. My heart feels like it's going to burst under that insatiable heated gaze of his.

"Leah," he utters perfectly. I wonder how many times he's practiced saying it.

"Were you waiting for me?"

He nods.

Branches shift in the breeze, revealing a glimpse of the kitchen window through the leaves. I move farther into the shadows, and he follows. "I'm not supposed to be here, so I can't stay long—"

He reaches for my hand, long fingers encircling my wrist. "Ss . . . stay. Pl—please."

Great. Like I can say no to that. Sensations start simultaneously in my stomach and hand, where his calloused thumb is creating friction on my skin, spreading out like spiderwebs until they meet in the middle, dangerously close to my heart. "Okay."

Worry fades from his face, replaced by the faintest of smiles. "Okay." His voice is coarse like gravel as he glances up at me from beneath his long lashes.

His hand slides down my wrist, his fingers intertwine with mine, and again I get the feeling that we've been in this moment before, lifetimes before, and that this is completely rational when I know it's not. Heat races up my arm, my brain zings, and thoughts scatter. Sanity screams as it sinks beneath the tide of emotions that rushes in as it always does when I'm beneath the shade of these trees. Maybe fear should be one of them, but I'm not afraid. I know the safest place in the world is right next to this boy, and crazy or not, I will follow him.

"Where are we going?"

He points forward, but his eyes keep drifting my way, like he's seeing me for the first time, taking in every detail, and wants to miss nothing. It's both flattering and unnerving and has the effect of a drug, leaving me exhilarated and wanting more with every lingering glance.

We follow a game trail I'm familiar with, his bare feet stepping lightly on soft pine needles that coat the ground. Instead of feeling awkward, I fall into place beside him, because this forest is my home too.

"How long have you lived . . . here?" I wave to the trees.

After another long glance he shakes his head, and I'm not sure if he's saying he doesn't know or doesn't understand my question. Before I can ask anything else, he lets out a shrill whistle. Nothing answers, and for a moment I'm convinced nothing is there.

Until a large, black head peeks around a tree a few yards ahead of us.

I gasp, pulling away, and he reaches out a hand, his eyes pleading for me to stay. I grab a branch to steady myself. It's also thin enough that I could break it off and jab something with it if I had to.

The boy waits, standing halfway between me and the young Sasquatch. It's hiding like *I* might jump out and eat it or something, not the other way around. Slowly, Baby Bigfoot emerges from its hiding spot. While it looks at him with trust, it watches me with anything but.

He holds out his hand, and it, no . . . *she* . . . takes it. I can see her clearly now. The fur-covered breasts that swell from her chest were indistinguishable from so far away, and yesterday I was too scared to notice.

I'm trying to decide if that makes her less frightening when he motions to me.

Surely he's joking.

I shake my head, mutinous.

His eyes narrow.

More head shaking on my part.

He sighs heavily and walks straight for me. I stumble backward, turning to flee, but arms come swiftly around me.

Before I can scream, his hand covers my mouth. I consider biting it, but, really, *imagine* the germs. I jerk my head back and it connects with his face. He groans in pain, hand sliding away from my mouth to cover his nose. "Let me go!"

His arms tighten as he utters a single syllable. "No."

I slam my boot heel down hard, but what I thought was his foot is only a root. He exhales loudly, and I can almost hear him say "enough." He lifts me up like a baby and swings me around to face her. The boy carries me like I'm nothing, and just as quickly deposits me in front of her.

"Are you crazy?" I hiss, pressed against him, terrified. But he's not letting me go. I can't believe I'm doing this. I can't believe I don't have a choice.

I finally find the nerve to look up at her. Hyperventilating is still a possibility, but whatever. This may be as close as I ever get to one again.

My brain takes in the fur, the build, the smell, and says "animal." But I see her face, and all thoughts of a simple animal are dismissed. The liquid brown orbs see all of me, and I feel as if every thought, every secret, and every sin is now laid bare before her. And she's accepting of them as no human ever could be.

She looks me up and down, fascinated by the buttons on my shirt. Her body is motionless, but I'm surprised to see her chest heaving quickly and her nostrils flared.

She's frightened.

The boy loosens his grip, his arm sliding down my left one and taking my hand. His fingers wrap around mine and squeeze when he finds them shaking. Then he lifts our hands and holds them out.

She watches warily.

I'm about to throw up.

She huffs, frowns, and raises her hand reluctantly.

jennifer park

When her fingertips graze mine, I stop breathing, entranced by the sensation of her skin, soft like warm leather.

God knows how long we stand like that, but she must decide that I'm fairly harmless.

Her next step puts her right in front of me, and both hands go immediately into my hair. My ponytail snaps when her thick fingers encounter the elastic band, and she sniffs and huffs around in the tresses for longer than I think is necessary.

I am going to smell so bad when this is over with.

She touches my shirt, plays with the buttons, and sniffs the fabric. Her jagged fingernails scratch at the fabric of my jeans and catch in the snags. She circles me, touching and feeling as she goes. I'm pretty sure there isn't an inch of me she hasn't investigated.

I feel mildly violated.

When she's done, she stands in front of me again. She's waiting, but for what, I don't know. "What is she waiting for?"

He jerks his head in her direction.

"You're kidding?"

"No."

"Great." This should be interesting.

I study her, trying to figure out how to go about this. It feels wrong to pet her like a dog or any other animal, but my fingers itch to feel her. When the boy nudges me, I go for the only thing that seems appropriate.

I gently lay my palm against her cheek. Our eyes meet, hold, then hers droop and finally close. She sighs heavily as I slide my hand down the coarse, dark fur, and they open when my hand drops away.

That's all I can do. To do any more feels, I don't know, sacrilegious or something.

The boy steps forward, his chest brushing against my shoulder, and takes my hand again, and hers, and they sort of tangle together—black, white, and brown. My stomach does a strange, twisty flip, and all I can think of is how lucky I am to be here.

I should have realized by now all good things end.

"Leah!"

We freeze for the space of a second. It's surreal to hear another human voice in the silence of the forest, *my* forest, in the midst of such a moment.

Ben.

I can see his silhouette in the distance near the edge of the forest. How is he even here? Why? He calls my name again.

When I turn around, I'm alone. They're gone, the boy and the female Sasquatch, as if they were never here at all.

Maybe they weren't. Maybe I really am dreaming and none of this is real.

I glance down to see my shirt covered in black fur. I pluck a piece from the fabric and twist it in the sunlight.

As unhappy as I am that Ben ruined this, I can't help but smile as I walk to meet him.

jennifer park

chapter twelve

I snag a random handful of leaves as I go, hoping none of it is poison ivy.

Ben's eyes light up when he sees me, his hands in his pockets and a baseball cap on his head. "Hey, you. Your mom said you were out here but I really didn't believe her."

"Why?" I stop a few yards away.

"You know . . . Roberts' rules and all that."

"I needed leaves for art."

"Can I help?"

"I think I've got enough, but thanks. What are *you* doing here?"

Ben shrugs. "Dad needed to drop off some stuff to your dad, so I came with him."

"Oh. Is Dad back?" Because that is kind of important to know.

"No, not yet." He grins, eyes sparkling with humor. "I thought I'd check on you."

I try to read his face, to see what he's not telling me. "Why?"

Ben smiles wider, that cocky one that he wears so well. "Because if you're breaking the rules, I'd like to watch."

"It's a stupid rule."

He sobers. "Maybe. You're not afraid to be here?"

"I stopped being afraid a long time ago. It's just trees; there's nothing here."

"That's very adult of you."

"You should try it sometime."

"Ouch." Ben grabs his chest. "She has teeth and knows how to use them."

"Whatever." I punch his arm. "I'm not a child. Dad just can't see that. Living like it was yesterday is like breathing underwater. It's suffocating."

Ben kicks at a pinecone, his hands in his pockets. "I don't know, Leah. He's your dad. He's just worried and overprotective." He reaches out and touches my nose with a fingertip. "If you were mine, I'd be protective too."

"Well, I'm not yours." I swat his hand, but instead of dodging, he grabs it and links his fingers with mine.

"You could be, if you wanted to." Ben's eyes hold mine.

"What are you talking about?" I stall, heart in my throat.

"You know." Ben glances down at my lips as he pulls on my hand, until I have to take a step toward him or fall against him.

We're a breath apart, and instead of closing my eyes like any sane girl would do, I'm trying to rationalize this, because this is the boy I've wanted, who now wants me, and for some reason, it's not enough to make me surrender.

The rock comes so close to my face that I feel the wind from its wake. "Ow!" Ben yells. "What the hell?" He spins around until he picks up the rock where it fell by his shoe. It's barely more than a pebble, but there is a cut across his forehead, just above his eyebrow.

jennifer park

"Who . . . who threw this?" he calls into the forest.

Silence answers him.

I know the forest isn't empty. I hear the familiar knock on the tree, and another one answers it in the distance. They didn't leave me after all.

Ben lets out a string of expletives when he wipes blood from his face. At first I think he's angry, and it's not until his eyes flash to the trees behind me that I see the worry.

"Did you see that?" he asks.

"Yeah, but there's no one here, Ben. You don't think maybe a bird dropped it or something?" I glance up into the trees, mind scrambling for a believable explanation. "Look, a couple of squirrels are running around up there. That's probably where it came from."

Ben stares at me, that intense look from the other night at the party, like he's got something on his mind. "Yeah, maybe, if squirrels can throw a rock like Aaron Fletcher's fastball."

I stare, confused.

"You know, the boy on the freshman team," he clarifies.

"Come on." I strain to control the quiver of my voice. "I've got what I need and you definitely need a Band-Aid."

We're quiet as we walk across the pasture. Every few feet Ben glances over his shoulder, and I pretend not to notice.

In the kitchen, Mom's welcoming smile disappears when she sees Ben's face.

"What happened?" Ben's dad says, getting to his feet, his coffee cup rattling on the table.

"I was following Leah out of the woods, and a branch

snapped and hit me. It's nothing, really. Just a scratch." Ben plays it off so well, but I catch a glimpse of the look he gives his father, one of shock laced with fear. But it's not possible that Ben could suspect what really hit him. I think if he did, he wouldn't be so calm about it.

"Well, it looks like a little more than a scratch." Mom frowns. "Why don't you let me get you a bandage?"

"Thank you, Mrs. Roberts." Ben takes the chair she offers next to Sheriff Hanson.

I glance down at the leaves in my hands and walk out onto the back porch, laying them with the others. I can see Ben and his dad talking, leaning close with their heads together. Though the back door is open, I can't hear them.

"Leah, did you get what you need?" Mom asks when she returns to the kitchen.

"Yes."

"Well, come in and shut the door. Your father and Matt will be home soon. Sheriff, would you and Ben like to stay for supper?"

"Would it be too much trouble? I'd like to talk to Michael about a few things."

Mom smiles. "I'll set two extra places."

After Mom patches up Ben's cut, he follows me to the living room and takes the spot on the couch beside me, instead of the recliner he usually tries to snag from Matt. "Are you okay?" he asks, turning so that he faces me.

"Me? You're the one that got smacked by a ninja squirrel."

Ben laughs, then reaches for my hand. He turns it over,

tracing the lines of my palm, and it's so surreal that it's like watching someone else's hand and not mine. "I think we were having a conversation earlier."

"What?" I blink, trying to focus on his voice and not what his fingers are doing on my skin.

"About us? You and me."

"You and me," I repeat.

My hand disappears between both of his. "Leah."

"Yep?"

"You look a little freaked-out."

"You're holding my hand."

"Is that bad?" He rubs his thumb over my wrist like he knows exactly what it's doing to me.

"I'm not . . . Yes, it's freaking me out. You've been to my house a million times, and you always sit in *that* chair." I point to the recliner. "But now you're sitting here, holding my hand, and it's really hard to absorb right now."

Ben leans back with a grin. "You're not going to make this easy, are you?"

"You're Ben Hanson. I thought everything was easy for you."

"Not you."

"And is that bad?" I throw his question back at him.

"Not at all. The best things are the ones that are hard to get."

"You think I'm playing hard to get?"

"No. I think you are being you, and that's exactly what I want."

"Why now?" I ask the one thing I really need to know. "Two weeks ago, you didn't look twice."

Ben shakes his head. "It was the bikini."

I jerk my hand away and spring off the couch, but Ben is faster, already anticipating my reaction. "Come here." He bursts out laughing, grabbing me around the waist. "I'm just kidding with you, Leah Roberts." He pulls me back down with him, eyes dancing as mine burn. "I just wanted to see the look on your face."

I glare, embarrassed that I reacted the way he expected. "And are you happy now?"

"No, because I didn't answer your question. It was the other night at the party. I know it sounds cliché, but seeing you in the firelight was like seeing you for the first time. You were just you, without everything else that usually goes with you." He nods toward the kitchen, where we hear Mom and the sheriff greet Dad and Matt. "And I realized I didn't really know *you* at all. And I want to."

Ben's hands slide from my waist, and he pushes himself to the opposite end of the couch just before Matt walks in. "What are y'all doing?" he says, dropping his backpack to the floor.

"Just talking," Ben says easily, though his grin suggests we were conspiring against the world.

"Dude, what happened to your face?"

Dad walks in behind him as Paul Hanson explains what happened to Ben. My dad levels a cold stare on me, like it's all my fault. "Why were you out there?"

"Leaves. I needed them for art class."

"And you don't think we have enough around the house?" He gestures grandly with a sweep of his arm.

"I needed a lot. We don't have that many different trees around the house."

Dad sighs heavily. "It's as if these rules mean nothing to you."

My face burns as I stare at the ground. "It was just a few minutes. Mom said it was fine."

The look he turns on Mom is both bewildered and furious as heat rises in his face. "But *I* didn't. That's the point. You've gone too far, and you continue to do it over and over again."

"Michael," Mom warns.

"She could have gotten what she needs here, Nora. She needs to understand that what I say goes in this house."

Mom's eyebrows raise. "This is not your church. This is our house, and I let her go because I wanted to. She was in my sight the entire time, and Ben was with her."

Mom doesn't look at me, but I wonder who else besides us realizes she just flat-out lied.

Dad's face goes blank. "Paul, I believe you have something for me you wanted to discuss?"

"Well, Michael, it can wait . . ." He glances between me and Dad.

"No. No, we'll take a look now. Nora, call when supper's ready." Dad's voice is formal, as if he's addressing his congregation and not his family, and he didn't just embarrass me in front of Ben and his father.

I turn and head for the stairs, pretty sure I may never come down again, leaving Matt and Ben staring after me.

chapter thirteen

Mom picks me up from school the next day with red eyes and a coffee cup.

"Hey." I slide into the passenger seat and toss my bag in the back.

"How was your day?" She takes a sip before pulling out of the pickup lane.

"Fine."

"How was Ashley?" Mom spent a while with Ms. Hutton on the phone last night, since Ash is taking this harder than usual.

"She didn't come to school."

"Oh. I was wondering. I'll call her mom tonight and check on her again. Do you want to stop by?"

"No. I'll call her later. She was pretty worked up yesterday." And likely doesn't want to talk to me yet.

"Okay. How was Ben?"

"Fine." "Fine" meaning he walked me to my classes and sat with me at lunch like he belonged there.

She glances at me as the car pulls out onto the highway. "Should I ask any more questions, or is everything going to be *fine*?"

My smile is rueful at best. "Possibly."

Her smile fades when she looks at the clock on the dash. I

know what she's thinking. We have two hours to go home, eat supper, and get back in the car for Wednesday-night church. She takes another long sip of coffee. "I made meat loaf."

"Sounds good. Matt will be mad—you know it's his favorite."

"We'll save him some," she says. Matt usually rides home with Ben on Wednesdays after practice and then comes to church with him, since Dad is too busy to get him today.

"We could always skip." The words are out of my mouth before I can stop them.

Mom is silent for a moment. "He'd be mad."

"Do you care?" God, I need a filter for my mouth. What is wrong with me?

Part of me expects Mom to rail at me, stop the car, or do something dramatic, like when she's mad at Dad, but all she does is consider. "Maybe the meat loaf wasn't good after all."

It takes me a second to catch on, because I can't believe my mother is saying to lie about food poisoning to get out of church. Suggested by none other than the preacher's wife.

"On one condition." She glances at the clock again. The electric dial flashes "3:30" in glowing green. "I want to go to the deer blind."

"Um . . . what?"

"I want to see it."

"Oh." I stare at her, dumbfounded. "I don't . . ."

"You were there a few days ago. You should be able to drive us back, right?"

"Well, I guess?"

"That's the deal, deer blind or church. Take it or leave it."

the shadows we know by heart   121

I'm not sure what a heart attack feels like, but I think I'm having one. I want to put my hands over my ears and huddle down in the seat, except I'm driving and that might kill us. The Ranger is so loud, we might as well scream our presence to the forest.

I've almost hit a few trees because I can't stop looking around us. I thought about saying no, or chickening out, but this is just so out of Mom's character. My mother has never set foot in the woods. As far as I know, she couldn't care less about nature and trees; "hates it" could be a better description. Forget that we are breaking Cardinal Rules here. What could she possibly want to see the deer blind for?

The farther we drive, the less prepared I feel. We have nothing; no cell phone, no weapon, not even a big stick. Not that it would do us any good. I have no idea what we'll do if we get there and find we are not alone and under attack again.

When the deer blind finally comes into view, I spin around, facing the Ranger back the way we came before cutting the motor. If we have to run, I don't think I'll have the clarity of mind to put this thing in reverse. "Here we are."

Mom sits quietly for a moment, her eyes scanning the area around us. She pauses when her gaze lands on the rocks near the front wheel. They look out of place just lying there. Of course, that's because they were thrown here.

Mom looks away. "I've never been out here before."

"Why did you want to come now? You hate hunting, and you've never liked the woods."

jennifer park

"I used to."

I stare at her.

"Your father used to take me hunting when we were young. We probably spent half our lives in the woods when we were dating."

I don't speak, because I already know what changed, and why.

"You know I even killed a deer?"

"Really?" This time I can't hide the shock. I can't even picture the event in my mind.

"It's why . . ." But she shakes her head, pressing her lips between her teeth as she looks around. She slides out of the Ranger and walks up to one of the rocks. It's about the size of a baseball, one of the bigger ones. I can see a scrape of red paint across the top.

Mom nudges it with her toe, watching as it rolls a few inches across the flattened grass. She looks up and stares into the trees, wrapping her arms around her waist. "Were you scared?"

So I guess we're getting right to the point. "Yes," I answer, sliding out to join her. More so because I knew what was throwing the rocks.

"And you didn't see anything?"

"I'm not sure. I didn't see anyone throwing them."

She nods, silent for a moment. "But you saw something?"

Good grief, she's intuitive. "I wasn't near them when it happened. I was walking around over there." I point to where the boy and I were hiding from the Bigfoot. At least it's the truth, or most of it. I spot the shrubs where we crouched down out of sight, and I can almost feel his arms around me.

Spots of color burn their way onto my cheeks at the memory, but Mom's not watching me anymore. She's eyeing the ladder to the deer blind, and before I can blink, she's halfway there. I wish I knew what she was up to.

Mom scales the ladder and peers out from one of the windows. Matt and Dad got most of it cleaned out before we were *encouraged* to leave. Mom goes to each of the three square windows cut into the plywood, staring for several minutes out of each one. I'm tempted to ask her what she's looking for, but I'm afraid I'll sound like I know. Or maybe I've already messed up. Maybe I should have protested coming here in the first place because *supposedly* some crazy person in the woods threw rocks at us and it's not safe for either of us.

I'm not truly afraid like I should be. I wish I knew if Mom could see it. She's not exactly afraid either.

So many secrets.

I wonder what it feels like to have none.

The tree knock in the distance cuts that thought short. I force myself to look up casually at Mom, just to see if she noticed it. Her face is turned in the direction I think it came from, but her expression is blank. A few seconds later, another one answers it, this one even farther away.

I shuffle my feet around in the grass, feigning ignorance. I'm not sure how long I'll be able to stand here if the knocks get closer. Because acknowledging them will be acknowledging that something is *making* them. I saunter back to the Ranger, trying my best to look bored. When a third knock echoes closer, this time on the other side of the clearing, I reach down and pluck a strand of grass, seriously considering my options.

"We're going to have to leave soon if we want to beat the dark." It's not a lie. The sun has dipped far enough that we probably have thirty minutes left of visible sunlight.

Mom doesn't answer. She's staring in the direction of the last knock.

"I'd rather not hit a deer. I think one of the headlights is out, anyway." Hopefully we'll be back before I have to turn them on and reveal that they probably are, in fact, both working.

I slide into the cab as she turns away from the window and comes down the ladder. My hand is on the key, my foot tapping on the accelerator. She stops again at the base of the tree, hugging herself. When I hear a branch snap nearby, I crank the motor. We have to go or I'm afraid we're going to have another round of rock throwing. I put it in gear, and as Mom slides into the seat, I see a flash of dull silver peeking out from underneath the edge of her sweater.

I'm pretty sure my mother has a gun sticking out of her jeans.

If I wasn't already freaking out about our situation, that alone would have done it. Mom hates guns. Never touches them. And she's wearing it like it's a part of her, which worries me more than anything.

"Let's go," she says, snapping her seat belt and holding on to the side as I hit the gas. I drag my gaze away from her and focus on the trail, praying a rock doesn't come flying out of the shadows.

We're halfway home when I slam on the brakes.

A young pine tree, maybe twenty feet tall, is lying across the trail. It's not dead, but it will be. We sit for a moment, staring at it. There is no logical excuse for its presence here. At least, not for a human unfamiliar with monsters.

I cut the motor.

The forest is deathly silent as we get out of the Ranger. This close to twilight, the crickets should be going crazy by now, but the distant call of a hawk only serves to magnify the quiet.

It's obvious the tree has been pushed over. There's no clean cut that would have been made by a machine or tool, just jagged pieces of bark and wood ripped apart, like the open mouth of a sharp-toothed animal or one of those deep-sea fish that dangles a light in front of its mouth. Right now I kind of feel like Marlin and Dory, completely at the mercy of the environment and its hidden predators.

"We're going to have to move it," Mom says. "Unless you think we can drive through the trees."

"Trees are too dense." I glance around, trying to see a path that will get us through here without going too far away from the road. Hopefully that wasn't the objective of this "accident."

"Maybe a bear?" I say, trying to come up with something logical.

"Maybe. Come on, help me." Mom motions me to follow and we line up side by side along the trunk. As we begin pushing, the slender tree bends under our weight. Fighting for each tiny step, we win a few inches at a time, the wood snapping with each shove. The air smells like fresh-cut pine, and sap is working its way over my fingers and hands. The green needles are sticking through my clothes and piercing my skin where I have nothing to cover it. Mom keeps blowing needles out of her face, but neither of us stops.

"I think it's far enough," I mumble through the branch in my face. We've pushed it up until it's nearly parallel with the road, enough that I can drive over the end of it.

We turn in opposite directions, me to the left, and her to the right. I'm glad, because I know she would have seen him if she had turned my way. The urge to scream is so strong that I can't stop the moan that escapes me as I meet his stare not more than thirty feet away.

"Leah, are you okay?"

"Fine, just a leg cramp." I swallow over the fear in my throat as I walk the few steps to the driver's seat. The hardest thing is taking my eyes off him to face forward and start the Ranger. When the motor breaks the silence, I want to scream again. He's not even trying to hide. Just standing there, all eight feet of him, watching us.

The Ranger lifts as Mom's side goes up over the end of the tree. The limbs scratch and scrape the bottom, and a new fear envelops me when I think about what damage they're doing to the underside, potentially jarring something loose, and then we'd really be stuck here. With him.

When the last tire rolls off the tree and everything sounds normal again, I shudder in relief. This time I don't look back. I don't want to know how close we came. All I want is to get out of here.

That was our second warning. I don't know if we will get a third.

chapter fourteen

Ashley's bounced back from her depressive state with enough enthusiasm to make me wonder if she's on something. She's been off and on antidepressants for years, so it wouldn't be surprising. Or maybe it was the aspirin and the energy drink she chugged outside before school this morning.

"You want to go out tonight?" She spins around in her desk to smile at me, wearing a short white skirt and furry Uggs. No Goth girl today. The pink streak in her hair is now aqua, along with new blond highlights instead of the normal brown.

"It's Thursday."

"I know, but it'd be fun."

"It's *Thursday*."

"What is your point?" She taps yellow-and-blue nails on my desk.

"I have several. Homework. Dad. Grounded. Dad. Thursday. Dad."

"So sneak out."

"Are you listening to yourself?"

"I am, and I think you don't want to have any fun."

"You take anything else with those aspirin?"

Ashley's eyes widen, then narrow. "No. I had a headache."

"So completely normal *you* is asking me if I want to go out on a Thursday?"

"Fine. Forget it." She turns around.

"Do you want to talk about it?" I tug on her hair, feeling guilty that I'm not willing to risk my dad's anger to make her happy.

"There's nothing to talk about, obviously, since you haven't called me lately."

The truth of her words hits me. She's right, I haven't called her. I haven't even thought about it, and that's the worst part. I let my hand fall from her hair in shock, realizing how absolutely low I've sunk into my web of lies. I can't even remember to be there for my best friend when she has a breakdown. *Shit. So how do I say "Sorry, Ash, I forgot to call you and check on you because I've been hanging out with a Bigfoot and a wild boy"?* I don't. That's the center of my problems. I have no excuse because no one can know about the real one. "Ash, I'm sorry. I didn't think . . . I just didn't think. Stuff's been going on at home—"

"Like what?"

Don't lie. She can tell. "Mom and Dad have been acting weird, and Dad yelled at me in front of Ben and his dad . . . the usual."

"Weird how?"

So we're not dropping this conversation. "Mom wanted me to take her to the woods, to Dad's deer blind."

Ashley whirls around, ignoring the bell and the rise of students around us. "What? Why would she want to do that?" she says, alarmed.

"She just wanted to see it. I don't really know why."

Ashley stares through me, until we are the last ones in the classroom. At least her anger at me has faded, though.

"Come on, time for lunch."

"I'm not hungry." Her voice drops.

"Well, don't eat, just sit with me."

"I think I'm going to lie down in the nurse's office. My headache's back."

"Are you sure?" I grab her arm, not believing her.

"I'll see you this afternoon." She twists out of my grasp, gathers her things, and walks away.

Suddenly I'm not hungry either. I pass the cafeteria and head toward the library. I have questions that need answers.

Our only computer at home is in Dad's office, so there's no way I can search there for what I want to know. I enter my student ID, then google "missing persons." I don't type Zavalla, specifically, because I know what will show up. It will show up inevitably, I know, because they were missing for days before their bodies were found, but I'd like a few minutes before their faces appear.

Very few children are listed in the various articles that appear, and even fewer boys. I narrow it down by age; the boy can't be older than twenty or so. As expected, two familiar names pop up, and I skim right past them. But I'm left with nothing that helps. Dead end there.

I type in "Bigfoot." The results are endless. Pictures, videos, articles—I could sit here for days combing through the evidence, fakes, and theories. Undiscovered primate, wild humans, cavemen that survive in secret, aliens, descendants of Cain, and the list goes on and on, each theory more wild than the last. They can communicate telepathically, use mind control, make themselves invisible, teleport, have been seen many times surrounded by lights in the sky like alien reports.

It's just too much. All I can gather from all of this is that *no one* really knows what they are, and any time someone claims to have a body, it disappears, or it's proven to be a hoax. Hair samples are really from bears or contaminated with human DNA. The government knows, the military knows, and everything is covered up. Logging companies have contracts that specifically state that they are not allowed to mention Bigfoot or Sasquatch to anyone if they see them. You can find a footprint but not the animal that made it. Cell phone pictures and videos are distant and grainy at best or cut off too soon or catch the image too late.

But there are hundreds of eyewitness accounts. Thousands. So I am not alone, but after my encounter with Baby Bigfoot, I think I might be unique.

"Is Leah Roberts in here?"

I close out of the computer so fast my hands are shaking by the time Ben walks over to the computer tables. "Hey, Ben."

"Hey." He pulls out the chair next to me and sits, his knees on either side of mine. "I missed you at lunch. Where's Ashley?"

"Headache. She's in the nurse's office."

"What are you doing?" He peers at the screen, a suspicious edge to his voice.

"Nothing much," I say, trying not to sound defensive. "Just research for homework. The home computer's not always free."

the shadows we know by heart

Ben nods, accepting my answer. "I have a question for you."

"Okay."

"There's this thing, Saturday night? I was wondering if you'd want to go with me."

"You mean, like a date?"

"Yes, like a date." He reaches for my hand, sending warmth streaking through my body. His eyes hold mine, and once again I'm reminded that this is what I've wanted.

"What's the thing?"

"Another party, same crowd."

"I don't know if Dad will go for that."

"He won't be home, if that's what you're worried about."

"I'm not sure what bothers me more, that you're encouraging me to sneak out again or that you somehow know my parents' schedule before me."

"Dad said they've got plans that night. That's all I know."

"Well, if it's true, then I guess I can come. I'm sure Matt will want to go."

"Can I come pick you up?"

"That's a little pointless, don't you think? Matt can drive us there."

"It's not a problem. I want to." His hand slides up my arm, scattering my thoughts like a cue ball break shot on a pool table. But beneath the rush of feelings and warmth, there is a tiny thread of doubt. What does he want? I've always been in front of Ben, so why is he just now seeing me? This is almost too perfect to be real.

"Okay," I say, suppressing the hesitation because I'm interested to see where this is going.

jennifer park

"Great." He stands, pulling me up with him. "Come on, I'll walk you to class."

"I think you're acting like my boyfriend."

"I'm not acting."

"So what is this, then?"

"*This*"—Ben reaches down for my books—"is you and me. Us."

My brain is spinning, and I'm afraid I might say something stupid next. "What if I don't want *us*?" Too late.

Ben's smile turns mischievous and he drops our books on the table. He slides one arm around my waist, and the other takes my hand, like we're about to waltz, then pulls it down and tucks it behind my back. "I think you do, Leah Roberts."

"You seem to know everything."

"I know a lot about you. More than you think." He grins.

"Like what?" Again, the uncertainty blooms out of the mist of warmth spinning in my mind.

Ben hesitates, and I know whatever he's about to say, it's not what he's meaning. "That you're going close your eyes in three seconds, and then smile in seven."

I'm too distracted by what he's not telling me to notice that he's pulling my face toward his. "Are you about to kiss me?"

"Um, I was?"

"You're not sure?"

"I am sure. Are you?" he asks, our noses nearly touching.

"I don't—"

His lips silence mine. My body floods with sensation, but it's more about being kissed than who is kissing me. Of all the

the shadows we know by heart

times I'd imagined what this moment with Ben Hanson would be like, I never thought it would feel this . . . disillusioning.

After a few moments he pulls away, eyes warm as he runs a hand down my cheek, and I smile, because it's the only response he needs, and the only one I can manage.

"Ben kissed me in the library."

Ashley sits up so fast she nearly smacks me in the face. "Ohmygodareyoukiddingme?"

The nurse looks up from her desk with a frown.

"I'd be happy to give you details, unless you still have a head-ache?"

"I'm feeling better, Ms. Helen, I'll go back to class now!" Ashley hops off the bed, grabs her stuff, and literally drags me out of the office. "Spill. Now. Don't leave out a single detail. I demand it." She pulls me into an alcove and corners me.

"It's really your fault it happened."

"I'm so sorry I enabled the moment we've been dreaming of. You can buy me a thank-you gift later. Talk."

"He asked me out to a party Saturday night, said he's picking me up, and that's about it."

"Sure. That's it. Except for the kiss!"

"I told him he's acting like my boyfriend, and he said he's not acting." Ashley grabs my arms and sucks in a breath. "I told him I might not want him for a boyfriend, and then he kissed me."

"How was it?" She squeals quietly.

"Nice," I say, feeling like there's more to Ben's interest in me than simple chemistry. But maybe I'm just being skeptical.

jennifer park

Maybe it's all the years of being seen as a Roberts that has me uneasy about this.

"Nice? It's Ben Hanson; it sure as hell shoulda been better than *nice*."

It was nice. Perfect, as far as first kisses go. And as I tell Ashley everything I know she wants to hear, I try to remind myself that Ben is *the* guy, and he wants me. Just like I've always wanted. Maybe I should let the wariness go and just be happy, for once, that this is something I don't have to hide or lie about.

Except I'm not sure it's a place I truly want to be.

chapter fifteen

I've managed to beg out of going to Matt's football game today, claiming homework, but I'm really just not in the mood to sit for four hours in a crowd. Oddly enough, Mom and Dad both seem okay with the idea. Just the usual reminder from Dad about staying in the house, and *don't you dare* go into the woods just because Mom bent the rule and let me get leaves a few days ago.

I'm betting Mom didn't tell him about our adventure in the forest. Once we got home, she never said a word to me about it. Not the fallen tree or the wood knocks, almost like breaking Dad's rules was nothing to her and shouldn't be to me either. I'm still not over the fact that she had a gun. And Dad bought her lie of bad meat in the meat loaf that made us sick as easily as he buys mine. I guess that's where I get the gift.

I toss my history book on my bed and grab a pen from my desk. A flash of color outside catches my eye.

There's another apple sitting on my windowsill.

It takes only a few more seconds to see the shape melded with the upper reaches of the magnolia tree outside.

The boy's eyes glow in the late-afternoon sun as he watches me.

The car doors slam and his gaze follows Mom and Dad down the driveway before flashing back to me.

I hesitate. I shouldn't do this. I should want to be a normal girl with normal problems. I should be in that car going to watch my brother and sort-of boyfriend play. I shouldn't be hoping that a wild boy from the woods might magically appear in front of my window, just like I knew he would.

But life hasn't been normal in years.

I grab my hoodie off the back of my chair and he moves, swinging out of the branches like a primate.

When I fling the kitchen door open, he's standing there waiting for me, a single white flower in his hand. I stare, struck by the familiarity as a memory surfaces, of another boy, and another flower, over a decade ago. "Thank you." I take the delicate stem, absorbing the shock when our fingers brush. Light plays across his bare skin and makes his long brown hair glimmer. When he tilts his head, windswept strands fall across his face. My fingers flex at the thought of touching them, but that would require bravery. Standing here gaping is about all I'm good for at the moment. And there is *so much* to look at. He has like zero percent body fat. None. Flames race up my neck and cheeks, and his eyes narrow inquisitively.

Come on, you can do this. I step out carefully and close the door behind me. "Hi."

"Hi," he replies, and the ease with which he does leaves me smiling.

"Co—come?" He gestures to the trees.

"Come with you?"

The boy nods, long strands of hair falling across his face. His smile is soft, and when he holds out his hand, I don't hesitate.

Our fingers slide together, and his hand is warm as it envelops mine, like an extension of my own. Again, I'm reminded of the puzzle he fits; if only I had the rest of the pieces.

When he tugs, I go, without a second thought for anything I'm leaving behind, and we don't stop running until we reach the shelter of the forest. He leads me down the trail and deeper into the trees, where the birds call and deer scatter, and the only human sound is that of our breath and beating hearts. I'm not afraid of him, or of anything, here beneath the trees. But maybe I should be afraid for myself.

Because the thought of him letting go of my hand is enough to send waves of fear coursing through my body. So much so that I thread my fingers through his, and he tightens his grip on mine. The walls are falling down around me, pushing me closer to the human embodiment of everything I love about the forest. Leah is gone, and in her place is a girl walking with a boy who feels like home, the way it was before everything fell apart.

The sensation of a hungry blue jay among a flock of butterflies is swirling around in my chest. My body is shaking, and beads of sweat are forming along my neck and face. It feels like the flu but I'm afraid it's something much, much worse. Our shoulders brush, pinning our hands between our hips for a moment, and my heart drops. My arm burns from the contact, and all I want is more. My entire world revolves around our linked hands. I am exquisitely aware of every point of contact between us, every inch of his skin touching mine. My mind is consumed by it.

jennifer park

The boy pulls me deeper into our world, until the forest becomes clear of the thick underbrush. Ferns cover the ground between the tall pines, in their last days of life before the cold sets in.

When the knock sounds from only yards away, I jerk to a stop, unintentionally pulling my hand from his. Baby Bigfoot's face is peeking out from behind a tree, so still she could be a statue, just another part of the forest. Even from here, I can see her large eyes watching us. The boy walks back to me, a smile playing at his lips as he reaches for my hand. The fading sunlight catches his eyes, setting them alight with glowing flecks of golden amber scattered across the deep emerald shade. "S . . . safe."

"What?" I whisper.

His gaze is amused, but a determined focus is still there. "You—are . . . safe." He pulls our linked hands up and presses them to his chest.

"I believe you."

His smile fades and his eyes hold mine with an intensity that makes my heart do somersaults. The boy nods slowly, reaching out to brush a strand of hair away from my face once again. His fingers lightly graze my skin, tracing a path along my cheek and into my hair, running down the back of my ear before dropping away.

My entire body feels like it's wired for sound, and the slightest spark could make me come undone. When my brain recovers from the contact, I get the feeling the action is more about touching me than moving the hair.

"Okay, let's go." We walk hand in hand to meet her. As we get closer, she lifts her face and sniffs the air, slowly coming out from behind the tree. I wrap my hand around a bicep that could easily be steel instead of muscle, closing the narrow distance between our bodies. A sense of the surreal creeps over me as I watch him lift his hand to touch her outstretched one. She shuffles closer, her gaze wary, as if I'm the thing to be feared, and not her.

I hold out my hand, just like he did, and after a moment's hesitation she touches it. I can't stop the smile that splits my face, and she attempts to copy me, baring her teeth. I laugh as she huffs with excitement, overcome with something close to joy. It's been so long since I've felt it, and a sudden wave of emotion hits me, leaving tears in my eyes. I brush them away, and she watches intently.

The boy steps out of the way and eases his hand from mine when Baby Bigfoot starts to circle me, inspecting my clothes and sniffing my hair. This time I know what to expect, so her explorations aren't as unnerving. She pulls the apple from my hand and eats it without hesitation. When she's done, she steps back and looks at him, something unspoken passing between them.

"Now what?" I ask.

"F—fun."

"I'm sorry, did you just say 'fun'?"

The boy nods, and all I can think is that whatever happens next, no one will ever believe me.

jennifer park

chapter sixteen

"You're joking, right?" Two pairs of eyes whip my way, and the boy places a finger over his lips. Baby Bigfoot gives me a frown. "This is such a bad idea." That announcement earns a sigh from the giant creature next to me.

"You do see all the guns lying around, right?" A massive furry hand drapes itself across my face, pressing against my mouth. "Mmno." I pull her hand away, rubbing my sleeve over my lips. "When was the last time you washed your hands? Like ever?" I hiss.

We all three duck behind a fallen tree when the hunters in the clearing glance around. We are likely going to die out here, and I try not to think about the irony of it. Two men, both middle-aged, have set up a hunting camp. Two small tents sit near a dying fire, and they busy themselves with cleaning up their supper. They lock all their cooking supplies in the back of a pickup with two shiny new Yeti coolers sitting in the back of the bed. Again, more irony.

One man zips up the tents, while the other loads gear and guns onto the back of a four-wheeler. A few minutes later they leave, the rumble of the four-wheeler fading into the distance. We stay where we are until long after the sound fades. When Baby Bigfoot moves, the boy follows her. "What do you think you're doing?" I blurt out when they leave. "We can't just go into their camp!" Realizing they are completely ignoring me, I hurry after them.

The boy leaps in one smooth motion onto the back of the truck and flips open the Yeti lids like it's nothing new. Baby Bigfoot is playing with the zipper on a tent. The boy pulls out water bottles and a plastic bag of fruit. I peer inside, noting he doesn't touch anything that's been processed. Deli meat, cheese, bread, he leaves it all. When he moves to the next cooler, he whistles. Baby Bigfoot strides over and, with a gasp that screams of humanity, pulls a severed deer head from the cooler. She holds it by the horns, staring into the lifeless eyes of what was a very impressive buck. Her thick fingers trace lines down its face, almost petting, and then with a frightening growl she turns and walks toward the forest.

"Where's she going?"

He nods toward the trees, so I follow her. Not far from the camp, she kneels down and places the head beside her, carefully resting it against the trunk of a tree. Grabbing a fallen branch, she begins to dig into the soil at the base of the pine. Once the ground is broken up, she uses her hands, scooping great heaps of red dirt up from the ground to place in piles around her. I kneel beside her, put my hands in the hole, and dig. She watches me, but I focus on the dirt, pulling rocks and roots when I find them, until there is a hole the size of our kitchen stove between us. I'm pretty sure we just dug a grave.

Baby Bigfoot grunts, reaches for the head, and pauses. She stares at me, human eyes contemplative, and then hands me the remains. "You want me to do it?" Her gaze never wavers, so I place the buck's head down into the ground.

I know it's just a deer, like all the others Matt and Dad bring home every winter, but this feels different. She cares about this animal, even though it's dead, even though she can't bring it back. I blink furiously, knowing I'll just get dirt all over my face if I have to wipe away tears. After adjusting the antlers until they are completely beneath the surface, I glance up for approval. She answers by pushing a mound of dirt back into the hole. A few minutes later there is nothing to show we were even there. Pine straw covers our footprints, and any of the dirt we didn't get back into the hole.

Baby Bigfoot reaches up and pulls on a tree branch until it breaks enough that she can bend it. After tearing off the small branches at the end, she angles it down toward the ground and pushes the end into the dirt. She steps back, studying the formation, and then brushes off her hands.

She stares down at the ground, at the spot where the deer is buried, and against my better judgment, I take her hand. I squeeze, she squeezes back, and I follow her away from the grave. The tears come, and I wipe them away with the hem of my T-shirt.

The boy's got a pile of things ready to go, but Baby Bigfoot walks by him and heads for a tent. She slowly slides the zipper over, releasing the tent flap, and then crawls inside. The boy shakes his head and motions me in behind him. She's sitting in the middle of a sleeping bag, and I can't help but laugh out loud at the ridiculousness of it.

"I think we've probably broken a few laws by now, not that either of you care."

Baby Bigfoot reaches for a duffel bag tossed in the corner. She rustles around in it for a moment, then pulls out a pile of clothes. She gives them a sniff, then a toss, and reaches back in and produces a plastic bag of toiletries, including a hairbrush, a toothbrush, and toothpaste. The boy takes the tube of toothpaste out of the bag but shakes his head when she tries to hand him the toothbrush as well.

She stares at it, turning the orange-and-white handle over and over. Her fingernail flicks at the blue bristles, and then I know what is coming next.

She licks it.

I close my eyes in sympathy for the man who is going to wonder where his toothpaste went tonight. I should probably take the brush and toss it when she's not looking. I'd likely be doing him a favor.

Next she pulls out the hairbrush and hands it to me. "Thank you." I take it and put it in my lap, not sure what to do with it. She grunts expectantly, and I glance at the boy. "She wants me to brush my hair?"

He shakes his head.

"She wants me to brush . . . ?" I let the question hang.

He points to her.

"Seriously?" It's like this is turning into a damn slumber party and all I can think is, what if those men come back and find us here? I mean, they'll have a heart attack for sure, but they might shoot her before they do.

But what the hell.

I scoot forward and pretend this is nothing but normal and I'm not about to actually brush Baby Bigfoot's hair. I mean, she's all hair. Am I supposed to groom her like a dog?

I start with her head, pulling gently when I encounter a tangle and praying she's not tender-headed. The boy slips out of the tent and hurries across the camp into the other one. I continue to run the bristles through her black hair, hearing her breaths grow deep and heavy. "Hey, Bee, are you falling asleep?" The name feels right the second it rolls off my tongue. So much easier than saying Baby Bigfoot to myself all the time. At least one of them should have a name.

Her head droops as I continue long strokes down the back of her head and neck. She's nothing but hard, heavy muscle beneath all this hair. She could probably snap my neck with a finger. Just as I'm convinced I put her to sleep, the boy whistles and she's on her feet in an instant, crouched like a bear, making the tent seem even smaller. The sound of a motor whines in the distance. "Oh good, we're all going to die." Bee crawls through the opening and I follow, tucking the brush with her hair away in my back pocket. She joins the boy as they gather up their treasures: the food from the cooler, the toothpaste, and a book, and then we hurry out of the campsite. Once we are behind our fallen tree, he runs back with a pine tree branch and moves around the camp, sweeping up where our footprints leave evidence. He even stops to snag a tuft of Bee's hair from where it caught in the tent zipper.

By the time the hunters return, we are long gone.

the shadows we know by heart   *145*

We walk in silence, which gives me time to justify what I just did. We destroyed a hunting camp. We stole food and personal items. We buried a deer head. Bee *licked* a toothbrush. Basically we're forest pirates. That will look so good on my rap sheet when I'm sent to juvie.

"Do you two do that a lot?"

"Yes."

"And you've never gotten caught?"

He thinks for a moment, then shakes his head. "No."

"What do you do with all the stuff? Where do you keep it?"

He stops, and Bee does too. I can see Mr. Watson's pasture in the distance, hazy in the dusk of a setting sun. They've brought me home. I'm suddenly not ready to leave.

"I . . . sh-show you."

"Now? It's getting dark." I've been in the forest when it's dark plenty of times, but always on the other side of night, when the day is coming, not leaving. When he begins walking toward the house, I stop. "Wait. No, I want to go."

His eyebrows raise like he's questioning my judgment.

"Yes, I'm sure. Let's go."

Wood snaps behind us. Even as we turn around, the boy is already pushing me behind him, and a growl forms in Bee's throat.

The male is standing there, not ten feet from us. The setting sun reflects in his eyes, lighting them afire. Bee and the boy stand still as statues, waiting. A voice, soft and unintelligible, drifts on the wind. I don't realize it's coming from the male until Bee answers him. It's like listening to someone talk

jennifer park

from far away, hearing a voice, recognizing the rise and fall of cadence, but too far to make out any specific words.

They are talking to each other.

Bee goes quiet, looks at the boy, then me. Slowly she walks away, toward the male, and then into the woods beyond. But he stays, watching us still. With a reluctant set to his shoulders, the boy turns around.

"You . . . go home."

As much as I want to argue with him, plead with him to come with me, I don't. I'm too busy fighting the fear that threatens to swallow me every time I look into the male's eyes.

"When will I see you?"

He shakes his head. "Go."

"Tomorrow?"

"No." He turns me around and walks with me until we reach the pasture.

"When?" I'm on the verge of begging.

"Go."

"Dammit, is that all you can say to me? I don't want to go, and I don't want you to leave." The male roars from the forest, and I can't stop the tears that roll down my face as my body starts to shake. "I heard you!" I scream back, and the boy grabs me by the shoulders.

"Go, Leah." His eyes plead with me.

"Fine. Go back to your dad or whatever the hell he is. I'm gone." With every step I take away from him, my body screams at me to turn around, to run back and apologize, but I'm angry. The kind of stubborn anger that I know I'll regret later, but

I'm trying to make a stupid point that he probably doesn't even understand.

I know this is my fault, that I'm the one who has intruded on them, who sought the boy out. But being with him and Bee is unlike anything I've ever experienced. It's more than just being in my forest, and being myself, the one I keep hidden from the world. It's being that version of me and having someone else see it too and accept it without question.

More and more, it's getting harder to leave the trees and go back to the old me. I don't fit into her shell as easily as I used to. I don't like the weight of her baggage, the expectations placed on her, the rules she has to follow. The forest is freedom, and the boy is now part of that. But even he now comes with boundaries. I'm being forced away from him by something I can't argue with or lie my way around. Something I can't even speak to, much less reason with. My claim I think I have on this boy is so strong that I can't dispel the jealousy that wraps around me like a second skin.

Sharing him is not something I'm sure I'm willing to do anymore. And he's not even mine.

jennifer park

chapter seventeen

By Wednesday of the next week, I'm quite certain I'm getting exactly what I deserve for being a jerk to the boy. He hasn't come back.

"You're acting a little less Leah this week." Ashley pops a handful of Cheetos into her mouth and passes me the bag.

"I'm fine."

"But see, here's the thing. We're sitting here, watching football practice for the third day in a row, something neither of us cares about, because Ben asked you to, and you don't really seem excited about it."

"Well, like you said, it's football practice."

"Yes, but you're dating Ben Hanson and it's like you don't care."

"What do you mean?" I shove some Cheetos in my mouth and try really hard to look like I don't know what she's talking about.

"Come on, Leah. You've got the thing you've always wanted, at least since we've been in high school, and you don't seem happy about it. Ben is your boyfriend. You should be on cloud nine or something. Smile all the time. Or at least when he looks over here every five seconds. Coach has already yelled at him twice about it."

"It's just . . . different from how I imagined it."

Ashley turns on the bleachers to face me. "What? Disappointed he's not riding on a unicorn and surrounded by a choir of singing cherubs? Leah. He hangs all over you, drools when you speak, and can't wipe that stupid, gorgeous grin off his face whenever he looks at you. What more could you ask for?"

"Nothing. Ben's great. And you're right, he is the perfect boyfriend." I paste the happiest smile I can manage on my face, wanting nothing more than to tell my best friend what's really wrong, knowing I can't because a dark voice in the back of my mind taunts that she wouldn't understand why I've kept it from her.

Ashley stares way too long. "Something's wrong with you."

"Nope."

"I'm going to find out what it is."

"No, you're not, because there's nothing wrong."

"You've never been able to pull a lie past me so don't start now." A horn honks from the parking lot, pulling her attention away. "Mom's here. I'll call you tonight so we can finish this mind-numbing algebra homework."

"See you later." I wave, ignoring the knowing stare she gives me as she stomps down the bleachers in a short skirt, combat boots, and pigtails.

The algebra homework in my spiral is mostly Ashley's work. I copied, and I don't really care if I get the concept. I tell myself I'm overthinking this, and that he's not mad at me or trying to punish me for being mean. I've punished myself enough. Especially since the forest has been silent since they left. No knocks, howls,

jennifer park

screams, or any apples left at my window. Yesterday a herd of deer were eating the apples on the stump that I left over the weekend as a peace offering. It's been years since that has happened.

He's gone.

I pushed him away. Got too close. Went too far. The reasons go on, but the conclusion is the same. He's gone, and my fear is that he won't ever come back.

And that's not the worst of it.

The night he left, I was sifting through my bookshelf, searching for the devotional someone gave me years ago that I never use, except to press flowers in. As I was flipping through, looking for a place to press the white flower he gave me only hours before, I came across a forgotten memory.

Another white flower.

This one given to me by Reed, during that last camping trip, right after he saved me from the snake. Ashley and I were collecting them to make necklaces, and Reed brought me the biggest he could find.

I never used it. I saved it, tucking it safely away until I could get it home and press it within a book.

And as I was looking at them both, side by side, new and old, something forbidden entered my mind. A tiny thread of suspicion, something so devastating that if I followed it to its source, it might shatter my world and that of those closest to me. But it's not possible. It can't be. That hope died ten years ago.

But what if? *What if?* The words whisper to me, even now. And every time, my heart stops.

A shrill whistle signals the end of practice, and Ben jogs over to where I sit. "Hey, you. Have fun?" He leaps over the low cyclone fence separating the bleachers from the track like it's nothing. Ben charges up the steps, pulls off his helmet, kisses me on the cheek, and kneels down on the step below me. I'm not used to this kind of attention. It makes me uncomfortable, but not enough to tell him. Besides, to everyone else, there is no reason why this relationship shouldn't exist.

"Um, yeah. Got most of my homework done." I pat the spiral, feeling a little guilty.

"You don't like football, do you?" He grins.

"Don't say it out loud," I whisper. "You know it's a crime."

"Especially in Texas," Ben whispers back. "It's like one of the Commandments."

I can't help but smile at how easy we are together, wishing it was enough, that it was still what I truly wanted. "You looked good, though. Why was the coach yelling at you?"

Ben blushes. "I missed a pass from Matt."

"That doesn't happen often," I say, baiting him.

"Well, this girl I really like was laughing to her best friend, and it was distracting."

"Well, maybe I should stay away from practice. Wouldn't want you getting in trouble over me."

Ben grabs my hand and pulls me down beside him. "Don't you dare. I like you here. Especially right here," he says in my ear, wrapping his arms around me.

"Matt's watching us."

Ben looks up at the emptying field. "He's probably waiting to chew me out about that pass, too."

"Then I guess you'd better go."

"Will you miss me?"

"Maybe."

"What? Come here." He turns my chin up and kisses me, lips tasting like salt. This should be turning my brain into mush, but all I can do is try to rationalize why I'm not melting down to my toes. After a long minute, Ben pulls away, tucking my hair behind my ear. "Now will you miss me?"

"Definitely not."

"Okay, we'll continue this conversation later." Ben grabs his helmet, then pauses. "You haven't been back into the woods, have you?"

His question takes me by surprise, and he notices my hesitation as I try to process why he would even ask me. "Um. No? Why do you ask?"

"Just some weird things happening out there. Some campers reported their stuff missing last weekend, and Dad was talking about it. Just, you know, want you to be careful."

"It was probably those rabid ninja squirrels. Why stop at throwing rocks when you can raid a campsite, right?" I say, trying my best to sound like he's worrying for nothing.

Something about his smile seems forced. The next second, it's as natural as can be. "Oh, hey, we're still going to the thing this weekend, right?"

Surely he's not talking about—

"The homecoming dance, remember?" he prods.

No. "Oh, yes, I think?"

"Did you forget?"

the shadows we know by heart

"Did you ask me?" Because I have no memory of it.

"Monday. At lunch." Ben stares. "You did say yes."

"Right. I did. Yeah, we're going."

"Just checking. You didn't mention it today." His eyes narrow, like he's wondering what's going on in my mind. I've noticed it's a look he wears when he thinks I'm not looking.

"Sorry. I'm just distracted." But I did agree to go. I've been so caught up in my other life, plus the memorial at church is next week as well. Still, I hate formal dances, so what was I thinking?

"Oh. Yeah. Sorry." His sympathetic look nails it. The anniversary, the one day of the year we publicly acknowledge the loss, ripping the wounds open again, giving ourselves another twelve months to reheal before doing it all over again. I love my life.

"Ben!" Matt yells.

"I'll see you later," I say.

Ben waves, walking slowly backward down the steps, watching me until I grin. "There's that smile." He vaults over the fence again and jogs back to the field house. Matt punches him in the arm and gestures wildly, but whether he's talking about me or the practice, I can't say.

Ben laughs all the way across the field.

Whatever I may have thought about him in the past, regardless of my crush, Ben has been almost perfect. The initial doubt I had about his intentions has faded, though sometimes he still looks at me like he knows something I don't. Still, that cocky, smug boy who used to crash on my couch and toss popcorn at me and call me "little Leah" has disappeared.

jennifer park

In his place is a real, decent guy who looks at me with something that verges on adoration.

It scares the hell out of me because I'm responsible for that, and I never meant for it to happen in the first place. A month ago, sure. But now? No, everything has changed. I've changed. I know I'm probably leading Ben on at this point, but if I break it off, I can't give a legitimate excuse for why. It will draw too much attention, and I'm afraid someone will figure out my secret. Ashley would never let this go, and eventually I'd crack. This double life will eventually catch up with me, likely with disastrous consequences.

But even knowing that, knowing what I've initiated, both in the forest and out, all I want is to see the boy again, apologize for what I said, and go back to where we were.

And if that's out of my reach, then I'll risk anything to get it back, no matter the cost.

chapter eighteen

A week has passed since I've seen his face. It keeps me awake at night, leaves me restless and drifting during the day. Yesterday I finally used the memorial excuse as an explanation for my behavior. Ben was understanding, even brought me flowers at school this morning.

But I don't know what I'm doing anymore. Everything feels wrong, like I've gone too far with the lies, and I'll never get out of the pit I've dug.

It's nearly eleven when my family gets home from Matt's game. I pleaded sick, desperate to just be alone for a while, so anxious I haven't been able to do anything but sit at my desk and stare at the window. Mom and Dad's voices reach up through the floorboards from their room, then fade into silence. I can hear the click of Matt opening the refrigerator door. I should go down and ask him about the game, but I can't move from this spot. From my desk I can watch the forest, the field, and the apple tree as the moon fades in and out of the clouds, losing track of time. Matt eventually goes into his room, where the sound of Halo reaches my room through two closed doors.

At midnight, when my eyes are beginning to burn from staring, shadows move near the house. I jump up, thinking it's the boy, but it's the last thing I expect. Mom and Dad walk into the blackness, toss some bags into the trunk of the car, and leave, turning on the headlights only when they near the trees at the end of the driveway.

I don't even know how to deal with what I just witnessed. They left, in the middle of the night, without a word to us. As if they didn't want to be seen. I'm trying to decide whether to tell Matt when another shadow moves outside, slipping over the fence.

It's him. *It's him.*

Still dressed, I tiptoe down the stairs and hurry out the back door, barely slowing to close it.

When I leap off the porch, he's running as fast as I am.

I literally throw myself into his embrace. I don't care about anything else when his arms wrap around me like they were made to fit there. My face is buried in his hair, pressed against his shoulder, and nothing in the world feels as right as this madness.

"I thought you weren't coming back," I mumble against his skin. "I'm so sorry for what I said. It was stupid, and my fault, and I'm just so *sorry*."

He holds me at arm's length. "Leah?"

"Yeah?"

"You thought I wouldn't come back?"

"Yes. Because I said— Wait. Did you just . . . You just asked me a question. In a complete sentence!" I slap a hand over my mouth and glance at the house in elated horror.

When I look back, he's grinning. "You . . . want to get out of here?"

the shadows we know by heart

All I can do is nod in shock. He takes my hand and we run across the field, until a shadow greets us at the edge of the trees. "Bee." I reach out to touch her palm with mine, her dark eyes reflecting starlight.

She drops her hand and walks away into the night. He tugs my hand to follow, but I stop. "Where have you been?"

"Away. Not safe."

"What do you mean? Safe from whom?"

He stares, like he knows the answer but isn't going to tell me.

"Okay. Why can you speak? I mean, you know, better. What happened?"

His shoulders relax. "I practiced."

"You practiced," I repeat. "With who?"

He points to Bee's fading silhouette.

"She . . . Please tell me she didn't actually talk back?"

"She listened."

"I don't understand. If you didn't know how to talk . . . ?"

"The words were always in my head. I can read, and Bee and I take books when we find them. It's just . . . saying them out loud took practice. It's been so long, and I wanted to get it right."

"So if you remember the words, do you remember who you are?" *Because I'm afraid I do, even though it's not possible.*

He's quiet for a moment, his face hidden in shadows. "Some things are gone."

"But someone must have said the words to you. Your parents?"

"I remember nothing but them." He nods in the direction Bee went. "They are my family." Disappointment floods me,

jennifer park

cutting deep, even though I know what I hope isn't conceivable.

"Your family kind of scares the life out of me sometimes."

"He won't hurt you."

"Then why does he keep warning me away?"

"He's very protective. They work hard not to be seen."

I guess Dad isn't the only overprotective father around here. And neither of them wants me in the woods, another thing they have in common. I can't blame the Sasquatch for wanting to protect his family; I just wish he could get his point across without frightening me to death. "But I've seen them many times. For years."

"Because you were meant to." He laughs softly and pulls me into the shadows. Home is now gone from my mind. I'm alive and free, just another piece of the forest.

It's strange that in this moment, one of Dad's sermons comes back to me. It was one of those times where I drifted in and out, catching the barest phrase here and there in my boredom and impatient desire for the clock to strike twelve.

The concept has never really had this sort of clarity until now. Here in the pitch black of night, I should be afraid. But even knowing I am now far from home or anything familiar, the words of my father hit me from out of nowhere, and they are more comforting than I ever thought they would be.

I can only try to imagine Dad's face if I told him where I was when I finally grasped one of his most valuable concepts, something I'm not even sure he gets, or at least he hasn't in a long time. Because as I hold the boy's hand, following the footsteps of a Bigfoot as she leads the way through the trees, this is the phrase that keeps running through my mind.

This is how it must feel to walk by faith.

To walk *blindly* by faith, because there is literally no other description for what I am doing. I mean, I could walk into a tree in two seconds and not even realize it. I can't see *anything*.

But I trust this boy, and, Heaven help me, I think I trust this creature that leads us deeper into the woods.

At some point I simply close my eyes, letting the feeling of complete and utter surrender wash over me. With the loss of my sight, every other sense is on high alert. The wind lifts my hair as it drifts through the pines, carrying the faint scent of rain and earth, and the heavier scent of animal. The ground is soft beneath my boots, an endless path of pine needles and ferns. An owl calls from somewhere ahead, answered by a distant pack of coyotes, their cries sending chills down my arms. A symphony of crickets and frogs rises up around us, so loud that I want to cover my ears, and the only answer must be water.

Just as I hear the steady drip, confirming my suspicions, we stop.

For a moment nothing happens, until I realize my eyes are still closed. I open them and am greeted by two sets of eyes peering at me, one filled with amusement, the other curious. We are in a narrow clearing, and above, millions of stars shine down on us.

I glance past Bee to see a darkness behind her, a black space in the otherwise moonlit forest. "What is that?"

jennifer park

"A cave," he whispers.

"There aren't snakes down there?"

"Nothing, I promise." We begin to walk down a rocky slope. "Careful, the rocks," he says as he navigates it with ease, but I can barely stand, even holding on to him. Baby Bigfoot just clomps down the slope like it's a casual stroll, her massive shape making it to the bottom before I'm even halfway down.

The faint quarter moon catches her eyes as she watches my progress. When she makes a huffing sound, I swear it sounds impatient.

"I'm doing the best I can here." I slip, going down on one knee and both hands as rocks scatter around me. Before I can scramble to my feet, hands wrap around my waist. I am lifted to my feet. And then off my feet.

"Hey! What are you—" My words are cut short when I am slung very unceremoniously over Bee's shoulder. She takes two leaping strides, my nose banging into her shoulder with each one, and then reaches the bottom.

I mumble a grudging "thank you" when I am on my own feet again, smelling less than desirable now. We are standing in something that looks more like a grotto than a full-blown cave. A small, glass-like pool sits in the center of the rocky hollow, reflecting the stars above like a mirror. Along the opposite side, a deep depression in the rock is protected by a low overhang, dripping with moss and vines. "What is this place?"

"Sometimes home. She likes the water." The boy leads me carefully around the pool until we reach the shallow cave. The lichen and moss are thick along the ground and create a sort of hollowed-out bed. One big enough for a couple of Bigfoot. Bee sits down, patting the ground around her until she shifts into a comfortable position, and then leans back against the wall. Her hand reaches out and pats the ground next to her. I sit, and the boy follows, placing himself just far enough away so that we don't touch. Bee scooches closer, taking my hand and holding it loosely.

I am going to need a serious shower by the time I get home. Bee's intelligence is obvious, and I can't find the line that says, *This is an animal, not a person.* She has a way of expressing her feelings that blows my mind. Emotions move across her face as easily as they do his. Her dad may scare the life out of me, but they are far from common animals. The question is, what exactly are they?

"This is unreal," I murmur. Bee stares out at the still, black water, her gaze unblinking. Suddenly she releases my hand with a grunt of excitement, leans forward, and points. The reflection of a plane crosses the pool, the blinking red light signaling its course across the sky. When it leaves, Bee leans back, her gaze steady again. A few minutes later, when another plane appears, she does the same thing.

"How do you communicate with her?"

"We just . . . know each other. I don't need to talk to her to tell her what I'm thinking."

"And do you know what she's thinking?"

"She's usually hungry, so it's easy." The grin in his voice is obvious.

We watch her for a while, and I use the time to get my

jennifer park

thoughts together. I've got fifty thousand things I want to ask him, but I don't want to overload him with questions either. I'm still in disbelief that he's talking so easily now. He must have talked Bee's head off to be so eloquent in such a short time. How can he not recall learning the words or remember the voice that first said those words to him?

"You've never talked to anyone else? No one other than me?"

"No."

"Have you ever wanted to? You've seen campers and hunters before. You've never wanted to go up to them and ask for help?"

He sighs. "I never wanted to be a part of what they were. The forest is my home. She is my family." He gives me a sad smile, and I wonder if it's painful not to remember what made you human.

A satellite comes into view, the tiny star tracking its way across the reflection of the pool. "Look, Bee." I nudge her and point to the light moving across the water. "See the satellite?" She leans forward, a picture of complete curiosity, eyes steadily following it. Even after it disappears from view, she stays like that, waiting for the next one.

"Why me?" I ask, as if it will answer everything.

For a while he's silent, staring at the mirrored sky with Bee. "You were the first one I wanted to see . . . *me*."

"I definitely see you." I glance down at his bare chest and realize what I said. I turn away, feeling heat flood my face, my heart rate accelerating at the increasing tension between us. I force my brain to think, to find some other question to ask him that might ease this tension building inside me. Unable to stand the feeling of him watching me any longer, I glance over to find him grinning.

"What?" I say, unable to stop the embarrassed grin from spreading across my face.

"You," he says, his tone suggesting he understands why I'm blushing.

"What do you mean?" I run my hands over my face, hiding.

"You say what you think." He moves closer.

"I shouldn't. I usually have a filter, or I try to. But . . . it's like you said. This forest is my home too. I don't have to pretend here. It's always been that way. This has always been the place I can run to, to escape my family and all the expectations that go with my life."

"Why do you want to escape?"

I stare at him, wondering if I spoke the words, what would happen. What if I told him the story? What if I told him that I'm afraid I know his name and that to speak it out loud would be devastating? Because if I'm wrong, it will tear me apart, and if I'm right . . . If I'm right, I don't know what that means. The consequences are too vast to comprehend.

"I feel like this is spinning out of control. There is so much at stake. I shouldn't even be here." It's only when I see his face that I realize I spoke the words out loud.

His eyes are locked on my lips, and a rapid progression of emotions moves across his face. It's the vulnerability that tugs at me, makes me curl my hands into fists to fight the urge to touch him. "You don't want to be here?"

The look he gives me is so unsure that I grab his hands and

jennifer park

turn toward him, my knees pressed against his stomach. "That's the whole problem. There is nowhere else I'd rather be than here. I think about nothing else when I'm with you, and nothing but you when I'm not. There are things I can't ignore in my other life, but I swear it can all go to hell as long as I can be with you. And that's not normal, right? It's crazy. I'm crazy. And you're . . . just . . . so damn beautiful." Once again I cover my face in horror, completely mortified that I said that out loud. "I've got to stop talking," I groan.

"Leah," he whispers, pulling at my hands.

"No," I mumble. "I'm embarrassed."

"Of what?" I can hear the smile in his voice and I press my hands harder.

"What I just said. I'm so stupid."

"Look at me, Leah."

Finally I do, because he says my name like no one else. Like a gift, something precious. All traces of humor are gone from his chiseled face. He reaches out a hand to skim my cheek, his fingers sliding down my skin to rest on my collarbone. I can feel my pulse beating an erratic rhythm beneath his fingertips, and he slides one finger along the ridge of the bone.

One second I feel like I could melt into a puddle and join the pool below, then next I'm frozen, my body humming with energy, hands shaking, and head spinning. When he tilts his head, watching me in that curious way of his, I don't stop myself. I reach out to move the hair that falls across his forehead. His eyes close, and he exhales like he's been holding his breath forever, his body as still as the black water beside us.

the shadows we know by heart

The boy *is* beautiful. The layers of sun, wind, earth, and rain that he wears only enhance his features, rather than mask them. Every wisp of scent I catch of him only draws me closer, a magnetism I can't escape. He is the forest embodied; mist and soil, trees and air, all combined into this heady scent that is distinctly him.

"I think"—he turns my hand over, running a calloused finger across my palm—"you're anything but crazy."

I watch in breathless fascination as he slowly traces each of my fingers with his own, leaving trails of fire in his wake, making me believe it would be a relief to combust into flames and simply cease to exist.

The only thing he's touching is my hand, and I feel like I could die from the sensation. What would happen if I felt like that everywhere? What if he *kissed* me? My heart stutters, sending a wave of something close to nausea through me. It's like the drop that waits at the top of a roller coaster, the unbearable rush that is unavoidable, but you know it's coming and there's nothing you can do about it.

I feel like I'm dropping, but the fall is endless.

His eyes are black in the darkness, and rivers of chills course over my skin. The corner of his mouth lifts, and he looks positively wicked. He brings my hand to his mouth, brushing his lips across my achingly sensitive palm, and then to each fingertip, his touch barely more than the brush of a butterfly's wing. I suck in a ragged breath and press my lips together.

God, just kill me now because I won't survive this.

"Leah . . ." he whispers. I can see his hesitation and a sudden flash of uncertainty that melts what is left of my shattered heart. "You . . . You're brighter than the sun, darker than the night, and more beautiful than anything I've ever seen."

"That's . . . that's really good," I say breathlessly.

"I read a book or two." He grins. "And I might have practiced that line with Bee."

"I'm sure she appreciated it."

"She probably thought I was crazy."

All I can do is stare. This is bad. This is so bad in so many ways, and each one has the potential to end terribly, leaving me broken and ruined.

He wraps his hands around mine. "Or maybe we're both crazy."

What would my life be like if this were what I chose? I would be Jane, living with Tarzan and the apes. I would fall into this world and happily never return, if it meant being with him forever. But the reality of that is unlikely, no matter how much I wish it. And if Tarzan came out of the jungle to follow Jane into civilization, would we still be the same? And would he be happy with his choice?

Feeling a sense of bravery I wish I'd been born with, I lean forward, meeting him halfway, shoving all my doubts and fears deep inside and locking them away. The fire ignites in his eyes, reflecting the stars above, and he reaches out and wraps his hand around my neck, his fingers threading through my hair as he pulls me in. "Crazy could be a good thing," I whisper.

He presses his forehead gently to mine and I close my eyes, submitting to the overwhelming rush of emotions that threatens to wash away all sense of reason. My own hands are shaking when I reach forward, touching his shoulders and then sliding them down his arms. My fingers dig into his biceps, and his curl deeper into my hair. The rubber band pops, and his shaky sigh of relief rushes across my face when the mass of hair falls around us. I can feel him smiling as his nose brushes mine and his fingers wrap themselves eagerly into the freed tresses.

Somewhere above us, a branch snaps.

Our eyes flash open simultaneously.

With a soft growl, Bee springs to her feet and walks out of the grotto in seconds, her steps terrifyingly silent for her size. After a moment the boy presses me back against the wall. "Don't move." With a single look of warning for me to stay, he leaps to the edge of the pool and, on soundless feet, runs around it and up the incline into the darkness.

As I watch him disappear, I realize absolutely nothing about that was human. He moves like a cat, or maybe a mountain lion would be more accurate.

He's been out in the wild a long time.

I have no problem staying put because there is no way I can even begin to imagine where I would go. I'm lost and directionless down here and should have grabbed a flashlight. But that would have involved using intelligent thinking, and that's something I haven't done in a while. What *was* I thinking? What am I even doing here?

No, I'm not thinking because I've completely lost my mind. I can see clearly now, thanks to the jolt of fear.

A pebble tumbles down the incline. It breaks the glass-like

stillness of the pool, sending out a ripple of tiny waves that lap at the rocky edge. I drag my gaze up and wish I hadn't.

A pair of yellow eyes watches me from the lip of the ravine. The wolf lets out a low growl and takes a cautious step forward, sending a wash of tiny pebbles scattering down the incline. I tuck my feet beneath me, ready to move the second he does. I wonder if the pool is deep enough to submerge in, or if I'll just slow myself down and make it easier to be caught.

I don't have time to think about it, because without warning the wolf springs, diving down the slope and reaching the base faster than I can push to my feet. We stare at each other, and I can see the size of him now, lanky but tall, and easily big enough to take me down. I slide my hands along the wall behind me, looking to the right, where I hope there's enough room for me to run along the pool. The last place I want to get caught is here in the shallow cave.

I take a careful step, at least hoping to keep the pool between us, when he takes a step into the water.

Not good. At all. I take another step, hoping he'll follow me and sink into the deep water. The wolf growls again, and this time his steps are confident as he slinks closer. And he doesn't sink. The water can't be more than a foot deep at most.

I grab a handful of rocks at my feet. I'm not getting out of this. He watches my hands, snarling when I raise my arm. I can almost see his legs bunching up for the leap across the water.

I tilt my arm back, my eyes burning, a prayer on my tongue and a million regrets in my heart.

As the wolf lunges, a blur flies across my vision and takes me

the shadows we know by heart   169

to the ground. I feel the impact of the wolf on top of us as I am crushed beneath the boy. He lashes out with a flash of silver. The wolf yelps in pain but comes back with a vengeful snarl, his white teeth snapping near the boy's face. I try to scramble out of the way, but we are already pressed up against the wall of the cave and there's simply nowhere left to go.

That's when the roar echoes from the forest. A massive shape flies out of the trees, dropping the entire distance to land in the middle of the pool with a splash that sends water spraying everywhere. Bee launches herself into the fray, wrapping her arms around the body of the wolf. The boy pushes off me, whipping his blade again with snakelike reflexes. The strangled cry of the wolf makes my skin crawl, gurgling and desperate.

And then it's stopped short with a snap.

There's nothing but silence for a moment, as if the entire forest is holding its breath in expectation. Then the wolf's lifeless body drops to the ground with a crunch of gravel. Bee lets out a deep, territorial growl of satisfaction, nudging the wolf with a massive foot. If I wasn't already on the ground, this would probably be the moment I dropped in shock. I feel like I've run a marathon. My body is shaking uncontrollably, breaths coming in harsh gasps.

The boy kneels, wiping his blade across the fur before sliding it into the leather sheath at his calf, his movements quick and efficient. "Leah?" He spins around and reaches for me, running his hands over my face and neck with frantic, searching caresses. "Are you okay?" Finding no damage, he slides them down my arms to grab my hands. I wince when his fingers slide over my palms, embedded with gravel from the fall. The worst injury is my ribs, where I can already feel bruises forming, but I'll go to my grave before I lift my shirt to check the damage in front of him. "Here, hold still."

I can't help the hiss of pain that escapes me when he delicately brushes the gravel away. I was wrong; it does hurt as bad as my ribs. He makes a noise in his throat, similar to the growl of the Sasquatch behind him. His brow furrows in anger as he holds my palms closer, blowing the pieces away with heavy breaths. As if in defiance of the pain, chills drift casually down my body as I watch him. Only a few stubborn rocks remain, and he looks at me questioningly.

I nod, biting my lip. "Just do it."

His lips twist into a smile, then the frown returns as he plucks the remaining rocks quickly out of the skin. Before I can finish my cowardly groan of pain, he pulls me to the pool and submerges my hands in the icy water. Once he's satisfied that I'm either clean or in enough pain, he releases me. "You'll live." I stand quickly, moving away from the water, away from him, away from all of it, only to trip over the carcass behind me.

I don't even hit the ground. He looks down at me, grinning as I lay in his arms a few inches from doing even more damage to my body.

"Don't even say it." I glare at him.

His eyes soften as his gaze drifts down. He slowly slides one hand away from my back, the other still cupped beneath my head. He peers down at me, his eyes drinking me in, fingers brushing the hair from my face. "You're sure you're okay?"

When he runs a thumb across my bottom lip, eyes so full of longing, something shifts, settling deep inside my bones with an irrevocable finality.

"Yeah, I'm fine."

I'm at the edge. If I go over, there will be no going back.

Maybe I don't want to go back.

Maybe what I want is what waits at the end of the fall.

chapter nineteen

I wake to the feel of morning light dancing across my face. It's strange, considering my bedroom window faces the west. I open my eyes to see a canopy of trees peeking beyond a stone ledge above my head.

Am I dreaming?

I turn my head and bump noses with *him*. He's watching me through lazy eyes heavy with sleep, a smile playing at his lips. His arm shifts beneath my head, bringing my face closer to his. A bare foot runs up my calf.

Oh. Wait. What?

The events of last night hit me like a rock. It's morning and I am nowhere close to my bed.

Holy crap.

"Morning," he says.

"Morning? Ohmigod we fell *asleep*!" I scramble to my feet. "You have to take me home! My dad is going to *kill* me!" My eyes are burning, and I'm afraid I might actually cry I'm so scared of what's going on at home. Mom's probably beyond hysterical by now. I am so stupid to pull something like this after everything we've all been through. If Dad doesn't kill me, Matt will. What if they've called the police? I can just see everyone at our house, combing over every inch of our property and surrounding forest. The helicopters, the dogs and horses, just like before.

"Leah? What's wrong?"

"Please, I have to go."

"I'll take you home." He grabs my hand and leads me along the rocky edge of the pool. I look back, remembering Bee, but she's already gone, only a wide depression in the ferns showing she was ever there.

Once we climb up the slope and reach the soft, needle-coated floor, he drops my hand and starts to run. I curse the fact that I'm wearing boots and sprint after him, figuring it's only the beginning of my punishment. Blisters are nothing compared to what is coming.

By the time we reach the edge of the forest, the sun hasn't risen above the tree line yet, and my house still sits in the early morning shadows. We are greeted by silence; no sirens, no helicopters, and no screams.

Is it possible?

Surely I have not gotten this lucky. No earthly way. "I can't believe they aren't up."

"You should go."

"Yeah," I agree, but my feet remain still.

"I'm glad you came with me." He looks up through his lashes, a blush across his face but a dark light burning in his eyes.

Sweet baby Jesus.

"Me too." Does he have any idea how I am about to say *screw it all* and walk back into the woods with him? No. Nope.

I can't do that. *Remember Matt and Mom and Dad. Turn around, and walk away.* "I wish I could stay."

"Then stay," he whispers, and it's a relief when he pulls me back and wraps his arms around me, burying his face in my hair.

The sound of a slamming door breaks the moment like shattered glass. Through the trees, I can see Matt on the back porch, his arms crossed as his head turns from one side to the other, looking.

"I've got to go." I push away from him, or I'll never leave.

I know he can see it. His lips quirk up in a halfhearted smile, but his eyes are heavy with sorrow. "Leah." He says my name like a prayer, and I can hear everything he wants to say but won't.

I nod. I have to go and it's too late for anything else. But still, I don't want to walk away. I don't know if I can.

He takes my shoulders and spins me around, giving me a gentle push. "Go." I take one step and then another. I don't look back. It will break my heart if he's watching me, and break it if he's not. And either option will cause me to turn and run back to him, anyway. So I walk through the field, the last sprigs of leftover Bermuda grass leaving drops of dew on my jeans and soaking the surface of my boots.

I can tell by the set of Matt's shoulders and the heat working up his face that I'm about to find this conversation unpleasant. "Have you lost your damn mind?" Matt says as he meets me by the fence. "Where the hell have you been?"

"I just went out for a morning walk."

"You're a shitty liar, Leah."

the shadows we know by heart   175

"What are you talking about?" I laugh shakily. "I've only been out for a little while."

"I slept in your damn room all night waiting for you to come back! Come up with another excuse," he hisses, grabbing me by the shoulders.

I stare, shocked that he knew I was gone all night and didn't say anything about it. "Mom and Dad don't know?"

"No, and you're damn lucky they aren't up yet to figure it out."

Okay. Evasive maneuvers, then. "Why didn't you wake them up? Weren't you worried?"

"Scared shitless, Leah. Thanks for asking. But they'd be worse." Matt crosses his arms, his face red and angry. "Like I said, no matter what I went through last night, it was better than telling them. I figured you'd snuck out with Ashley and I'd at least give you the chance to get back home before they woke up. You owe me regardless. And you can start by telling me where you were." Matt reaches out and grabs my shoulders again, and I realize just how lucky I am that he's the one who is greeting me instead of Mom or Dad.

I throw my arms around his neck in relief.

He resists, muscles stiff, back straight, until finally I feel the tension leave his body and his arms wrap around me. "I'm going to kill you if you ever do that again," he mutters, chin resting on top of my head.

"Deal," I murmur back.

"You still have to tell me where you were."

"Would you believe me if I told you I got lost?"

"Not really. You've lost your mind, Leah." He pushes me back, holding me at arm's length, the edge in his voice gone, leaving nothing but fear. "Of all the things to go and do, you thought walking into the woods and not coming back would be the smartest? After everything?"

After everything. He's right, it was the worst thing I could have done. And I would do it again in a heartbeat, so what does that say about me?

Maybe we're both crazy.

"I don't . . ." He runs a hand through his blond waves in frustration. "Just go. Go take a shower. You smell like an animal. Where did you even sleep, by the way?"

"I found a deer stand. Turns out it wasn't too far from the house. Just got turned around in the dark."

"Why? You know the rules. Sneaking out with me is one thing, but going there alone . . ." He points to the trees.

"I saw deer in the pasture and I followed them. I just went too far."

Matt eyes me distrustfully, but what else is there for him to suspect? He doesn't know about the Bigfoot, and he doesn't know about the boy. It's a completely legitimate excuse.

Except he knows it's just that, an excuse.

"How'd the game go?" I ask, desperate to turn his attention to something else.

"We lost, thanks for asking."

"Sorry." I stare down at my boots, feeling smaller by the second.

"Kelsey and I broke up too."

the shadows we know by heart

"Why?"

"She wanted more." He shrugs.

"More? More than what?"

"Doesn't matter. Apparently she's already got some guy from Huntington going with her to the dance tonight."

"So you're not going now? But we were all going together."

"I'm not going to a dance solo, Leah. I'm not that desperate."

"Ashley's going. We could invite her along and neither of you would show up alone."

Matt frowns. "Ashley? I don't know."

"Why?"

"She's like family."

"So? Ben is practically family, and we're . . ." I wave my hand, not sure what word I'm looking for to describe us now that there's not even room for him in my head.

"You're . . . what?" Matt's eyebrows rise.

"Not that. Jesus."

"Look, I'll think about it. Go shower," he says grudgingly. "And use extra shampoo." He sniffs my hair with a wrinkled nose. "You seriously smell. What'd you sleep in, a pile of wet animals or something?"

"Yeah, something." *You have no idea.*

Guilt overwhelms me as I stomp up the steps, pausing to wipe the grass from my boots. As everything I should be doing or should have done comes weighing down on my shoulders, I realize one certain fact.

I should have stayed in the woods.

❧❧❧

jennifer park

"You didn't sleep much last night, did you?" Ashley leans forward to stare at the magazine I'm pretending to read, but I swear she's really just sniffing my hair for the fiftieth time. She doesn't say anything, though, not anymore. Not after she made me rewash it the second she walked into my bedroom to get ready for the dance. She's agreed to go with Matt, but I know she thinks she's just a stand-in.

"No, not really."

"So you thought walking outside last night and running into a skunk was a good idea?" She sniffs loudly this time, frowns, and sprays a burst of air freshener she confiscated from the bathroom.

I cringe as the cold drops land on my skin. "He was by the apple tree. I didn't see him."

"Until he saw you. This would be funny if it wasn't such a disaster." She scrunches her nose. "What about your clothes? Did you chuck them?"

"Not yet."

Ashley turns away with a grimace. "I'll be right back," she announces, and then walks out of my bedroom without a backward glance. She says something to someone in the hallway, and suddenly Matt appears.

"How's it going?"

I wait until I hear Ashley's footsteps on the stairs. "Fine, but we'll never get ready until she stops making me wash my hair."

Matt smirks, but his eyes are humorless. "It's no less than you deserve."

"I know." I glance down at my folded hands, remembering

how dangerous it actually was last night. I almost got attacked by a wolf. A real, live wolf. Matt would die. He would kill me first, then he would die.

"Here." Ashley bursts back into my room, not even sparing Matt a glance. "Vinegar and baking soda." She shoves the white bottle and orange box into my hands. "Go scrub one more time. I just can't stand it and Ben will notice." Matt rolls his eyes and slips out of the room. He doesn't see Ashley watching him leave.

I stumble over the pile of towels littering the bathroom floor, a sea of green-and-yellow cotton, and crank the shower knob. Ashley's right, I do still stink. I can smell my hair every time I take a breath.

It smells like Bee.

A skunk would have been worse, but not by much.

Ashley is sitting in my desk chair when I walk into the bedroom, staring out the window with a distant frown. I twist the towel around my hair one more time before yanking it out. "I think I got it this time. If you don't mind the faint vinegar smell."

She continues to stare out the window.

"Ash? Earth to Ashley? Don't you want to smell my hair, since all of this is your idea?"

"Shh!" she hisses, waving at me to come closer.

My stomach drops, cold drifting over my damp skin as I edge closer. What am I going to see when I look out the window? Better yet, what am I going to have to explain for damage control? "What is it?"

"I see something. Out there." She points to the trees, near the stump.

"What, like an animal? It could be Old Man Watson."

"No, he's by his barn, working on that ancient tractor. This is something else." She leans forward, her nose nearly touching the glass.

"A deer?"

"Maybe," she says doubtfully. "But it looked bigger. It just won't come out of the shadows long enough for me to get a good look." Ashley sits back in the chair. "You know, I can't look at the forest without . . ." She stops, and I know where she's going with that sentence. The forbidden zone.

"I don't know why it got to me this time. Kelsey and them, on the track. I mean, it's not the first time someone has accidently, or even purposely, brought it up, but I . . . I don't know. It just bothered me. Reed and Sam would be graduating this year with Matt, and sometimes I can't believe they're not here. I still look for my dad to be sitting in his rocking chair when I wake up in the morning, sipping coffee and watching the news."

I stare out the window, seeing nothing but memories.

"You really can't talk about it, can you?"

"If I don't talk about it, I don't have to deal with it."

"You'd think I'd be the one like that, wouldn't you? But I don't have anyone to fill the gaps like you. You still have a brother and father. I guess that's why I think about it so much." She taps her fingernails on my desk absently. "Does Matt ever talk about it? I mean, he lost his twin brother . . . I don't know, it just seems so unreal sometimes."

"It's real enough to me. You held my hand through three funerals. Have you forgotten that?"

"I haven't forgotten anything. But don't you ever get tired of being a Roberts like I get tired of being a Hutton? This town will never forget us. I just want to be anyone else but Ashley Hutton. I want to go somewhere no one knows my name or face."

"The way this house is, it might as well have been yesterday."

"Yeah," she says quietly. "I know. All the more reason for us to leave next year. Haven't you been looking at colleges? We could go together, you know. Can you imagine us as roommates? Think of all the awesome clothes you'll have!" Ashley spins around in the chair, her arms thrown up in excitement. "Seriously, though, think about it, Leah. We could go anywhere. Just pick a place. I can get a marketing degree anywhere."

"Marketing? That's what you've decided on?"

"Yep, it's the one thing I could think of that won't do me any good if I live in this town. Therefore, I must move on to bigger things."

"I think nearly anywhere is bigger than Zavalla."

"True, so it shouldn't be too hard." Ashley peers at me. "You are leaving, right? And I don't just mean driving down the road to the junior college. I mean leaving, as in only-coming-back-on-important-holidays kind of leaving."

"Of course," I say. "There's nothing here worth staying for." The words feel like ash on my tongue, and if I could unspeak them, I would. It doesn't matter that it's a lie. It feels like a betrayal. Because I know now, no matter what happens, I'll

jennifer park

never leave this place. My future is now entwined with his, for better or worse. I may leave this house, but it won't be by car, to a dorm room, or even another home.

It will be by my own two feet, on a well-worn path through the forest, to live beneath the stars in a world that is completely my own.

chapter twenty

Sam is ten minutes older than Matt. It doesn't matter to me, since they're both older than I am, but they argue about it endlessly. "I'm older, so I go first." Sam pushes Matt out of the way, stumbling past him in tall cowboy boots.

"No, I'm taller, so the biggest person goes first," Matt argues.

"Well, Reed is older and taller than both of you, so he should go first," I say, pulling on their shirts as we hike through the trees.

"Yeah, Reed, you go up there." Ashley pushes her brother to the front of the line. "That way the ghosts can get you first."

Matt and Sam stop cold, and I run into them. "There aren't ghosts," Sam says. "That's kid stuff." But he's no longer trying to get in front of Matt either.

"Well, I'm sure something's living in Aldridge. It's still got buildings, so something probably lives there."

"Could be Bigfoot," Dad calls out as he and Mr. Hutton follow in our wake. "Or maybe vampires."

"Vampires aren't real either," Matt says, pushing ahead. "Come on, Reed. I'll race you there."

Matt and Reed take off, tearing up the trail toward the town. "Hey, wait for me!" Sam yells, in the middle of dumping a rock from his boot. By the time he chases after them, they're already gone around the bend ahead.

"They're totally going to get lost," Ashley says, reaching back to grab her dad's hand and letting him swing her forward and into a twirl, like a dancer.

"Let them run," Dad says. "They need to burn energy and I'd like to be asleep before midnight."

"Did we bring the marshmallows?" I ask.

"Sure did." Dad ruffles my hair. "I wouldn't forget my favorite pumpkin's favorite treat."

"Thanks, Dad."

By the time we reach the town, Matt and Reed are already inside one of the buildings, yelling and laughing. But Sam is standing just outside, arms crossed, eyes wide.

"Hey, buddy, did you catch them?" Dad asks.

Sam shakes his head.

"You okay? Did you get hurt?" Dad walks over and grabs his shoulders.

Sam shakes his head and mumbles, "No," then walks into the ruins where the boys are.

"Hey, guys, I brought the spray paint," Mr. Hutton says, tossing his backpack onto the ground. While the boys rush to get their cans, I walk into the building. Vines trail up the walls like an indoor garden, reaching for the sunlight that pours down through the caved-in roof. The only solid wall has been covered in spray-painted names, the vines ripped away to reveal gray stones that are now a rainbow of colors. Matt and Reed rush to it, while Sam trails behind. It's so out of character for him that I ask him what's wrong.

He glances around, and then shrugs. "Nothing."

the shadows we know by heart

"Then why are you acting like something's wrong?"

Sam waits until Ashley walks by, then continues. "I just . . . I thought I saw something."

"What? Where?"

"In the woods. When I was chasing Matt, I got another rock in my boot. I stopped to get it out, and when I looked up, something was watching me."

"Like an animal?"

"I don't know," Sam whispers.

"Well, what did it look like?"

"Like . . . a person covered with fur. Taller than Dad."

"Are you sure? That sounds a little weird. I saw a tree back there that looked like a person reaching up into the sky. It was probably something like that. Shadows, maybe."

"Maybe."

"Are you going to tell Dad?"

"No, it's stupid." He shakes the bottle of spray paint. "Just forget it."

Ashley's stomach growls as the smell of pizza wafts into the room. "Is that pizza?"

"Matt's probably having a snack." I dust my cheeks with Ashley's blush, barely enough to notice.

"You think he'd share?"

"You know we're going to dinner in two hours, right?"

"Yeah, but I'll be nervous. I don't like eating on dates."

"Since when?" I gape at her.

"Since now."

jennifer park

"Oh." Right. Because it's with my brother. "Well, let's go make him share."

Matt's sitting at the kitchen table when we walk downstairs, while Mom stares at the oven, mitt on her hand and a blank look on her face.

"That's the best thing I've smelled all day," Ashley says, giving me a wicked smile. I glare at her but smile anyway. It seems like the paste for my hair finally worked.

"Hello, girls. Would you like some pizza?" Mom says absently.

"Yes, thanks for letting me come crash this weekend, Mrs. Roberts."

"Nora, sweetheart, always Nora to you." Mom comes out of her fog long enough to smile. "Pizza is almost ready, and I've already got cookies made. If you need anything else, I'm sure you can find it."

"Are you going somewhere?" I ask.

"Yes, actually," Dad says suddenly, appearing from his office with a stack of file folders in hand. Mom glances at him, her level stare meeting his. I'd swear something passes between them. "Your mother and I will be in late tonight. The Becker family invited us over for dinner." Dad glances down at his watch. "Nora, you should probably get ready."

"Oh, you're right," Mom says as she glances at the clock on the wall. She pulls the pizza out and places it on the stovetop, steam rising up into the vent. "Leah, cut this for me. I completely forgot the time." Mom lays the pizza cutter on the counter and tosses the oven mitt beside it.

"Sure, got it," I say, watching her carefully. She's hurrying,

the shadows we know by heart

but in a good way, like she's excited about this. The last time I checked, she wasn't too crazy about having to have dinner at other peoples' homes. "Have a good time."

Ten minutes later they pull out of the driveway.

"Ben's on his way over," Matt says, eyeing my wet hair.

"What?" I choke down my bite of pizza. "He's not supposed to be here for another hour."

"He wanted to come over early."

"Okay, we've got work to do." Ashley grabs her drink, holds one slice with her teeth, and grabs a handful of cookies.

"You want a plate?" I ask.

"Nommgud," she mumbles, taking the stairs two at a time. A few seconds later her voice calls back clearly, "Get up here, Leah!"

"Kill me now." I drag myself out of my chair, grabbing one of Mom's homemade chocolate-chip cookies. "Okay, wish me luck."

"You're going to run out, eventually."

The look he gives me tells me he's not talking about Ashley.

"This dance is kind of lame," Ashley says, sitting next to me at one of the tables that line the cafeteria. Matt and Ben are at the buffet table, loading up plates of snacks to bring back to us. My feet are aching in these shoes, and I dread getting up again to dance, mainly because I almost can't look Ben in the eye without this overwhelming guilt.

"Well, it's a homecoming dance in the cafeteria. What do you expect?"

"More. Of everything."

jennifer park

"You've been dancing with Matt, though. Isn't that good?" *Isn't that what you've always wanted?*

"It's fun, I guess. He's not really into it, though. He got kinda pissed when Kelsey walked in with that new guy."

"If he wanted to be with Kelsey, he would. He wouldn't even care if we weren't at a dance where she could show off her new date so soon."

"But that's just it. He doesn't seem to care. About anyone."

"Come on, Ash. You know Matt. That's just how he is."

"But why? Maybe he's more messed up than either of us, and we just never realized it."

I'm still thinking about what Ashley said when the boys arrive at our table.

"Okay, we've got a destination." Ben points to a group of boys standing near the spiked punch. "Charlie Becker said his parents are out of town tonight."

"Wait. Are we leaving?" I ask.

Ben smiles, glancing at my feet. "Do you want to dance again?"

"Please, no. But . . . the Beckers'. That's where Mom and Dad are. Didn't they say they were having dinner at the Beckers' house?"

"Well, Charlie said they're gone. His mom is visiting her mother and his dad is going hog hunting with friends. It's just him and his sister."

"Are you sure they said Becker?" Matt asks me.

"Of course, I mean, I think. You didn't hear him say that?"

"Maybe, I don't know. It doesn't matter, does it? They won't be back until later, either way."

chapter twenty-one

It's past midnight when we get home, and Mom and Dad still aren't back yet. Matt parks the car, and Ashley and I head for the door. "We smell like a bonfire." I glance over my shoulder, expecting Mom and Dad to come driving up any minute.

"Well, who knew the wind would be so bad? It's about to rain, anyway."

"We're going to have to wash our hair again. I don't want them asking questions in the morning."

"Fine, you go first," Ashley says. "That way I don't have to hurry."

Ten minutes later, I switch places with Ashley. Just as she turns on the water in the shower, I hear tapping on my window when I walk in from the bathroom. I freeze, wet hair dripping into a puddle on the wooden floor, the dropped towel lying in a useless pile alongside it.

Thank God I put on my pajamas in the bathroom. I will never *not* do that again.

The boy's silhouette is framed by the curtains, and after closing the door, I rush to the window. "It's late," I whisper nervously. "Were you waiting for me?"

"Yes."

"I . . . went out with some friends." I jump when lightning

splits the sky in the distance, but it doesn't faze him. His faint smile and green eyes flood me with a rush of memories from the night before. It must show on my face, because his smile widens. So when thunder drums around us and fat drops of rain start to fall, showering with relentless ferocity, I do the most stupid thing I can think of. "Come in?"

I stumble away from the window after nearly slipping on the puddle of water beneath it. The boy slides into the room with sinuous grace, and for a moment I seriously question my sanity. He takes up way more space than I anticipated. My room has suddenly shrunk now that he's standing in it. While he looked lean in the woods, now he looks broad and agile, like a living piece of the forest standing here in stark contrast to my colorful, girlie room. When he shields his eyes, I immediately turn off the overhead lights, leaving only the bedside lamp on.

Panic sets in, and my heart feels like it's going to race right out of my body. He doesn't move, or at least his body doesn't, but his eyes are zipping over everything in my room, taking it all in faster than the lightning strikes in the distance. I try to look at everything from his point of view, and suddenly feel childish. There are at least twenty stuffed animals on the bed and around the room, posters of favorite childhood movies and TV shows plastered on the walls, and even a few toys that remain on shelves, untouched for years but too sentimental to trash.

And there's also my pile of dirty laundry in the corner that smells like Bee, along with my clean laundry from yesterday piled on my desk to fold. Most noticeable is the bright yellow bra lying on top. If I can't move my cement legs to hide it, I'm going to pretend it doesn't exist.

"I definitely need to redecorate," I mumble to myself. "Serves me right for not doing laundry today." He glances at me in his perusal of the room, and I swear he smirks.

What must he think of all this?

What do I think of all this?

I think I just let a wild boy from the forest into my bedroom on a Sunday and I'm probably going to hell for it.

Or maybe that's just my father talking in my head.

Curiosity satisfied, he turns to me, eyes drifting down. The corner of his mouth ticks again, and something flickers in his eyes.

I glance down, and my mortification is complete.

Oh. Of course I had to put on these pajamas. I cross my arms and fight the urge to swear. I'm throwing them away. I absolutely don't care that my deceased great-aunt gave them to me three years ago for my birthday. Nope. Don't care.

Sparkling pink unicorns.

Something about this situation is on the verge of hysterical, and the desire to laugh is overwhelming. The window is still open, and rain is starting to trickle in, the widening puddle creeping across the floor to merge with the one from my wet hair. I pick up the towel and toss it toward the window, hoping it will land in the right spot and catch most of the rain. I'm afraid he'll feel trapped if I close it. The last thing I want is for him to leave.

He moves toward me without warning, and well within my range of personal space. I can feel his breath on my face as

jennifer park

he reaches out to touch my hair, and the damp strands leave his fingers shining. "I missed you." His whispered voice drifts across my skin.

"I missed you too."

With a smile he presses his forehead to mine, our fingers finding each other and twisting together.

"How long have you been waiting?"

"Forever."

I swear my heart is going to burst right out of my chest. The sound encompasses me, as if it's echoing around the room. He looks at the door, and I realize the dull thrumming isn't coming from me.

Someone is knocking.

I know I've waited too long to open it.

"Hey, Leah, you're not asleep yet, are . . ." Matt freezes with his hand on the doorknob, his mouth hanging open.

The boy spins around in one fluid movement, moving me behind him to face Matt, a deep rumble in his throat.

"What the—"

"Matt!" I hiss. "It's not what you think." I wrap my hands around the boy's arm, wishing Matt would shut the door. I scramble around to place myself between them.

"Are you—? No, you've got to be—" I slap a hand over Matt's mouth and jerk him in by the shirt. He's so shocked he doesn't put up a fight. I close the door as quietly as I can, twisting the lock.

But then Matt moves.

He lunges at the boy and just as quickly ends up on the

floor, staring up at the ceiling with the breath knocked out of him. The boy moved so fast I barely turned in time to see him flip Matt like a toy. "Matt! Are you okay?"

Matt groans as he glares daggers at the wild boy hovering above him. For a long moment there is only tense silence. I'm not sure I can explain my way out of this. "I promise, it's not what you think," I say, bending over to reach for Matt's hands.

"I'm not thinking much of anything right now, Leah, so if you'd like to fill in the giant empty space between my ears, that would be helpful."

"Matt," the boy says, and I can see something flickering in his eyes.

"Yes, Matt. My brother," I say, wondering if he's putting the pieces together or if he remembers them to begin with.

I pull Matt to his feet and he steps back toward the door, taking me with him. "Well, now that we know who I am, who the hell are you?"

"He doesn't have a name, Matt."

"Come again?"

"He's from the woods—seriously, don't look at me like that—and I don't know his name because he doesn't remember it."

Matt looks him up and down. "Assuming I believe any of what you just said, what's he doing in your room? With Mom and Dad not here." He pauses. "On a *Sunday*."

"I know, I know, I'm going to hell. I've already established that. Matt, you can't say anything."

"You've got to explain this." Matt steps forward, studying the boy as much as the boy is watching him. "Now."

jennifer park

"It's complicated."

"I've got time, ironically enough, but you've got, mmm, maybe five minutes until Ashley walks in here and shit really hits the fan."

"You're not going to believe me."

"I'm pretty open to options at the moment." His laugh is hollow.

"Matt, please, it's not funny."

"It kind of is, if you step back and look at it. At least, until one of the parental figures walks up here and we all die."

"Okay, fine." I take a shaky breath. I've never said the words out loud before. Now I don't have a choice. "You know that big tree stump at the end of Watson's hay field? The one next to the woods?"

"I think so, yeah."

"Well, a few years ago, I started putting apples out there, you know, to see if deer would come eat them."

"Okay."

"Well, it wasn't deer that came and ate them."

Matt is slowly nodding, waiting. "And?"

I have to say it, but even in my head, it sounds ridiculous. "It was . . . Bigfoot."

Matt snorts so loud he starts coughing.

"Be quiet! "

"Are you serious?!" His cough turns into a laugh, and he covers his mouth. "I'm sorry, Leah, but that was the last thing I was expecting to hear. You're kidding, right?"

"I'm not lying, Matt. I've been watching Bigfoot or Sasquatch or whatever you want to call them come to that stump and eat apples for years. There were always three, until a few weeks ago, and then I saw him with them."

"Him? What do you mean, he was with them? Wait, oh my God, we're actually talking about Bigfoot."

"Please be serious for a second. I'm not lying about this. I swear."

Matt's gaze levels on the boy. "How old are you?"

"I . . . don't . . ." His voice is unsure. "I don't know."

"And you don't know how you ended up in the forest? How you ended up with . . ." Matt sighs. "Bigfoot?"

"No. I can't remember." The boy's eyes glaze over as he stares into the distance. He shakes his head, and I would give anything to know the memories he's got locked away.

"He's a little dirty." Matt eyes the long tangled hair that drapes around the boy's shoulders, then looks down to his mud-crusted feet, his nails stained from years of going barefoot. "No, never mind, a lot." Matt steps closer to him, still keeping a hand on me. "Leah. Have you really looked at him?"

"What are you talking about?" Matt's faster than I am. It's taken me weeks to see what he's seen in five minutes.

"He looks . . ." Suddenly Matt shakes his head and steps back. "Nothing. I just thought he seemed familiar."

Familiar. The word rings in my ears, the puzzle piece flashing in my mind. *I know. And that's what makes me afraid.*

"I don't know what to do."

"You should turn him in to the police."

"No!" I say, then lower my voice. "No. They would take him away. He would hate it."

jennifer park

"You seem to know him well," Matt says wryly. "Does Ashley know about him?"

"Of course not. No one knows. And you can't tell, especially not Ben. He'd likely go ballistic."

"He'd do more than that. What are you doing, Leah? From what I saw when I walked in here, Ben's feelings are the last thing on your mind."

I glance down, guilt washing over me. "I know, I just don't know what to do."

"You do the right thing."

"I don't know what that is anymore."

"Maybe call your boyfriend and tell his dad there's a wild boy living in the woods that needs help?"

"No. That's not happening."

Matt shakes his head, looking at me with something close to pity. "So what, you're just going to let him go? Keep sneaking into the woods to see him and, oh my God, is that where you were the other night?"

I point my finger at him. "Not. A. Word. It was late and I fell asleep. Nothing happened, end of story. Look, I haven't figured this out yet, but calling the police isn't the answer. There're too many complications."

"Damn right. No one's going to believe where he came from anyway. I don't even know if I believe it."

A piercing call comes from the forest, louder than the pounding rain. Matt's eyes are huge as he watches the boy move to my side. "What was that?"

"They're calling him."

the shadows we know by heart

The boy reaches out and takes my hand, his fingers wrapping around mine, sending heat spinning up to my head. In the next moment he's gone, disappearing into the torrential night. I stand there, unable to close the window, until my pajamas are just as soaked as the floor. Matt stands motionless by my side, both of us flinching each time a call rings out in the night, until finally they are silent.

chapter twenty-two

I wake to Ashley snoring in my ear. Half of me wants to roll over and go to sleep; the other can't stay here a second longer. This secret is pulling me in ten different directions. I'm relieved that Matt shares it now, but he's rational; he won't let me drag this out forever. He'll make me face it and deal with it eventually.

What I really want is to tell Ashley. I think she would take my side and understand why I can't tell anyone who might do something about it.

And Charlie Becker was right. His parents were gone.

Which means my parents lied.

I slide out of the bed, cringing when my feet touch a puddle of water that Matt and I must have missed. Ashley continues to snore, rolling over to take my spot immediately.

The first thing I notice when I hit the stairs is that the house doesn't smell like bacon. It's also quiet. Treading softly, I enter the kitchen to find a large box of grocery-store doughnuts sitting on the kitchen table.

I imagine if someone walked in right now, they'd see me staring at the box like it's an alien or something. It's not that I mind the doughnuts, but I can't remember a time in my memory when Mom didn't cook on a Sunday morning.

The coffeepot's on, so I know someone is up. Dad's usually dressed and sitting at the table right now, but he's nowhere in sight.

I grab a glazed and walk out to the porch, tucking my feet beneath me on the faded wooden glider. It's cloudy this morning, the scent of rain still in the air, and everything glistens with last night's downpour.

I can't imagine sleeping in the rain. I don't know how the boy stands it, whether he slept in the grotto or somewhere else.

The back door opens and Ashley walks out. "I thought you were still asleep?"

"You took the heat away." She sits beside me and pulls her feet up. "How about that epic Roberts breakfast in there?"

I hold up my doughnut. "This could be a first."

"They must have stayed out pretty late."

"I guess."

The coffeepot rattles, and I look back to see a kitchen full of people. Mom and Dad have appeared out of nowhere, dressed and ready to go. Matt is standing by the coffeepot, watching them with squinty eyes.

"I guess it's time to get ready. I didn't plan on sleeping so late," I say.

"Oh! That's right. I've got the car."

"Got to pick up your mom?"

"Yeah. Save me a seat if we're late."

I follow her back into the house. "Morning, Ashley, Leah," Mom says, filling a to-go cup.

"Morning!" Ashley says, sprinting up the stairs.

jennifer park

"Morning. Did you have fun last night?" I ask.

Mom hesitates for a second. "Oh, yes. It was a lovely dinner. Did you kids have fun at the dance? You'll have to show us pictures later."

"Yeah, we had a good time." I almost say it. It would be so worth it to see her face when I tell her. But then I would have to admit where we were after the dance, and I would get into trouble with Dad all over again. Why lie? What could they be doing that requires the preacher and his wife to lie to their children about where they go on a Saturday night? Or why they've been coming and going so late at night without telling us? And why my mother looked so comfortable with a gun in the woods?

Then I see the bandage around her hand.

"What happened?"

"Oh, cut it on a knife. I was helping Lisa in the kitchen last night. Look, your father and I are leaving early. Can you and Matt come by yourselves?"

"Sure." She lies just like I do, natural and effortless. What is she hiding?

"Great. See you soon." Mom smiles as she leaves the kitchen, accidentally brushing into Dad's shoulder. She mumbles an apology, grabbing his arm to steady herself, and a piece of paper flutters to the ground from one of the folders under his arm. Notes for his sermon, likely.

Dad doesn't notice the fluttering paper, not until it hits the ground by my feet.

My breath stills. It's a photo. Of *them*. Their last day. The camera must be set on a tripod, because Mark Hutton is there with Samuel and Reed, the vivid green eyes and dark hair of Ashley's brother sending chills down my spine. They're all smiles as the camera flashes, Mr. Hutton's arms around both little boys. The bright orange tent stands out starkly behind them, and the beginnings of a campfire off to the left.

Dad's hand snakes out to snatch it up, our eyes meeting for one split second, and then he places the photo back into a folder like nothing happened.

But not before I see what is there.

In the background of trees, within a black circle, like someone took a Sharpie and marked on the print, is a face. But it's not the faceless monster of my dreams, the one I was told committed the crime, some soulless sociopath that ripped our worlds apart.

It's not even a human.

It's a Sasquatch.

I don't remember getting dressed for church or saying goodbye to Ash, but suddenly I'm sitting next to Matt as he pulls out of the driveway. I'm having a hard time with coherent thoughts. Ideas form in my mind and dissipate within seconds, always replaced with that photograph. My parents know about Bigfoot. They would have to, if they have a photograph like that. But what else? And what do I not know that they do?

Matt clicks his tongue, in that way he does when he's bothered by something.

jennifer park

"What's wrong?" I say, more out of habit than actually wondering.

"You . . ." Matt taps his fingers on the steering wheel and shoots me a look. "You need to tell Ben."

"I can't."

"Why?"

"I'm afraid to hurt him."

"So you think it's better to string him along?"

"I'm not . . ." I begin, but realize he's right. "I know it's wrong, but I don't know what to say. How do I tell him the truth? I can't, not everything. Ben's not going to buy the *it's not you, it's me* line."

"It doesn't matter, Leah. You have to. And it's going to suck, but it's the right thing to do."

I can feel tears forming, but I blink them away. "He's been perfect. Beyond perfect."

"Which is why you need to do it now. It will only get worse the longer you wait. How long do you think you can keep this up without it all blowing up in your face? You're my sister, and I don't want something to happen to you."

He stares as I wipe at my eyes, but I cross my arms and stare out the window as Matt's words soak in and begin to eat away at my sanity. Hurting Ben is going to be awful. And it's all my fault. I don't want to do this, but now that it's in my mind, I can't let it go.

Matt clicks his tongue again, and I brace myself. "You know you're crazy, right?"

"God, again? Now what?" I throw my hands up.

the shadows we know by heart

"You say you've found Bigfoot, and now a boy in the woods who lives with them, and you really haven't told anyone. That's crazy, Leah."

"Who would I tell, Matt? Who would believe me?"

"Well, I do."

"You still haven't seen them."

"Yeah, but I heard that scream. It wasn't human, and I've never heard an animal make that kind of noise before. You saw how that boy ran away. He wouldn't have gone if there wasn't something there, right?"

"Right," I whisper.

"But we're talking about a human now. A missing boy, because that's what he is. Have you even considered who he might be?"

"I've asked him if he remembers, but he can't."

"Or he doesn't want you to know."

"What?"

"You don't recognize him, do you? You, of all people."

I stare at Matt, my body growing cold as the truth surfaces. Matt knows. I wait for him to say it, to say the name that's been floating in my mind for days now. But he's focused on the road, his fingers tapping a silent rhythm on the steering wheel as the car speeds over the slick blacktop. There's so much water you can't really see the rogue potholes that hide beneath the surface. Filled with water, they look like sheets of glass under the gray sky.

When the deer trots out of the forest and onto the edge of the road, Matt jerks the car. It's cliché, but I really can feel time

jennifer park

slow. In that moment, I'm aware. I see what's about to happen, and for one split second, time ceases to exist.

I feel the wheels lift off the pavement and slide onto the water as if I am part of the car itself. It's like the Tilt-A-Whirl cups at the fair, only times one hundred. We spin so fast I can't keep my eyes open. My heart feels like it's going to burst. We fly off the blacktop, career down into the ditch, and soar into the trees. Only it feels like driving down a mountain and soaring off a cliff. I see it, the one we're going to hit: a pine just like the others, but it will never look the same. I get one more glance at Matt before my head snaps forward, a rush of white balloon meets me, pain bursts in my head, and everything goes black.

chapter twenty-three

A few nights later, after the camping trip, Sam crawls into my bed, tears running down his face.

"What's wrong?"

"Matt wouldn't let me sleep in his bed."

"Why are you crying?" I scoot over to make room as he burrows beneath the covers.

"Bad dream."

"About what you saw in the woods? Again?"

"Yes," he sniffs, rubbing his hand across his face.

"You should tell Dad. He'll know what to do."

"Reed wants me to come with him this weekend camping again. I don't want to go, and Matt said he doesn't want to go either."

"Why doesn't Matt want to go? He loves camping."

"I don't know."

"You're not going to see it again, Sam. It wasn't even real. You saw something else, I promise."

"What if you're wrong? What if there really was a monster?"

"Monsters aren't real."

"Maybe it was a demon."

"Demons don't have fur." I laugh.

"How do you know? You've never seen one, just the pictures in Sunday school, and those aren't real."

"Because they're fallen angels. They would have wings, silly."

"I know what I saw, Leah."

"Just go to sleep, Sam. It'll be fine. There's no such thing as monsters."

The first thing I feel is my face. A feather-light touch whispers across my forehead and my cheeks and lingers on my lips. Something else burns, but I can't tell where it starts and where it ends. At times it's all of me, others it's focused on one bright point. That's how I see the pain, in light and dark. At the moment, my body glows like the sun.

Sounds are muffled and distant, but it seems like someone is calling my name down a long, dark tunnel. I am weightless, and the feeling of being wrapped in a warm cocoon makes me forget anything else but what that feels like and what I can do to stay inside it forever.

Minutes, hours, or days later, I smell rain. It tugs at my thoughts, but I fight to keep them away. All I need is this feeling. Nothing else matters. At some point the weightlessness ends, but the cocoon remains. It is ceaseless, endless, and it absorbs every errant thought before any can penetrate my mind and ruin my peace. I drift, unaware, warm, and content. My lips move, and something cool and wet trickles down my throat. I swallow and float back into my nest of nothingness.

The first person I find in the blackness is Samuel.

I can see him perfectly, as if a day hasn't passed, only he's not eight anymore, but older, and much bigger than me now. His face is beautiful, chiseled, his eyes a deeper blue than Matt's.

His hair is like mine, the color of dark beach sand, with bright blond streaks running through the long waves. Someone needs to cut his hair. Dad would never let him wear it that long.

He stares at me for so long but doesn't say a word. I try to speak, but my voice won't come. I want to tell him I miss him and that I'm sorry. That we're all sorry.

And we're all broken.

I used to go to bed and dream of what my family would have been like if Sam was still with us. Mom would be happy. Matt wouldn't spend his days being perfect and nights anything but. Dad would loosen his grip because there wouldn't be that ever-present fear of losing us.

I could've known what normal was, if there's even such a thing.

If only my voice would come, I could tell him I believe him now, about the monsters in the forest, even though it's too late. And that he's the reason I escape to the forest, so I can see him, remember him, and that for some strange reason I feel like watching the Bigfoot will in some way make up for my disbelief of his story. But the price will never be paid, because he's gone forever, and neither my lies nor my honesty about any of it will change that.

Too soon Samuel fades away. This time I call to him, but it's less than a whisper, and he leaves anyway.

When I find myself again, I'm overwhelmed by heat. It's no longer the comforting presence it was, but thick and oppressive. Something drips in the background, and heavy breathing echoes around me. I try to remember where I am, but

jennifer park

something about that terrifies me. As the warmth increases, so does this burning in my arm. The light of pain becomes focused now, along my shoulder and upper right arm.

Voices drift in and out, but it's meaningless chatter, just beyond my understanding, yet still familiar. I try flexing something, and my fingers are the first to move.

They clench fur.

Well, that's not right. I flip through the various reasons in my mind of why I would touch long fur, and I can't come up with anything rational. All my stuffed animals are short-haired. We don't have a dog. Matt's hair doesn't feel this thick. Not that Matt would be lying practically *on top of me.*

I let my fingers move again, testing the hair. It's coarse and slightly oily. There's a smell too, animal-like, musty, kind of like a wet dog.

My mind keeps hitting a wall. I know there's something I should remember. It feels imperative that I do. The only way to describe it is like continuously hitting the snooze button on a really important day, only to find you slept your way right through it, and now it's too late and everyone already left without you.

I think I'm going to be sick.

Heat rolls over me in waves, and sweat runs down my skin. I try to shift my legs, but they're immobile. I think I'm going to scream if I can't pry my eyes open, but it's like they're glued together.

Another scent hits me, wrapping around me with recognition, luring me out of the darkness. Fingers drift down my cheek, rough and soothing, smelling of pine and earth. The pain in my arm flares for a moment as I feel my blanket shifting, the fur drifting through my fingers.

Something breathes on my face. My eyelids flutter open. If my tongue wasn't so thick and my mouth dry like cotton I would scream.

Two large, liquid brown eyes stare back, sunken beneath a jutting forehead and black fur.

My blanket is alive.

Her warm breath blows across my face, her gaze watchful. I lift my head enough to glance down, even though the simple movement nearly takes my breath away.

Yep. Bee is snuggling me.

I groan with something between pain and denial. She shifts again, and fire lances down my shoulder. I scream, and suddenly he's there, looming over me, his face washed in firelight and panic.

"Leah? Can you hear me?" Even through the searing pain, my mind registers how easily my name falls from his lips. As the red fades from my sight, I can see him clearly now.

God, he should exist continuously in firelight and nothing else. He's like some avenging angel of the forest, with deep shadows and sharp planes creating a chiseled sculpture of perfection. His hard muscles flex as he pries my blanket off my body. She doesn't go willingly, and scoots close to my head, her steady gaze never leaving me. She twists strands of my hair around her thick fingers, eliciting a soft humming sound.

"Water," I whisper, my throat burning. I cough, clenching in pain, until he lifts my head gently, placing a cup of water against my lips. Before I think to care if it's clean or not, I gulp it down, sputtering when I swallow too fast. He frowns but doesn't take the cup away. His thumb drifts slowly across my cheek, and he stares at something above my eyes with worried intent.

I feel like I'm lying in the desert with a sunburn, but it's pitch black around the firelight.

Fever.

I don't remember being sick. But then, I don't remember anything before a few minutes ago. I can see a small fire licking the darkness just beyond my view. How? Why? Too many questions. I begin closing my eyes to shut them out but realize I can see a roof above my head.

Vines curl and stretch across the high ceiling, spreading down pale cement walls that are covered in faded graffiti. Tiny black things hang from the vines above, looking suspiciously like bats. One drops like water and swoops out into the night, through a massive hole in the farthest wall, blown there nearly a century before to remove logging equipment.

I know where I am.

To my left, on the closest wall, almost as if I knew they were there, I see the familiar scrawl of a handful of names in faded black spray paint, nearly crowded out by others. Even now my eyes find them easily, though I haven't been here in years.

Reed's name sits just above mine, joined by Matt, Ashley, and Sam. The Robertses and the Huttons, one of the last times we were all together. The line that surrounded the names is gone, overlapped a dozen times over.

I remember it like it was yesterday. I remember Reed helping me hold down the sticky spray knob on the paint can so I could do a barely legible version of my name. Dad took a picture of all of us together by our names, goofy grins and funny faces filling up the space around the painted concrete.

That's the dad I wish I had today. The one with the unfailing smile and ever-ready hug, who played the role of horse or bear when I wanted it, or hero when I needed it. The dad who wasn't afraid to let me push the boundaries and leap, as long as he was there to catch me.

I would give anything for that dad to come back and take the place of the one I have now, who's drowning in guilt and bitterness and trying to take the rest of us down with him.

But it's just a memory now. Like that photo, tucked away somewhere in an old, musty box.

"Why am I here?"

The boy frowns again, staring just above my eyes. Bee lets out a moaning huff, and he narrows his eyes at her.

"You don't remember?"

"No." My voice breaks, and he holds out another cup of water. "What's wrong with me?"

"You're hurt. I'm sorry, Leah. I found you first and couldn't leave you there."

I agree with the hurt thing. My arm feels like it's on fire, and it worries me that he keeps staring at my forehead. "What happened?"

He chews his lip for a moment, watching me, and I flinch when Bee accidentally tugs my hair. I can feel the tangle that she's made by twisting it over and over. He takes her massive hand and slides it gently out of the strands. He folds her hands in his, keeping them still, until she heaves a heavy sigh.

"Car crash."

"What?"

He leans in close, his green eyes glowing with reflected flame. "Your car crashed."

The memories hit me in a rush. The deer. Matt. The tree. Too fast. Too much. I try to sit up, but the action nearly makes my brain explode in pain. It feels like my arm is going to fall off if my head doesn't split open first. My breath leaves me in a scream, and when I slam my head back down on the concrete, I go willingly into the blackness.

It's not fever or the heat of flames that wakes me again but the cool sound of running water. This time I'm prepared. *Don't move my arm, don't move my head, just open my eyes and nothing should hurt.*

Hopefully.

I breathe deeply, inhaling the smell of clean forest air. My right hand tests my surroundings, feeling for anything that might tell me where I am before the shock of opening my eyes somewhere new and strange. My fingers encounter the feel of Spanish moss mixed with pine needles, the layers so thick that they protect me from the rocks beneath.

I can't hear anything over the rush of water. It's loud, and echoes around me until I can't begin to tell where it's coming from.

I might as well get this over with. Lifting my eyelids ever so carefully, I peer through the slits into late-afternoon light. It's the grotto. Except now there are a dozen or more thin streams of water flowing over the mouth of the cave into the pool at the entrance. The cave walls glisten with moisture, and tiny drops fall to the ground around me. I watch as one falls toward my face. I close my eyes but feel nothing. My eyes flash open. I should have felt that water drop. I reach a tentative hand up to touch my forehead, only to find some sort of fabric instead. My fingers trace the texture down and around, finding it wrapped completely around my head.

A bandage. Panic sets in. I remember now. The car crash, Matt, and then the boy. But where is Matt? Why am I here and he isn't?

I have to get up. I have to find Matt.

The pain in my head has reduced to a dull throb, and I don't use my arm as I push myself up to a sitting position. My head rushes and my sight swirls around me. Fingers dig into the soft ground, trying to hold my body still before I collapse again. All I can do is focus on breathing, in and out, one breath at a time. It takes a few minutes for the earth to stop whirling beneath me so I can open my eyes.

I slowly turn my head left and right, surprised to find I am alone. "Hello?" My voice cracks. There's no way anyone heard that over the pouring water. I put my lips together, take a deep breath, and let out a whistle.

Someone whistles back.

A silhouette shifts in the rays of the setting sun. The dark

jennifer park

shape drifts forward, and my heart sinks. It's too big to be the boy.

"Please let it be Bee. *Please let it be Bee*," I mutter over and over again. Because if it's *him*, I don't know that I will ever make it out of this cave. The fading light highlights the Sasquatch in an orange halo, softening the dark hair around the edge of its body. From this angle I can see it only from the waist up. It's not until I see the face clearly that I realize it's not her.

I dig my heels into the soft gravel and moss, using one hand to push myself back into the recess of the cave and sink back against the rocks, too afraid to even blink. A few feet from the edge of the slope, he stops. The creature stares down at me through the water, his face blurry, as I'm sure mine is to him. Blood pulses through my body, pounding painfully in my head. I have to tell myself he won't hurt me. I have to believe everything I've seen him do is just him trying to protect his family, and that if I'm not a threat, I'm safe.

Pebbles scatter over the lip of the grotto as he slides his toes over the edge. Where the hell is the boy? Why would he leave me here knowing his crazy Bigfoot dad is lurking nearby?

My fingers twist into the gravel beneath me, grabbing a handful in preparation. Not that it will do any good. Rocks press into my back as I scoot even farther away, my eyes never leaving his. Then, instead of slowly sliding down the incline like I expect him to do, he leaps. All I can manage is a horrified gasp before he's standing at the edge of the pool. *On my side.*

Bitter fear slides like ice through my veins. Where I felt only hot, pounding blood a moment before has now gone cold and numb. Air ceases to flow through my lungs, the muscles in my throat constricting beyond my control. Hair raises along my skin as he blocks out the light of the setting sun, converging on my hidden space.

A massive black foot slides beneath the sheet of water, followed ever so slowly by the rest of him. His large, dark eyes are so human it frightens me more than his nearness. Crouching down to enter the low space, he sits beyond my reach and just within the curtain of water. Wariness and suspicion emanate from every part of him, from his ready-to-flee legs bunched beneath him to the way his fur quivers with each heavy breath. He may be cautious, but there's no way he's as frightened as I am.

Around his wide eyes, tan skin gathers in deep wrinkles like sun-darkened leather. Wisps of coarse, shaggy black hair frame his face, and his fists flex over and over in a squeeze-and-release pattern. A wide, flat nose sits above straight lips, and every few seconds he lifts his face to sniff the air, nostrils flaring to catch my scent.

Time has stopped for me. I can no longer feel it passing, though the constant sound of trickling water tells me it must continue on. For all I know, we've been here for hours, just staring into each other's eyes, waiting. At some point my body starts to shiver, but whether from nerves or fever, I can't tell.

He reaches down, fingers sifting through the pebbles at his feet. He pulls up a handful of flat rocks and drops them into his palm. Then, one by one, he stacks them, until a tiny tower of pebbles sits between us. He looks at me, then at the rocks.

jennifer park

Then, after only a few seconds or maybe a million, he stands and walks away without a backward glance. In two leaping strides he's across the pool and then he surges up the incline, disappearing over the ridge within a few moments.

Just like that he's gone. I don't know what I expected, but it wasn't to be left alone in one piece. With a rock tower gift. In the silence of his departure, my body is tuned to every sound the forest makes. Every rustle of leaf or snap of branch has my nerves on edge. It's exhausting. I don't even realize I've fallen asleep until my eyes flash open.

Bee is staring at me, her humid breath falling heavily on my face. The sun has dipped below the tree line, casting a blue-orange glow over the darkening woods, and the sounds of twilight echo around us, magnified by the shallow cave.

A cool hand slips over my forehead, and I glance over to see the boy next to me. His face is in shadow, but I can see the frown on his forehead deepening the longer his hand remains on my skin.

"Where were you?" I whisper, because my voice has suddenly lost the strength to be any louder.

"Away."

"Why? He came, and I thought . . ." My voice feels thick like cotton, and a wash of heat runs over my skin.

"He was protecting you."

"You knew?"

He nods, his fingers sliding gently from my skin. I immediately miss the cold. The adrenaline that was keeping me from acknowledging the pain in my body has left, leaving aching agony in its place. I'm not sure what hurts worse now, my head or my arm. And where it doesn't hurt, it's gone completely numb.

"I have to take you home, Leah."

I drag my heavy eyes up to meet his. "Where is Matt? Is he . . . hurt?"

"No."

They don't know where I am. God, Mom is probably beyond hysterical. I try to stand. Big mistake. Something in my arm pops and white-hot pain is all I can feel. The boy yells, at me, at Bee, but it's incoherent as I fall down a dark tunnel into oblivion.

jennifer park

chapter twenty-four

I'm weightless once again. Only this time it doesn't come with the carefree nothingness of an unconscious mind. The memories are there, fighting to gain the forefront of my attention, but they battle against the excruciating pain of whatever's wrong with my head and arm.

Icy mist falls on my skin, and I can hear the rattling of bare branches as the frigid wind whips through the trees. The sound of runoff falling into the pool is gone. Where am I this time?

I realize I've been moving only when I suddenly stop. The motion makes my head swim with nausea.

"Leah?" The boy peers down into my face, sweeping wisps of hair from my skin.

"What?"

"Matt's here. He's going to take you home."

I have no idea what is going on, not until I look up at who is carrying me. Bee is watching me with a mildly possessive gaze, as if she might not let me go. Her warm fingers curl around my skin a little tighter when the boy motions at her to put me down. Her chest vibrates against mine with a warning growl. The boy sighs with impatience, gently peeling her fingers off of me. He lifts me against him, being mindful of where my injured arm is. A soft whimper escapes her lips when her arms fall away from me. My head swims, threatening to bring me down into the blackness again.

"Go," the boy whispers softly. Bee doesn't move. I can feel her fingers reach for my hair, twisting the strands anxiously. "Go," he says, pointing back the way we came.

With a huff she slowly turns away, her footsteps crunching on fallen leaves, the ground vibrating with her heavy steps. "She's mad at you." My voice sounds strangely delirious.

He puts a quick hand on my forehead. "It happens a lot."

"I like your voice."

"You're sick."

"You're getting really good at talking."

His hand presses harder. "Really sick."

"I wish you'd started talking to me sooner."

He lets out a frustrated sigh, not unlike the one he gave Baby Bigfoot a moment ago. "So do I," he whispers, his lips brushing across my forehead. He stops suddenly, listening. I don't know what he hears, because I can't hear anything over the hissing of leaves rushing across the ground around us. A high whistle sails from his lips, carrying over the sound of the wind in the trees. Suddenly, my world is flooded in light. Two shapes silhouetted from piercing headlights hurtle toward us. The boy stiffens, and I feel his arms move around me like he might run.

"Leah!" Matt's voice is raw, like he's been screaming or maybe crying. My relief is so strong that tears fill my eyes.

"He was supposed to come alone," the boy says, stepping back.

jennifer park

"Who else . . ." I stop when I see the tall shape next to Matt. Ben comes into sharp clarity, and then blocks the light out completely when he slides to a stop, his eyes shifting between me and the boy.

"The hell?"

"Just come on and help me," Matt says, his hands brushing my hair back, flinching when he touches the bandage.

I can't believe he's standing here. "Aren't you hurt?"

"I'm fine. Your side hit the tree. Jesus, Leah, I'm so sorry."

"Can you put her down?" he asks the boy. "I can't take her from this side. Her arm looks broken."

Slowly, reluctantly, the boy lowers me to the ground.

When my feet touch, I keep sinking. With a chorus of curses, all three of them reach for me. At least two smack heads. The boy swoops me back up into his arms, the look on his face daring anyone to protest.

"Who are you?" Ben asks, looking as if he'd like to snatch me away. "What is going on?"

"It's complicated," Matt says, waving the boy on. "Hurry."

"So you're okay with the fact that some nearly naked dude just walked out of the dark with your sister? 'Cause I'm sure the hell not." Ben reaches out to stop the boy and accidentally grabs my arm.

I bite my lips but a scream rips from them anyway. I hear a smack and a grunt, and then the boy's other arm loops under me again, a deep growl coming from his chest. Ben is doubled over holding his stomach and nose, blood gushing over his pinched fingers.

the shadows we know by heart

"Did you not see her arm?" Matt yells, grabbing Ben and shoving him toward the Ranger.

"I'm going to . . ." Ben gasps out.

"We've got to get her out of here, Ben." He turns impatiently to wait for us. "Just help me."

"It's fine. I'm okay," I whisper, feeling the tension radiating from the boy's body as he stares death at Ben.

"He hurt you."

"He didn't see. Ben wouldn't hurt me."

He snorts, eyes narrowing. "He's blind." The boy looks like he'd like to take another shot at Ben, so I say the first thing that comes into my head.

"Come with me."

That might not have been the best idea. His head jerks down, eyes widening as he stares at me in disbelief. "Just as far as the pasture," I say before one of us changes our mind. "You can get out before we get to the house."

The furrow between his brows deepens. I would think he was mad if it wasn't for his increasing heart rate, beating against my arm at an alarmingly fast pace. "You want me to?" The vulnerability in those eyes does strange things to my already pounding heart.

"Please."

He stares at me until warmth creeps up my face and it gets uncomfortable with the others watching. "I'll stay until you tell me to leave."

Something twists deep inside me. My vision blurs, but I can't tell if it's from the fever or his words. "And if I don't?"

jennifer park

His eyes shift from bright emerald to deep jade, and with a shy grin he carries me past Ben and Matt like they don't even exist. The boy doesn't hesitate when he walks up to the Ranger, holding me carefully as he navigates the backseat.

Matt hops into the driver's seat. "It's going to be rough," he says with a warning.

"Just go." I press my feet against the side bar, gritting my teeth in dread. Ben glances over his shoulder, eyes drifting from my head to my arm, and finally stopping where the boy's hands are wrapped around me. His head jerks back around when Matt cranks the motor and shifts gears. Ben will never understand this. I should have told him sooner. *He's going to hate me.*

We slowly navigate the turn, and I know Matt's torn between hurrying and not hurting me. I don't think it matters. This is going to hurt no matter how slow he goes. I can see the trail lit up ahead of us. It's wet enough that Matt's following their tracks from earlier, deep depressions still visible in the muddy ground.

The boy pulls my head close to his chest when the first good bump takes my breath away. I dig my nails into his arm, but he endures it and rubs small circles on my back. I know when a dip in the road is coming, because he increases the pressure just before it happens. He's completely at ease, though I know this must be strange for him.

It seems like hours, but before I'm ready, I see the lights of our house breaking through the trees ahead. It would be so easy to stay quiet, to let Matt take us right up to the front door and the boy carry me in. But I can't let anyone know about him. Not now, not like this.

"I've got cell service," Ben says, holding his phone up above his head.

"Call Dad first and tell him we're taking her to the hospital, then call yours."

"Where're Mom and Dad?"

"Out looking for you. Everyone's been searching for days."

"Days?"

"The car crashed two days ago." Matt drags a hand over his face. "You can't imagine . . ." His eyes are red when he looks back at me. "It's been a nightmare, Leah."

I think I might faint because I can imagine. Actually, the whole ordeal might be easier if I did faint. Like for the next three or four days. Long enough for Mom and Dad to calm down from all of this without me having to witness it.

Matt swerves to a stop in the backyard. Ben sprints around the house to get his truck, yelling into his phone, and Matt waits by the Ranger, arms out, ready to help me.

But the boy doesn't move.

In fact, his arms are like iron bands around me. I tilt my head back to see his face. "It's okay, I'll be back soon." I expect him to relent, because I'm sure that's what he's upset about.

Except he's not looking at me.

A gasp comes from the direction of the house.

I follow the boy's line of sight to the back porch. It's flooded with light, highlighting a figure emerging from the shadows. Ashley's horrified face appears, and her hands cover her mouth.

jennifer park

Something about the way she is standing feels wrong. I expect her to yell at me for being stupid and causing worry, or at least to run down and hug me until I scream. But all she does is stand and stare. Slowly her hands drop from her face and tears follow them.

"Ash? I'm okay." My words sound hollow and pointless. I don't even think she heard me.

Ashley steps down off the porch and the boy stops breathing. The closer she gets, the more I realize she's not looking at me either. Shouts abruptly come from the other side of the house, strobes of light tearing through the night from flashlights on the move, but Ashley ignores it all. She sidesteps Matt completely in her efforts to reach the Ranger. Shadows move around the house, and I see Dad followed by the sheriff and others.

For some reason Matt's suddenly frantic. He moves around Ashley and takes me from the boy's arms. "You need to go. Now."

I reach out and grab Ashley by the shoulder. "Look at me." I shake her, willing her haunted eyes to see me. "Ashley, what is it?"

"Reed."

That one word from her lips is enough to make me forget everything, even as people converge and chaos ensues.

"What did you say?" As if pretending I didn't hear her erases the truth that I've known for a while now. But hearing it, it makes it real, and for the first time the weight of it falls on me, more overwhelming than I imagined.

"It's Reed." The tears are pouring from her eyes as she points behind me. I turn around, wanting to see his face, to see if the truth is in his eyes as well.

But the backseat is empty. The boy is gone, back into the night from where we came.

chapter twenty-five

The hospital room is sterile and white and it makes me sick. Or maybe that's the dislocated shoulder, fractured arm, and gash across my temple. Either way, I crave green walls instead of white, and dark earth beneath my hands instead of crisp sheets. I'm on just enough painkillers that I can bear it.

I already tried pushing the little morphine button in my hand until I passed out, but it didn't work. I'm supposed to answer questions before they'll let me sleep.

"Leah, if you're able, I've got a few things to ask you," Sheriff Hanson says apologetically, pulling a chair from the hallway into my room. The other two are occupied by Dad and Matt, situated next to my bed between me and the dark window. Mom is perched on the foot of my bed, and Ben is hovering outside the room, his shadow pacing on the other side of the closed blinds.

"Go ahead, Sheriff," I mumble, wishing this was already over with. Dad's eyes flicker my way before drifting down to settle on the bright green cast now decorating my arm. I thought it was appropriate, though the nurse gave me a look when I asked if they had forest green instead.

"Do you remember the crash?" The sheriff pulls out a pad of paper and a pencil from the front pocket of his uniform. He resembles his son, with the same dark eyes, straight nose, and confident air that Ben wears so well. He flips the cover over and taps the eraser three times. His first two fingernails are stained brown underneath, and I stare, waiting for him to tap the eraser again.

He clears his throat, jolting me back to the question. "No. I mean, I remember before. It was wet, the road was slick. A deer came out. I don't remember hitting the tree or anything after."

"But you got out of the car? You were able to walk away," he says expectantly.

"I don't know."

"You don't remember if you unbuckled yourself and opened the door?"

Lie. Protect them. "I guess I would have if I made it to the woods."

Sheriff Hanson stares at me, only glancing away when Dad shifts in his seat. "Where were you when you first realized you weren't where you were supposed to be?"

I'm about to say Aldridge, the abandoned mill town, but he's not going to buy that. It's miles from where we crashed, and I likely wouldn't have been able to walk there fully healed in the woods, much less hurt the way I am. "I . . . I really don't . . ." I look at Matt, stalling.

He swoops in for the rescue, as I hoped. "Can't she rest for a while? She's been through a lot, and she obviously can't remember what happened. I mean, look at her head." He leans forward, elbows on knees, gaze intent on me, face taut with guilt and anguish. I can't imagine how awful he must be feeling, thinking he's responsible for all of this.

jennifer park

The sheriff waits for a nod from Dad. "Sure. We can do this later." He taps the eraser again, then flips the notebook closed and places them both back in his pocket. "Get some rest, Leah. I'll be back to check on you tomorrow."

Dad gets to his feet and joins him. "I'll walk you out, Paul."

They don't speak until they close the door to the room. I can hear their voices outside, and Ben is still there, peering in from the hallway. "I'm going to get some coffee," Matt says, giving me a pointed look before sliding out the door.

"How do you feel?" Mom asks for the gazillionth time, placing a hand on my arm.

"Tired. I wish I could sleep."

"I'll get the nurse. I'm sure she can give you something to help."

I reach out and grab her hand. "How's Matt? He's really not hurt?"

"A bump on the head. They released him shortly after they brought him here." Her smile is sad. "He didn't really give them a choice."

"So he could find me?"

"We've been terrified, Leah. I can't . . ." She stands suddenly, as if it's too much for her to sit here and talk about, and tucks my hand back under the blanket. "I'll be right back."

As soon as she closes the door, Matt appears, sans coffee cup. There is a light in his eyes that accelerates my heart. "What is it?"

"I got the details from Ben. He overheard them talking earlier while you were getting stitched up. The door was ripped off the car from the outside, and the seat belt was cut with a knife."

"Oh God."

"They know you didn't get yourself out of the car."

It's what he doesn't say that I need to hear. "And?"

"They found footprints."

I close my eyes, fighting the urge to rip the catheter out of my arm and demand Matt get me out of here.

"They think someone tried to kidnap you, and that you either don't remember or you're covering it up."

"That's ridiculous."

"Is it? I mean, he did take you from the car, didn't he? No one's going to believe he's harmless, Leah. Or the . . . others. They're planning to go looking for whoever took you."

"Did Ben tell anyone about him? Or Ashley?"

"They haven't said a word, but there's no way this will stay a secret."

"Where is Ashley?"

"She went home to tell her mom you were okay, said she'd be by later to check on you."

"I'm sure Ms. Hutton was upset. Did . . . did you hear what Ashley said?"

At that moment the nurse walks in. I can see Mom standing in the hallway talking to a new group of visitors laden with flowers. My room already smells like a garden. I glance at Matt when the nurse turns to my IV line, syringe in hand. The nurse checks a few more machines, tells me to rest well, and leaves quietly.

jennifer park

"Matt, you've got to get me out of here," I whisper through the haze of painkillers she just dumped into my IV.

Matt's white knuckles are fisted into my sheets near my waist. The beep of my heart monitor has steadied back into a quiet rhythm, and the tingling warmth of morphine spreads through my body like a wave. I'm afraid I'm going to sleep, and when I wake up, it will be too late to do anything.

"Matt, did you hear me?"

"I heard you."

"Then help me. What if they go after them with guns? I just need to warn him. They can get away from here, go somewhere safe."

"Why don't you want them to bring him in? He's a human, Leah, not an animal."

"It's his choice. If he wanted to come back, he would. It would be cruel to take him away, and imagine what they would do to Bee and the others. She'd never see the light of day again."

"Bee?"

"Bee. She's the one who got me out." The warmth is too comforting now. My eyelids are growing heavy with sleep. "He needs to know they're coming."

Matt grabs my hands. "Even if I agree, and I'm not saying I will, because you look like hell, how can I get you out? This is a hospital, and Mom and Dad are here around the clock."

"Call Ashley. This is her area of expertise." I glance past him at the window, already wondering how Matt is going to get me out of here. "Good thing we're on the first floor."

Matt rolls his eyes and shakes his head when he sees where I'm going with that. "I haven't had enough coffee for this."

"Just call Ash . . ."

Honestly, no one is more surprised than me to be lying in the backseat of Ashley's car when I wake up. The aged Accord is motionless, and I can hear distant voices, muffled from the closed car doors, but nothing else. I'm also completely underneath a blanket. Like someone doesn't want me seen.

Imagine that.

I slowly pull the blanket down over my eyes and peer out the window. All I can see are tall pine trees towering over the car in the morning light. A car door slams nearby, followed by Ashley's elevated voice. Whoever she's talking to is having most of their backside chewed off.

The next thing I know, the door beside my head swings open. *"Are you awake?"* Ashley says.

"Do I want to be?" I mumble beneath the blanket, tilting my head to see past her. Matt is standing behind her, his face red with rage. Before I can ask what's wrong, Ashley waves her hand at me to scoot over.

"Shake it off. You've got to see this." She plops down on the seat, barely letting me move my head in time. "Sit up, hurry."

"Geez, Ashley, have you ever just woken up from morphine? Give me a freaking minute." I struggle through the dizziness and sit up beside Ashley, leaning against her for support. "Where are we, by the way? And how did you get me out?"

"I pulled the fire alarm in the hallway."

jennifer park

I suck in a breath and start coughing. "You what?!"

"It was tricky getting your dead-weight ass through the window and over the bushes, but we managed it."

"You know they have cameras. Someone is going to find out what you did."

"Trust me, this is worth a little time in juvie." She slaps a thick file folder in my lap. Written on the outside in thick black marker is "work stuff." Innocent enough, until I open the cover.

I'm not sure if this was supposed to be the first page or if Ashley put it there on purpose. Either way, the lance of pain that shoots through me makes me glad I've still got the pain-killers flowing through my blood.

It's a flyer, one of the first ones made, when everyone thought our brothers were kidnapped. Sam and Reed stare back at me from their individual pictures, the ones made for the school yearbook with the blue backgrounds. Matt and Sam had the same blue striped shirt that year, and both wore them on picture day. I remember Mom laughed when they walked into the kitchen of our old home, twins down to their shoes. The last time I saw that shirt, it was being packed into a box the week before we left that house for good.

Reed looks just as he always has in my mind. A boy of eight, thick brown hair swept across his forehead, still long from the summer. I was there when Ashley's mom was threatening to cut his hair for the first day of school, and I remember how hard Reed begged her not to.

My eyes burn, but I flip to the next page. Ashley sucks in a breath at the photo of her dad with Sam and Reed in the woods. The next several pages are hard. More photos of the crime scene. I tilt them away, trying to protect Ashley from the sight of her dead father's body, but I know she's already seen them. Photo after photo of blood, destroyed camping equipment, and large rocks littering the ground. I've seen all this before, but it's still a shock.

It was late on Sunday afternoon when we knew something was wrong, long after they should have been back.

By five o' clock, they had found the destroyed campsite with Mr. Hutton's body, his head bashed in with a rock, and the boys gone. I can still remember with vivid clarity what those words felt like to hear. It was a nasty, violated mix of fear, gut-wrenching pain, and total helplessness that took root and never went away. I remember wanting to run, somewhere so far that I could escape the words I'd heard. *The boys are gone.*

I didn't know it could get worse. I didn't know that "gone" still meant "hope."

Not until four days later, when I heard the word "dead."

At that point I realized how much I'd lost. Our inseparable group went from five to three. We were told a man did it. They said they had evidence, but the man got away.

The bodies were unsuitable for open caskets. I didn't know what that meant at seven years old. I couldn't wrap my head around the fact that my older brother and my best friend were lying in cold white boxes at the front of our church and I couldn't even see them. The last time I'd seen their faces was when they were laughing in Mr. Hutton's truck as they pulled

jennifer park

away. It was closure I couldn't have. The funeral did nothing for me. I still waited for them to come home. In my heart those were just empty white caskets.

I come to the newspaper clipping, the front-page story of their deaths, with a drawing of a scruffy, bearded man at the bottom, the killer who was never found. There are only a few pages after this, and I suddenly wonder what I was supposed to see. "Why are you showing me this?" It feels like I've been staring at these pictures for eternity.

"Keep going," Ashley whispers, gripping my knee tightly.

I take a deep breath and flip the page over. For a moment, I just stare, trying to understand what I'm seeing. Then I feel the pieces fit together in my mind with a click so visceral I'd swear it was real. *"Oh my God."*

Ashley is silent, a tightening on my knee the only sign that she heard me. It's another flyer for a missing person, but this one has been altered. On the left is Sam's first-grade picture, and on the right . . . on the right is a computer-generated picture of what he would look like at twelve. And then another one at eighteen. It is so eerily close to what Matt looks like that it could have been his picture, except for the darker hair.

It's long in the picture, past his shoulders. Sam never wore his hair long. I can feel my brain on the verge of overloading. I slide the paper aside with a trembling hand, needing to finish this before I can't think anymore.

I know what's coming next. Somehow, I think I've always known. I look at Ashley and understand why. I love her like my own sister. We might as well be, for all we've been through

the shadows we know by heart

since day one. I love her thick brown hair and her stunning green eyes and the way her mouth quirks up when she's up to no good.

I think the first time I saw the boy tilt his head like Ashley so often does, something deep inside me recognized him.

But to acknowledge the truth would be to accept that all we've been told has been a lie, that maybe we suffered more than we had to, or perhaps not enough. Either way, I ignored it for the consequences it would bring. And now they've come, regardless, all because I couldn't stay away from the boy that was once my hero. The boy whose name I used to draw inside red crayon hearts, who gave me tiny white flowers and held my hand at the bus stop.

I move Sam's page aside and let out a ragged breath at what lies before me. Ashley sniffs, wiping at her eyes, the same ones that stare up at me from the page. The computer-generated picture of Reed is astonishingly close to the real thing. But the picture feels wrong. They've got him on a white background, when all I've ever seen behind him is green. The Reed in the photo has light skin and more bulk, like an athlete. The boy from the woods is all muscle, and the picture doesn't show how his tan skin glows when the sunlight hits it through the forest canopy or the way it highlights his sun-streaked hair.

It's close enough, though. Guilt washes over me. This is one secret that has come back to haunt me tenfold. "Ashley, I'm sorry."

Her hand slides from my knee. "Did you know?" Her voice is trembling with faint accusation.

jennifer park

I can't tell her no, because that would be a lie. Some part of me knew, but it was so small I could flip the switch, just like I did for everything else. But to say yes, it doesn't feel like the truth either. I've fallen somewhere in the middle, and it's not a place that I'm used to being. "I . . . I didn't *want* to know, Ash. I wanted something in my life that had nothing to do with . . . this."

I glance up at Matt to find him pressing the palms of his hands to his eyes. He doesn't move from that position, and I wonder if he's mad at me or just in shock. Ashley stares down at the picture of her older brother with tears in her eyes and nods, accepting my flimsy excuse. "But it has everything to do with it, doesn't it? You found the truth; you just didn't know it."

I meet her eyes, seeing the green flames that burn within. "So what do we do now?"

"Ben," Ashley barks. "Get over here."

Ben shuffles forward, looking both mutinous and broken.

Ashley glares up at him, meeting him stare for stare. "Tell her, Ben. Tell her the truth."

He holds my gaze for the longest time. "I knew."

"Knew what?"

"About this."

"How long?"

"That night at the party. I stopped off at the house before I met y'all there. Dad left the folder out. He didn't think I'd come back home so soon."

"Is this why you suddenly *saw* me? Because your dad wanted you to spy on me?"

the shadows we know by heart

"No, Leah, I swear. It wasn't like that. He just wanted me to find out if you'd seen anything in the woods."

"So you thought making me your girlfriend would accomplish that?" Suddenly my guilt for knowing I've been leading Ben on vanishes. He's been doing the same thing.

"It didn't start out that way. But I realized the only way to find out what you knew was to get to know you. I needed you to trust me. And I just . . ."

"What? Thought you'd kill two birds with one stone?"

Ben glares. "I fell for you, Leah. And that's the truth, like it or not. And apparently while you were falling for someone else."

Matt pulls his hands away from his eyes long enough to give me an *I told you so* look.

"Like you said, it didn't start out that way." I press a hand to my head, feeling the pain coming through. "I just . . . didn't know what to do. I thought you were a good guy who didn't deserve to get hurt."

"I still am, Leah. I care about you."

"Then why didn't you tell me? Why didn't you tell any of us? You've seen what's in this folder and didn't think we should know?"

"You found Reed and didn't think they deserved to know?" Ben points at Ashley and Matt.

"I wasn't sure! Why would I tell them if I wasn't sure? That would be horrible."

"But you suspected. And you kept it to yourself. Isn't that wrong too?"

I glare, the pounding in my head almost unbearable. "Leave

off, Ben. She already feels like shit and you're making it worse."
Ashley squeezes my hand and takes the folder from me. "If
we're doing this, we need to go."

Ben sighs, defeated. "We'll take the RZR. It's the only way
we'll ever get there ahead of them."

chapter twenty-six

"I still don't know what the hell you think you're going to do when we find him," Ben yells over the roar of his shiny black four-by-four RZR. "*If* we find him. This might as well be like searching for a needle in a haystack."

"It doesn't matter," Ashley yells back. "We just have to find him."

I glance at Matt, sitting next to me in the backseat. He looks somewhere between sick and mind-blown, and I feel the exact same way. Except my painkillers are starting to wear off, so I have the added benefit of cringing in pain with every bump we hit. The RZR is built for speed, not comfort, and Ben is making use of it.

"You said it was a cave?" Ashley asks from the front seat, grabbing for a bar when the RZR dips down a hill.

"Not a cave, exactly, more like a sinkhole or depression. But it had a pool at the bottom," I answer, watching the ground below us like I'm on a roller coaster.

"Yeah, I've seen that place," Ben says. "We tracked an injured buck there about three or four years ago." He looks at me from the rearview mirror, and I ignore the stab of guilt. Ben was hiding even more than I was, and he had so many opportunities to tell me.

"Can you find it?" Ashley says impatiently as she is flung around on her seat.

"Probably. It's not close to any of the trails, so it'll be a hike if we can't get the RZR through."

Branches slap at the bars around us as we whip through the trees. I strain my eyes for any sign of human or Bigfoot, but the forest is too dense here. I've been gone from the hospital for four hours now. My parents will likely never let me see the light of day ever again. Ben left his phone at his house so we couldn't be tracked, but who knows if Sheriff Hanson has any kind of traceable GPS device on this thing. Knowing what I know now, there could very well be one inside my cast. I just don't understand how he could have kept all this from us.

The brush suddenly clears up as we pass through an open fence, signaling the beginning of the national forest land. Ben jerks the RZR to the left, leaving the trail and tearing across the woods. Ashley squeals as we go over a fallen tree, launching us airborne for a few moments. I can't stop the grunt of pain when we land. Matt glances over at me, his gaze bordering on frantic. "You should have stayed behind."

"Not an option."

"We may never find him."

"You don't know—"

I never get a chance to finish. The first rock slams into the hood of the RZR, bouncing up and cracking the plastic windshield. The second splits it apart.

Ben swerves and Ashley screams as chunks of Plexiglas fly

everywhere. Matt throws himself across me as much as he can with the harness across his chest. We narrowly avoid slamming into a pine, but Ben overcorrects, and the RZR flips onto its side and slams against another tree. The roll cage is the only thing that keeps us from being crushed.

Ben cuts the motor, and for a moment all is quiet. Then the silence is ripped apart by an unearthly roar from only yards away. My side of the RZR is on the ground, and with some effort and only one good hand, I manage to unbuckle the harness and slide out. I thrust my fractured arm out to break my fall, forgetting about it in the drop, and scream.

"Leah, don't you dare," Matt groans as he fumbles with his harness. His weight is pulling against the straps, making it hard for him to snap it loose.

I don't answer him. I crawl out through the roll cage to check on Ashley and Ben, using my good arm to lift myself up. All I can think is that I hope they aren't covered in blood. "Ashley? Ben? Are you okay?" I whisper.

No one answers me. At first I think they're knocked out, but their eyes are wide open and their attention is definitely not on me. They're looking straight ahead with identical expressions of surprise and terror. I turn, knowing what I'm going to see.

The male stands motionless as he watches us, all eight feet of him poised and ready.

"Leah, what do we do?" Ben asks, afraid for the first time in my memory.

"It's okay, just don't move." I get to my feet slowly, ignoring the pounding pain in my head from the rush.

jennifer park

Ashley reaches for my hand through the bars. "Don't. Don't go."

"He won't hurt me." If I say it, maybe I'll believe it too.

"Leah, *the rocks*."

"What?" I try to pull my hand away, distracted by the Sasquatch. He reaches down and grabs a chunk of wood, then swings the heavy stick against the trunk of the nearest pine. The crack echoes through the forest and Ashley jerks her hand away to cover her ears. Within seconds it's answered. I turn toward the east, where the sound originated from. "Reed." The Sasquatch turns and walks away, in the opposite direction from where the sound came. In another minute I can't see him at all.

I start walking, my only goal to reach the source of that answer. "Leah! Where are you going?" Matt yells, still struggling with the harness. "Leah, stop! Dammit, Ben, give me a knife."

I can hear them grappling with the straps and the *cling* of metal on metal. My feet are running before I realize it. Ashley screams for me to come back, but I can't, not when he's so close now. I run until I can't hear them anymore.

"Reed!" I scream, knowing he'll come if he can hear me. Saying his name out loud is shocking, and for a moment I wonder if I've lost my mind and we're all wrong. I mean, I'm calling out the name of a boy we buried ten years ago.

I pick up a stick and start slamming it against a tree until it snaps in half. My good arm burns with the effort, and I throw the rest to the ground and wait.

Unable to stand still any longer, I start to walk, only running when my body can endure it. If I pass out, I wonder if anyone will ever find me out here. I think of the wolf at the grotto and wonder if I would die from the elements or from predators first.

"Leah."

I gasp, all too aware of how my head and arm are beating painfully in time with my heart. Turning slowly, I find him two steps behind, as still as the forest around me. I open my mouth to speak, but the words won't come. And there are so many of them. So many things I want to say to him, things that I never imagined I'd get the chance to speak. Now that I have it, I don't know what to do.

He looks older; I can see it in his eyes, the way he watches me. It's as if he's more aware now.

The skin of an animal is draped over his shoulders and wrapped around his body, brownish gray and smooth. It's familiar, like it might have been on the wolf that tried to eat me recently.

I run my fingers down the fur, just along his shoulder. He tenses, watching my hand in frustration. "You shouldn't be here." He frowns, and something in my chest feels like it's slowly ripping apart. I step back, but he reaches for my hand, pulling me close. "No," he says harshly. "That's not . . ." His eyes narrow on my green cast, and then he reaches out to touch the edge of the bandage across my forehead. They had to shave part of my hair to stitch it, which means my trademark ponytail won't cut it anymore. "You're crazy, you know that? You should be resting."

jennifer park

"I'll go," I say, remembering why I'm here in the first place. "I just came to warn you. The sheriff knows about you and the Bigfoot. He's here now, hunting them."

"Sheriff?"

"You need to leave. Take them away, somewhere safe." A branch snaps in the distance, but the boy seems unfazed.

"This is our home."

"I know, but the sheriff will kill them or, worse, capture them and take them away."

He smiles, like I've said a joke. "They can't be caught."

"But they can be shot."

Something flickers in his eyes, and he shakes his head like something's bothering him. Does he remember something?

"Reed," I say softly, squeezing his hands. His eyes widen like they did when Ashley called his name. "Don't you remember? That's your name. Reed. Reed Hutton. Your sister is Ashley, and we used to live across the street. You were best friends with my brothers, Matt and Sam." He jerks at Sam's name, blinking fast. "You went camping with your dad and Sam. And then . . ." I can't say it. Truthfully, I still don't know what happened.

I pull the crumpled photo I took from the file out of my pocket, the one of them all smiling in the woods with the distant face of a Sasquatch in the background. "You don't remember this?"

With trembling hands he takes the picture, leaning over it with a blank stare. I start counting seconds, getting really antsy when I get to forty-five. "Reed?" He doesn't answer. "Do you—"

"I remember," he whispers hoarsely.

"What do you remember?"

He shakes his head. "I can't . . . Just pieces, flashes. My dad . . ." He shoves the picture back at me, eyes full of anguish. "It wasn't his fault."

"What do you mean? Your dad's?" Before he can answer, a deep howl echoes in the distance, sending chills down my arms.

Reed pulls me close and whirls around, standing in front of me as he faces the direction of the noise. "Don't move." His voice is so quiet I can barely hear him, but I do what he says, staring over his shoulder at whatever is coming.

When the baying of hounds echoes from the same direction, I realize who the danger is from. Not the Sasquatch but the sheriff. "Run," I say, pushing at him. "You have to protect them."

"I'm not leaving you."

"I'll find my way."

He spins around, his face inches from mine and full of disbelief. Something snaps in his eyes, and suddenly the words flow from his mouth, like they've been pushing against a dam for days, or years.

"Leah. I thought of you and my family until I forgot I was human. Until I forgot there was anything else but *them*. And then I *became* them, and I was okay with that. Until I saw you. Then what I was wasn't good enough anymore. You've brought me back. I'm not leaving you again."

Reed reaches up and runs his hands down my cheeks, then

back over my hair. All I can do is shiver when his lips find mine. He's gentle, hesitant, like it's taking every ounce of strength he has to make it so. I slide my trembling hand to his shoulder and his lips press harder.

He's touching me like I'm the last girl on the earth, like his every breath depends on mine. When he breaks away, I hold on to him, fairly certain I'll drop to the ground if I don't. He holds my face so carefully, runs a thumb across my bottom lip, eyes full of longing.

"Reed, I don't know if you want to come back, but if they catch you, you'll have to."

"I'd stay here for you."

"But what about them? What about Bee?"

He's silent for a moment, a muscle ticking in his jaw. "I have to make sure they're safe. They . . . they are my family."

"Where will you take them?"

"There is a place, far from here." The baying of the hounds is growing closer. If I listen hard enough, I can almost hear voices yelling behind them.

"I wish I could come." I hold up my cast, trying to smile past the burning in my throat. This could be the last time I see him. What if he decides he'd rather be with them? I'd never be able to find him again.

"I'll take you home first. We can outrun them."

My eyes are starting to burn. "I will slow you down." My voice cracks. "I can't run like you."

"No, but she can." Reed looks over my shoulder with a grin.

the shadows we know by heart

I whirl around to see Bee. I will never understand how either of them keeps managing to sneak up on me.

She towers over me, staring down with large doe eyes, and pulls her lips back into a toothy grin.

"Oh."

When Reed laughs, I'd swear she does too.

chapter twenty-seven

We stop at the grotto. Reed slides down the incline and skirts the edge of the pool. "She's not going to put me down, is she?" I call out to him, snug as a bug tucked up against Reed's adopted Bigfoot sister. He shakes his head as he reaches up to a crevice in the back of the shallow recess, tugging at something shoved in a narrow crack.

I blink when he pulls out a backpack.

"What is that?"

He shrugs as he slides his arms through. "Stuff. Matches, books, toothbrush, clothes."

"You have clothes?" I nearly shriek. Bee huffs loudly at my hair. "I mean," I say in a less hysterical tone, "why aren't you wearing them if you have them?"

"They itch," he says evenly.

We crawl out of the grotto, and when they run again, Reed has to take three strides to Bee's one. The crunch of pine straw is everywhere, beneath her feet and against her body when she runs through the young pines.

Without warning Reed comes to a dead halt, reaching out to grab Bee's arm. She freezes, becoming as still as a statue, hunching down over me as her eyes scan the forest and her nose tests the air. The familiar sound of an aging tractor cranks in the distance.

The quick, metallic staccato is all the warning we get as I feel something whip past me and lodge itself into Bee's neck. She grunts and starts to growl but doesn't drop me. "Reed!" He jerks the dart out and takes me from her arms.

"Nobody move!" I recognize Sheriff Hanson's voice immediately, but the trees are too thick for me to see him.

Bee lets out a deep, guttural growl, pawing at her neck. Before I can blink, two more darts fly out of the forest, finding her chest. Reed gasps as she drops to her knees, her fingers too sluggish to find the darts and pull them out. I flinch at his scream of rage as he removes them, and position myself to block her from any more darts. Reed pushes me back and wedges me between them, protecting both me and his sister.

"Leah, get out of the way!" I freeze, confused by this new voice. Why would my . . .

Suddenly they converge, coming out of the trees like wolves to a dying fawn. "Surreal" doesn't even begin to cover what I'm seeing. Twelve bodies appear from the trees, all dressed in some kind of camo tactical gear, looking like an overexaggerated Hollywood version of Special Forces. Everyone has black Flir goggles propped up on the top of heavy helmets and thick bulletproof vests over their chests. I see rifles, guns, and knives wrapped around hips, and a few even have grenades strapped to their belts.

They form a wide circle within seconds, every eye and scope trained on Bee. Her head is resting against my back, her breath hot on my skin. Every few seconds a faint growl emanates from her, but that's all she can manage. When her head starts to slip to the side, I reach back to steady her, twisting my fingers in her hair. Her hands rest around my ankles now, her grip getting looser.

"Leah. Move, now," Dad says, taking a step forward, marking him as twelve on the clock of people around us.

"What are you doing here?" Anger overrides the shock at seeing him. He'll have to tranq me, too, before I move an inch. "Why are you all dressed like the damn military?"

"Leah, you need to get away from it. It's dangerous," Dad says, quieter this time. His eyes flicker down to where she's touching me, worry fleeting across his face.

"*She* isn't dangerous. You're the ones with the guns."

"Leah, please." That voice again. I was right. It's my mom. She's next to Dad, in the one o' clock spot, almost unrecognizable in her gear except for the hint of a blond ponytail.

"Mom? What is going on?"

"We're trying to protect you and find your brother."

"Matt's with Ashley and Ben. He's fine." I don't mention the wrecked RZR or angry Bigfoot.

She hesitates, her voice trembling. "Your other brother."

My mind shuts down. "What?"

"Sam," Mom says, her voice dripping with hope.

"Sam's dead," I say automatically. Because to acknowledge that Reed is standing beside me is to accept that Sam must be dead if he's not with him. That is why I was so afraid to believe that the boy could be Reed. Because the miracle of one boy coming back from the dead would be overshadowed by the fact that my brother didn't, and that my family still won't be healed.

"We never found their bodies, Leah. We knew they weren't dead, but taken, and we've been trying to find them for a decade. This is the closest we've ever come." The look she gives Dad is one I haven't seen before. Her tearful smile is full of hope, joy, almost, and he returns it. I've never seen either of them look at each other like that. Not in years. And the fact that they're doing it now, when they could never do it in front of me and Matt, sends me over the edge.

Something in my body snaps, like a string pulled too tight. "Wait. You two don't even like each other." Their heads whip around, and I know my words are the last thing they expect to hear. I should be overjoyed that they believe my brother is alive, but all I can feel is irrational anger. "You stay drunk half the time and scream at Dad the other half." I ignore her gasp and raise my finger at Dad. "And you? You act like there's nothing else in the world but your precious church and doing whatever you can to keep me and Matt under your thumb."

"Sweetheart—" Mom interjects.

"No." I ignore her, feeling the last ten years of pent-up emotion coming out whether I want it or not. "No, you've got to be *kidding* me. Everything we've been through has been for what, a complete lie? Why would you do that? Instead of telling us the truth, you've *ruined us*." My parents gape at me in shock. Surely none of this comes as a surprise to them. But we're in *my* forest, *my* sanctuary, and here, I only speak the truth.

"You think . . . ?" Mom's mouth works soundlessly. "I don't . . ."

jennifer park

"I can't even breathe Sam's name in our house, and yet you two have been searching for him all this time? How could you be so selfish?"

"We don't have time for this, Michael." My head swivels to the left, hearing Coach Banks at my eight o' clock. Why is my teacher here?

Understanding trickles through me as I begin to study the faces around me. Sheriff Hanson; Charlie Brooks, the owner of the local grocery store; and Keith Willis, my seventh-grade math teacher. I can name and place every other person here as well, because they've all got one thing in common.

They're deacons at our church, close friends of my father's for decades, faces I've grown up with, trusted.

Steve Becker is behind me, the man supposedly hog hunting instead of having dinner with my parents. They likely were *all* hunting. More of the puzzle pieces fit into place, and it makes me nauseous. My father has used his place of power to do this, to accomplish this. The only reason they would all be here, dressed like this . . . *prepared*, is if they knew what they were going to find.

"You knew about them? All this time?" Fury unfurls deep within my stomach, churning with the hurt and betrayal already there.

"We knew the boys were taken and we knew what took them. We just didn't know where." Dad's voice is tired, lacking any of his usual preacher tone.

Reed shifts, shaking his head slightly. Bee's head pushes into my back, almost asleep. "Reed, she's falling," I mutter, feeling the rest of her weight follow her head.

the shadows we know by heart

He spins around to catch her, gently laying her down on the ground behind us. He crouches over her unconscious form.

"Leah, please. Move out of the way and let us handle this."

Dad's pleading voice has no effect on me. "You let us sit through their funerals and think they were dead? Why would you do that?"

"Look behind you, Leah," Sheriff Hanson says. "Who would believe us without a body? We found the tracks of the male that killed Mark, the boys' tracks that ran into the woods, and eventually all three met up and disappeared at the river. Any strings I tried to pull to get government help were cut. We're not the only ones that know about them, and the government wants no proof made public that they do."

The male that killed Mark. The rocks. The final pieces click into place. Reed and Ashley's dad was killed by a rock to the head . . .

"It wasn't his fault." Reed's voice cuts through the silence.

"Reed. Come with us, let us take you home," Sheriff Hanson says.

Reed shakes his head, his eyes blinking fast. His breathing has accelerated, and his knuckles are white where he's fisted them in Bee's fur. "Dad didn't know. He thought it was a bear."

"Reed, what are you talking about?" I say quietly, wanting to touch him but afraid to move.

"Something was moving around the camp. We saw glimpses of it. Dad thought it was a black bear." He runs his hands through his hair, eyes wide and glassy. "He took the shot. But it wasn't a bear." His voice cracks.

jennifer park

"Reed?" He stares blankly ahead, the events of that day passing like shadows across his eyes. No one moves.

"He was angry, throwing rocks at the truck. Dad ran to start it up, to get us out. It was just . . . He should have stayed with us, out of the way."

"Reed, son, what are you telling us?" Dad asks as Mom reaches out to grab his arm.

"It was just a baby, no bigger than us. Dad shot their baby. The rock was an accident. We ran away, and he found us, carrying the body of his child. It was dark, we were scared, and . . . and after that, we took its place."

chapter twenty-eight

When I can breathe again, I have to swallow several times to keep from throwing up. It's horrible. A terrible, horrifying tragedy. All because of a mistaken identity.

I almost feel guilty for asking, but it's the first thing I want to know. "Is my brother alive?"

Reed continues to stare into his memories, almost oblivious to the barely bridled chaos about to explode around him.

"Reed." I place my hand on his shoulder, willing him to come back from wherever he is. "Is there a chance my brother is—"

"Sam's dead," Reed says, cutting me off, his voice loud and detached. "He got sick. He fell asleep and never woke up. It was years ago."

His words pass through us like a shock wave. Feet shuffle, gasps and whispers drift through the circle, and silence follows, heavy and still.

My parents' faces pale, and I can see the denial in their eyes. Dad shakes his head, like Reed said something he can't understand. A moment that resembles eternity passes, and then the stunned silence is broken. A ragged sob escapes Mom, and Dad pulls her to him, wrapping his arms around her. Was this was it looked like when they first heard Sam was missing?

As my parents slip over the edge into heartbreak, some-thing shatters inside me. I realize why the funerals seemed so surreal to me, why I never felt closure. Some part of me knew, deep down, that they weren't dead, that sixth-sense kind of thing that siblings share. It's why we could never heal, because it wasn't really over yet. And now, hear-ing those words that fall into my heart like stones, I realize what just broke.

Hope.

The shards rip me apart as they go, and when the tears come, it's not the healing ones I've come to experience within the forest. These burn with regret and endless pain. We're here, once again, hearing my brother is dead. Will the last ten years of my life repeat now that we're back to square one? I don't think I can endure it.

"That's it, then," Sheriff Hanson says quietly. "We're done." He motions to the men on his left, and they move forward, one of them unwrapping cable cord from a tightly wound roll.

"What do you think you're doing?" I say as threateningly as I can.

"We're taking Reed home."

And with those words, all hell breaks loose.

A scream of rage erupts from the trees behind us, and a young ten-foot pine tree, roots still intact, comes sailing across the clearing, taking out half the circle around us, including my father. Mom yells at me to run, swinging around to fire shots into the trees. Reed jerks me down and throws himself over me and as much of Bee as he can. The other men scramble to take cover behind the trees when rocks come flying along with chunks of rotted tree trunk.

"Stop!" I scream. "Stop shooting!"

There is a pause in the fire. I can hear shell cartridges fall and magazines loaded. "Leah, get up," Dad yells. "Get out of here."

"No. He thinks you've hurt Bee. *You* need to leave!"

"Michael, we need to get it done," Coach Banks yells.

The sheriff and two others rush toward us, dodging the nonstop barrage of whatever the Sasquatch can throw at them.

The sheriff and Keith reach for Reed, pulling him off us and pinning his arms behind him. Dad is next, and the fact that he doesn't want to hurt my cast arm is the only thing that gives me leverage. I twist out of his grip and roll over Bee, putting her between us. "Leah, baby, please, you've got to come with me."

"Why? So you can kill her? I'm not letting you." I see the knife in Charlie's hand as he tries to dodge around me and a kicking Reed.

"We're not going to kill her."

"Then why do you have a knife?" I point at Charlie. Dad moves while I'm distracted, sweeping me up in his arms and running to where Mom is. Reed lands a kick to Sheriff Hanson's leg, sweeping it out from under him and taking them all to the ground. Reed moves like an animal, like something born of the forest. With two swift jabs, he's incapacitated both men, leaving them lying on the grass. He spins on Charlie, and the blade flies, landing somewhere out of sight. When I look back, Charlie's just as unconscious as the other two.

"Nora, now," Dad says, wrapping his arms around me.

jennifer park

I watch as Mom gets to her feet, reaching for a gun strapped to her back. She swings it over with practiced ease, takes aim, and fires.

The scream dies in my throat as a dart imbeds itself in Reed's chest. He jerks, looking down in surprise. "Reed!" I yell as he slumps to his knees. "Mom, what are you doing?"

"What needs to be done," she says, and starts walking toward the Sasquatch still screaming at us from the trees, unfazed by his relentless show of aggression.

"Don't miss," Dad whispers, watching her walk away.

Mom slings the dart gun over her shoulder and reaches for the Glock at her hip. "Dad, what is she doing?" Dad doesn't answer; he just buckles down and holds me tighter, like I can even try to run now. Mom ducks out of the way when a branch comes flying toward her, crashing into a tree and sending splinters raining down on us. I feel nothing but disbelief when she raises the gun and takes aim. "Mom?" I yell. "Mom, please!"

She hits her mark.

Blood flies from his shoulder, and his piercing scream reaches down into my soul. It's the kind of sound you know will find you in your dreams.

Mom hesitates before her second shot. She edges back as he utters a guttural howl, a mix of pain and helpless fury. I think I'm screaming, but I can't tell. All I can hear is this tremendous rumbling. She raises her arms again, aiming for him one more time. The Sasquatch stops, suddenly as motionless as the rest of us. There is something so human in his gaze—acceptance, regret—that it stills my breath. Can't she see it?

the shadows we know by heart

Something moves out of the corner of my eye and Mom flies off her feet, the bullet missing its mark, tackled by a blur with blond hair and a letterman jacket. Matt twists his body so he takes the brunt of the fall, crashing among the debris and sending the gun flying. Mom lunges away from him, her goal in clear view. My brother wraps her up in a bear hug and kicks the gun away from her desperate reach. "Matt, let me go! You have to let me do this."

"You've lost your damn mind! What are you doing?" he screams, and the shock of his outburst reverberates through my parents.

"He stole my baby. He stole Sam!" Her voice is raw, her hands digging into the dirt as she inches forward. "And now I'll never get him back."

"What?" Matt freezes. "Sam . . . Sam's not alive? But the folder, his picture . . ."

"Reed said he died." Mom's voice breaks. "We thought he was with them. We've been trying to find him."

Matt's bewildered gaze finds mine. Suddenly my brother looks like a little lost boy. It's more than I can stand.

Dad's arms loosen when he feels the first sob rack my body. "Dad, let me go," I whisper, and he slowly relents. I crawl toward Reed, slumped on the ground beside Bee, my cast arm tucked to my stomach.

"He took your brother away from us!" Mom screeches, still trying to get the gun. The Sasquatch has become a blur of brown among green as tears streak down my face.

Matt snaps out of his fog, desolation replaced by fury. "He

jennifer park

took a lot more than that, and you and Dad never bothered to fix it," Matt yells. "You've forgotten about *us*!" Mom and Dad stare at him like they've never seen him before.

"That's not true!" Mom cries, reaching one last time for the gun.

"It is, or you wouldn't be fighting me for a gun when your daughter and Reed are both lying on the ground needing your help!"

I halt in my slow trek across the ground. The selfish part of me wants to see her face, hoping that his words did something to her, but I'm not prepared for the guilt I feel when I meet her eyes. I watch as my mother falls apart in my brother's arms, but I don't move. Her tormented cries fill the woods around us, masking the sound of the wounded Sasquatch retreating through the trees.

Ashley stands over Reed, her body frozen in disbelief. Ben moves off to the side, trying to wake the men Reed left unconscious. The scuffed-up RZR stands a few yards away, windshield missing. Bee's open eyes watch me, then she reaches out to place a hand on Reed's chest where he lies beside her.

Ashley places her hands over her mouth as Bee pulls the dart from Reed's body. She drops it to the ground and strokes his hair, just like she did to me. "Ashley, it's okay." I can see her frantic nod, but she doesn't look at me. She walks around slowly, kneeling at her brother's head. She moves the hair out of his face and her hand brushes against another one, large and black. She stills, and with tears streaming down her face, she slides her hand next to the one that's not quite human.

the shadows we know by heart

"Why didn't you tell me?" I flinch at the hurt in her voice.

"I didn't want them to get hurt."

"Well, that really worked out well, didn't it? How could you not tell it was him, Leah? Look at him."

I am, and it's twisting something inside me until I can't breathe. I want to reach out, touch him, and remind myself that he was mine, if only for a little while, but even that's been suddenly taken away. He's no longer the wild boy from the forest. He's Reed Hutton, brother to Ashley, and no longer my secret.

I never thought I would regret that. I'm happy my best friend has her brother back from the dead, but it has come with such a cost. Looking around this circle of lies, I wonder how much more we'll have to pay before these sins have been atoned. I realize my secrets pale before those of my parents. They have played their parts so well I don't even know them anymore.

"Ashley." Sheriff Hanson hands her a black-cased cell phone. "Call your mother. Tell her to meet us at the hospital."

Ashley takes the phone obediently. "Where are you taking him?" I ask, circling a protective hand around Reed's wrist.

"To the hospital you should still be in," he says ruefully. "But thanks to you, we've accomplished more than we hoped." He smiles warmly at me and nudges Bee with the toe of his boot. She jerks away from his touch and fury rises like bitter bile in my throat. I squeeze Reed's arm, willing him to wake up and protect his adopted sister.

"You're going to let her go." The threat feels empty, and we both know it.

"Of course we are."

jennifer park

The sheriff plunges a wide needle into Bee's thick skin. I watch her eyes widen in fear and pain as a tiny silver transmitter slides into her body. He jerks the syringe out and passes it to Jim Stephens, the local veterinarian.

"What are you doing?"

"Just protecting our evidence. The government doesn't allow proof to come to light, but we've worked too hard to let them just disappear again. Now that we'll always know where she is, she's free to go."

"You can't do this to her. She's not an animal."

Any hope I had of him undoing this unspeakable act fades as he shakes his head with a smile. He can't see the truth, only a trophy lying on the ground. "Well, no sense in wasting a lucrative investment. This is better than winning the lottery." He chuckles to himself. "And like I said, Leah, we couldn't have done it without you."

chapter twenty-nine

Within an hour I'm back in the hospital. Apparently a missing person or two is enough to warrant a helicopter ride. This time there's no chance of escape. I can see the shadow of a guard standing outside my third-story room.

But at least they've left me here alone.

Not on purpose, but I screamed at my parents until the doctor forced them to leave. Now everyone's on the first floor, either in the waiting room or with Reed. Everyone except me. I might as well be in jail, because that's exactly how I feel. This is my fault, all of it.

An apple sits on my untouched supper tray, glaring at me. How could something so innocent have triggered such a catastrophic series of events? Yes, I'm glad we have Reed back, but I never knew leaving those apples on the stump years ago would lead to this disaster. I've betrayed something precious, something that should have been protected, and instead revealed it to the malice of civilization. I've destroyed their world and very likely their existence. For all I know, the male Sasquatch could be dying somewhere in the woods from that gunshot, Bee is now on the sheriff's radar, and we get to relive Sam's death all over again.

A soft knock pulls me from my thoughts, and Matt walks

into the room. His face is drawn, and dark shadows pool beneath his eyes. "Hey," he says quietly, taking a chair from the wall and bringing it close to my bed. His jacket is covered in mud stains and pieces of the forest.

"You look awful," I say.

He gives me a humorless smirk. "So do you."

We stare at each other, and I'm the first to cave. "So."

Matt shakes his head. "He won't talk."

"To anyone? Not even his mom or Ashley?"

"No."

I'm dying to ask questions but afraid of the answers. What if he's angry at me for everything, for finding him, for making this happen? What if he forgets all that he's been through and becomes this different person? That would be the worst, I think, if what happened in the cave and the way he kissed me today in the woods were all just a memory. That he might never look at me again like I'm the only person in his world. I was, for a little while. Now I never will be again.

What I wouldn't give to erase time. It's bitter, this truth of reality. I regret so much and there is nothing I can do but lie in this sterile bed and live each moment over and over, trying to find the path I should have taken, to decide which decision was the wrong one.

"It's not your fault."

I close my eyes, wishing so hard that was the truth. "But it is."

"No. I'm the one who got you out of here. Had we not done that, none of this would have happened."

"They'd still be hunting them."

"Yes, but maybe they wouldn't have found them."

"Because of me. He was taking me home because he couldn't leave me in the woods like I wanted. He should have gotten away."

"Reed could never leave you when we were little. You should've known he wouldn't start now."

"And look what happened because of it. Everything's so messed up now." I press my hands to my burning eyes. "I can't fix this. And it's not even over yet."

Matt looks out the window. His fingers tap silently on his thigh, keeping time to the muscle twitching in his jaw. "They're not going to let him go."

"What?"

"Reed. I heard the sheriff talking about setting up cameras around Ms. Hutton's house and posting a deputy there to watch Reed for a while."

"They're just going to lock him in the house? It will drive him crazy."

"Until they make him go to school."

"School?" My thoughts scramble. Reed, *my* Reed, go back to school? No way. In fact, I can't even begin to imagine it. He would have to wear actual *clothes*, for one thing, and cut his hair for another. I mean, he can't just waltz into precalc and honors English at Zavalla High School like every other senior, whether he's eighteen or not. He hasn't been in school since he was in the second grade.

I can almost see this dark future unfold as Reed becomes more human, as he molds himself into something civilized and

jennifer park

leaves the forest behind. He will find that there are other trea-sures in this world than what the forest has to offer, and he will leave me behind.

I try to picture him walking me to class, in place of where Ben was days ago. That will never happen. I don't want it to happen. This is not his world. "No," I whisper. "They can't do that."

"They've got a shrink here who says it will help him, even-tually, to socialize with his own peers."

"That's ridiculous."

"Why?"

"He doesn't need to be socialized like some animal. He's sur-vived out in the wild for ten years. What on earth is he going to have to talk about with people like Kelsey Wright? Reality TV, football, or prom? He can't relate to anyone, because no one understands what he's gone through. He's eighteen, for God's sake, and if he wants to walk back into the forest, no one can stop him."

"Why don't you tell me how you really feel?"

"You don't—"

"Kidding, kidding," Matt utters dryly, holding up his hands.

"Mom and Dad?"

"Sitting in the waiting room."

"Doing what?"

"Nothing. They're just sitting there looking guilty. Mom paces a lot, walks to the elevator, and then turns around. I think you got your point across to her earlier."

"Too little too late."

"They're going to come back up here eventually."

"Screw them."

Matt purses his lips and studies me. "Have you tried to look at this from their point of view?"

"What? Are you taking their side now?"

"No. I'm just as pissed as you are, but have you? Pretend you have a kid. Pretend he goes missing, and you know what took him. Wouldn't you do anything it took to get him back, no matter how long it took?"

"Yes, but I wouldn't have lied about it or done what they've done to us."

"I know, they've screwed up. But think about it Leah—all the not talking, the way Mom used to get mad for no reason and take it out on Dad—"

"The drinking," I interject.

"Actually, you got that one wrong."

"What? Then what the hell has she been drinking out of that silver flask?"

"She apparently has severe allergies to hay grass and pine trees and is on some pretty potent meds."

"That's so . . . somewhat believable, I guess."

"Yeah, she used to keep it in the plastic bottle from the pharmacy but said it kept breaking on their hunting expeditions. Said the flask was easier to use."

"Hunting expeditions?"

"We also have spent an alarming numbers of nights alone in our house while they go out searching and collecting data."

jennifer park

"Parents of the year." But it explains a lot. All the pieces have fallen into place. But the picture isn't what I expect.

"Seriously."

"Has anyone said how long I have to stay here this time?" I lift the lid to my dinner tray, making sure it's still the disgusting food I thought it was. I'm not disappointed.

"Mom's been lobbying with the doctor every time he walks by. I think he finally agreed you could leave in a couple of days."

"I figured she'd want me locked up in here for a week."

"She feels awful, Leah," Matt mutters.

"She should. She's a cold, heartless monster with a gun."

"She apologized."

"It doesn't matter. She shot him. He could already be dead." I wince when I knock my cast against the side bar of the bed.

"He took her child."

"Why are you taking her side?!"

"Because I'm trying to keep the shreds of this family together, and you are making it very difficult." Matt slumps back against the chair beside my bed and runs his hands through the mess of curls on his head. "You have the right to be angry, Leah. Just don't make it permanent."

I glare at him, knowing he makes sense and hating him for it. I'm not ready to forgive, and I will never forget.

chapter thirty

I'm changing into my going-home clothes when there is a
knock on the door.

"Just a minute," I call, jerking my sleeve over my cast. It definitely slows everything down when I have only one hand to use.

"Can I come in?" Ben stands at my door, hands in his pockets.

"Sure." I open it wider to let him in, cringing at what I
know is coming. I've been waiting for days for him to come to
my room, and he waits until now to do this.

"Don't look so excited to see me." He tries to smile but fails,
just as I do. "I guess we need to talk."

"Yep." I stare at him, seeing the many sides of Ben. The
beautiful boy always out of my reach, the sheriff's son who did
what his father told him, regardless of how it would affect me,
and then the way he looked at me on the bleachers, like there
was nothing else in the world but me.

"Look, Leah, I—"

"Wait." I stop him, needing to speak before I lose my nerve.
"I'm sorry for what happened, and I should have said something before things got as far as they did."

"It's a little late for that, don't you think?" His voice is cyni-
cal, and it strikes a chord of anger.

"You lied too, so don't pretend this is all on me."

"I'm not. I know what I did." He grimaces, then pulls the baseball cap from his head and twists it angrily. "But does it even matter now that I fell for you?"

"Ben . . ." I whisper, swallowing against the burn in my throat. "It wasn't real. Maybe it felt like it, but you know it wasn't. Neither of us was honest through all of this. We both had our secrets to protect, and we played the game."

"So you're saying you felt nothing? Did you ever care?"

"Of course I cared. You were the one thing I've wanted for years. And then suddenly you were there, wanting me back. Or at least acting like it."

"It wasn't all an act. I think you know me well enough by now to see that." He shoves the hat back on his head, eyes burning. "And you still choose him?"

I ignore the question. I'm not talking about Reed, not to Ben. "You weren't even in it for me at the beginning. Admit it, if your dad hadn't put you on the trail, you never would have pursued me."

He's turning it over in his mind, and it actually hurts, even though it's likely the truth. For a short time it did feel real, whether it was or I just wanted it to be, and that hurts worse than the lie. "You don't know that for sure," he says, but even he can't hide the doubt in his voice. "It could've worked out."

"For how long? Eventually something like this was going to happen. We were never meant for forever, Ben."

"It's funny that I had to pretend to like the old you, only to find that the real you is the kind of person I wanted to be with."

His words tug at my resistance, but I push the walls higher.

I can't break now, not when everything is falling apart around me. "Regardless, we both lied, and now it's done."

"So that's it?"

Be brave. "That's it, Ben. I'm sorry."

"So am I," he says, his sad smile chipping away at my heart. I'm drowning in guilt, and I want to let it swallow me and end this agony. He's just as much a liar as I am, but he's still Ben, one of my oldest friends.

Another knock sounds at the door, and I answer it, finding a woman standing in front of me and Mom and Dad across the hall behind her.

"Hello, Leah, I'm Doctor Clark. Can I speak with you for just a moment?" I glance down at the photo on her name tag. Same brown curly hair, same black-rimmed glasses, and "PhD" at the end of her name instead of the usual "MD."

I glance back, but Ben is already moving. "It's fine. I think we're done here." He brushes past me, shoulders hunched, leaving me sinking in emotions I wish I didn't have the ability to feel.

"Um, sure, come in," I say, and shut the door behind her without looking at my parents. I haven't decided when I'm going to speak to them, but I'm not in a hurry.

"How are you doing, Leah? With everything?"

"Everything?" I perch on the edge of my bed, and she takes the chair. I notice the clipboard she's carrying and the pencil stuck behind her ear. She looks sincere enough, but I feel like she might be referring to any number of things.

"Your ordeal of getting lost in the woods after your car accident."

jennifer park

"Oh. I'm fine. The doctor said I can go home today." I point to my bag, wanting her to understand that my staying here is not an option.

"That's wonderful. I know you must be ready to get out of here."

I sit silently, waiting for the punch line. She continues to smile at me, her eyes glancing over everything from the stitches on my forehead to my bare feet and chipped blue nail polish. "Leah, I have a favor to ask of you."

"Okay."

"The boy that was brought in yesterday, Reed Hutton?" Her smile fades a little, and my stomach clenches. "He's in a very . . . delicate place right now."

"What do you mean? Is he okay?" I hop off the bed, my eyes on the door.

"Yes, he's fine. As healthy as can be expected, actually."

I stare blankly at her. "Then what?"

"Physically, there is nothing wrong with Reed. Mentally, there's nothing really wrong either. But he's going to need time to adjust to his new life, and we feel that right now it would be best for Reed to have minimal contact with anyone but his immediate family."

"I'm sorry, 'we'?"

"Yes, I have advised Ms. Hutton and she agrees that it would be best, just for the ensuing days and weeks, that his contact with others be limited."

"Why are you telling me this?"

"Pardon?" She smiles, raising her eyebrows.

"You came up to my room, personally, to tell me this. My parents could have done that, so why are you here?"

Her smile remains in position, as if it's a permanent fixture on her face. "I was informed that you and Reed had a special connection. You might remind him of things that we are trying to help him through."

"This is about me, isn't it? All of this, about limited contact with others, that's all just to keep me away from Reed."

"Of course not, Leah. We are just trying to do what's best for him."

"Did the sheriff put you up to this?"

"Excuse me?"

"Sheriff Hanson. Is he the one who wants me to stay away? He has no right to tell me anything. He's the reason we're here to begin with."

"What are you talking about?" She leans forward, nudging her glasses higher up on her nose.

I hesitate. She wouldn't know any of that, not if Reed's not talking, because I know the sheriff and my parents won't say anything about what's really going on.

"Leah, if this is about—"

Another knock. It's the nurse, here to collect my discharge papers. Mom and Dad follow her in, keeping their distance as the shrink looks back at them. "If you feel the need to talk to someone, anyone, here's my card. You've been through a lot the past few days, and I know you'll have a lot to think about when you get home." She holds out a cream card on thick, textured paper. I make no move to accept it, so Mom hurries

jennifer park

forward with a "thank you," takes the card, and retreats back to the wall.

"Well, Leah, take care of yourself." Doctor Clark walks steadily out of my room, leaving it cracked enough that I can hear her talking to someone waiting outside. I walk quickly to the door, listening.

"Yes, I informed her," she says quietly. The other voice is muffled, too soft for me to recognize. When Doctor Clark leaves, passing the window between my room and the hallway, another person follows her. Through the partially closed blinds I see Ashley walking away, without even a glance toward the glass between us.

It wasn't Sheriff Hanson who wanted to keep me from Reed.

I don't see how I can feel more pain than I already do, but it comes anyway, like a knife in my heart. My best friend is the one who wants me to stay away.

After that I know I sat in a wheelchair to be taken to our car. I know I climbed the stairs to my room with Matt's arm around me. Then, nothing.

When I finally wake, it's dark through my bedroom window, and the bedside clock says three in the morning. Rain is falling outside, growing louder like the rush of waves with each gust of wind. The cold is pressing in, and it's likely all this water will freeze by morning.

I feel like the forest is screaming at me through the downpour. It's too easy to imagine I hear Bee calling through the wind for the brother I took away from her, mourning the father she could have already lost.

The morning comes swiftly, the sun catching on the frost and lighting up the world like a landscape of diamonds. It's the kind of beauty that should make my heart lighter, but it's never felt so dark. There is brightness all around me, but I am blind to it.

I could stay in bed all day. I've got the reasons, just not the temperament. Anxiety rolls through me, calling out for me to act, to do something. The drive is there, just not the way. There's a likely chance that anything I do right now will only make things worse, but the thought of doing nothing, of accepting this, is terrifying.

Whenever I change thoughts, Reed always sneaks in first before anything else. He's everywhere; standing at the foot of my bed, crouched outside my window, hiding in the magnolia tree, and running through the pasture from the woods.

I can't escape my thoughts. I can't pretend he should mean nothing now that I can't have him.

He's the one thing I can't lie about, even to myself.

The door opens quietly, and Mom pauses when our eyes lock. "I didn't know you were awake."

"Will you leave since I am?" She doesn't blink, but I know that hurt her. I'm just mad enough that I don't care.

She comes all the way in and pushes the door closed behind her. "I know you don't want to talk."

"You're right, I want to scream."

"But we can't keep doing this."

"You should have thought about that before you fired that gun."

"Can you even imagine what it feels like?"

"To be shot?" I hold up my arm. "I have a decent idea."

"No." Mom sits on the edge of my bed. "To lose a child."

I glare at her, unable to find a suitable retort that won't make me sound like a monster. We are talking about Sam, after all.

"I know you're angry, and you have every right to be angry. About *everything*." She places a hand on my cast. "But we did what we believed was best for you and Matt."

"How can lying to us be best?" I'm proud that I don't shriek like I want to.

"You had closure, Leah, however painful it might have been. I've never had that. All these years, the agony of not knowing has slowly eaten away at me, until I've become someone I don't even know anymore. There have been times . . . There have been times when I've wished he was dead, that we had found a body, and it all could have been over with."

My eyes widen at her confession. But I also *see* her, this open honesty, and I can't look away.

"It's torture, Leah, of the most awful kind. It has brought out the worst in your father and me. I know it has, because I see how you and Matt look at us, how you hide things from us, and I don't blame you. And now that Sam is really gone, it all seems for nothing. We've devoted our lives to finding him, sacrificed everything, even the both of you. I thought if we could just get him back, it would fix everything, and we could go back to being *us*." She runs her hands through her hair, eyes wild. "Now it's over. And what do we have to show for it? Nothing. Nothing but a family that is still broken after all these years."

"Was it worth the closure?"

Mom stares through me, a ghost of the person she was in the

woods. "I don't know. I can't undo any of it, so I don't know if it even matters. And we're done with Bigfoot. The hunts and the late nights, all of it. There have been so many times over the years when we've gotten close to them but they would disappear, and it was like losing Sam all over again. Those were the hardest times, when I would lash out at your father. It was never his fault, but I needed someone to blame."

"But he let Sam go with Reed and Mr. Hutton. You never blamed him for that?"

Mom smiles, her face full of bitter irony. "That's what's so terrible. Your father told him no."

"But Sam didn't sneak out. I stood in the yard with you and Matt and watched him go."

"No, he didn't sneak out."

I watch the agony pass over her face and realize the truth. Tears streak down her cheeks, and her hand starts to quiver on my cast. I can't help myself. I reach out with my good hand and take hers. Mom sobs, placing a hand over her mouth as the tears start in earnest.

"I let Sam go." Her body doubles over. "It is all my fault, Leah. He wanted to go so badly and I couldn't tell him no. I did it behind your father's back, and he never got to tell Sam good-bye."

"Mom, I'm . . ." I don't know what to say, because "sorry" doesn't even begin to cover it. As suddenly as her racking sobs began, they suddenly stop.

"I didn't shoot the Sasquatch because he's a monster, Leah." She grips my hand so hard it scares me. "I shot him because *I'm* the monster."

jennifer park

chapter thirty-one

When I finally find the nerve to drag myself downstairs, I'm surprised to find Matt, Mom, and Dad sitting around the kitchen table. I guess some habits are hard to break or maybe the only thing we have left.

A platter of bacon, eggs, and toast sits in the middle, looking very untouched. I slide into my chair, glancing at each of them in turn. Mom looks broken and hollow, her eyes as red as I've ever seen them.

Matt gives me a halfhearted smile, slowly dragging a piece of bacon across the table. He's already got enough to build a miniature log cabin on his plate, but he doesn't seem to be eating any of it.

Dad sits staring down at his cup of coffee, hair in disarray, T-shirt and shorts rumpled from sleep. I don't remember the last time I saw him in his pajamas. He never leaves his bedroom unless he's fully dressed. He even has his glasses on, the ones he uses only when his contacts are out. It must be Saturday for him to even consider looking like this.

"What day is it?" I'd like to know for sure that I've still got two more days before I have to show my face in school. I'm sure there's some story I've got to learn, to recite to whoever asks about Reed. But it's the questions about Sam

I'll hate the most, why one boy returned and not the other.

"Sunday," Matt answers. My wide eyes move from the clock on the wall that says nine thirty back to Dad, who hasn't even acknowledged that he heard Matt speak.

"But . . . Dad, why aren't you at church?"

Dad blinks and runs a hand through his disheveled hair. He sighs, peering down into his coffee cup again, like it might have the answers he's looking for. "What's the point?"

I know my jaw just dropped. "I'm . . . what?" I glance to Matt for an explanation, but he shrugs and goes back to building his bacon empire. Mom must have cooked everything we had left.

"What do you mean, 'what's the point'? Dad, you're the preacher. I don't think church is optional for you."

"I called Kevin."

I'm sure the associate pastor was thrilled to get that phone call, right after he picked himself up off the floor from shock.

"So, what, you're depressed? You and Mom didn't get to kill the monster so you're just going to live in your pj's?"

"It's not that," Dad whispers, his unblinking gaze zeroed in on that coffee cup.

"Then. What?" I say loudly, getting very close to completely losing it. And if Matt drags one more piece of bacon . . .

"How can I stand there and preach to a congregation about truths that I don't even know if I believe anymore?"

"So since you've lost your son for real this time, you've lost your faith as well? I think you're missing the point of all that, Dad."

jennifer park

"You don't understand," Dad says, like I'm missing a simple concept.

The resounding crunch when I slam my fist onto Matt's bacon tower is so satisfying I wish I could do it again. Dad's coffee sloshes over the side of his cup, breaking his concentrated gaze as the dark liquid runs for the edge of the table. Adrenaline courses through my body when I find I have everyone's undivided attention.

"What I understand is that you've spent the last ten years searching for the son you lost, instead of giving a damn about the two children you still had. You messed up, Dad. And maybe this is what you get, justice instead of mercy."

Dad blinks, looking up at me, like he's seeing me for the first time.

"Maybe if you'd started with the truth, you'd never have lost the rest." I should feel guilty, but all I feel is unholy anger that will not be silenced until this is done. We're already broken; the worse thing now is that we will just splinter.

I stare at Mom and Dad, wishing I could stop myself, wishing their tears made me feel remorse. "You've done this, both of you. You have destroyed us." I head for the door, not caring where I go, just as long as I get out of this house.

"It's not their fault."

Matt's voice stops me cold. I let my hand drop from the doorknob. "What?"

Matt is silent.

"What are you talking about, Matt?"

"It's my fault."

the shadows we know by heart   281

"Matt?" Mom says in a small voice.

"Sam knew you wouldn't let him go camping, Dad, because he'd miss church on Sunday. He was the one who told Reed no when he asked us. But . . . but I knew why he really said no." Matt crosses his arms, looking like he'd rather be facing the Sasquatch than sitting at this table. "He was afraid. He told me he was scared of going camping, that he saw something big in the woods that day at Aldridge. A monster covered in fur."

Matt pulls his knees up and puts his elbows on them, his hands locked tightly in his hair, the shadows of demons in his eyes.

"Son?" Dad leans toward him, but Matt flinches away.

"I called him a sissy, or something like that. I . . ." He squeezes his eyes shut. "I dared him to go alone. I told him he would never be brave unless he went camping with Reed without me."

Matt's words are met with shocked silence. Even I didn't see this coming.

"He begged me to come. He was crying when I helped him pack his clothes. I laughed at him, told him the monsters in the woods were going to get him if he didn't stop crying, that he would never be my brother again if he didn't do it."

I watch in detached horror as the perfect facade that is Matthew Roberts crumbles like a riverbank in a flash flood.

Matt's voice breaks, his eyes full of tears. "I'm his twin, for God's sake. I should have been there with him!" The last grip Matt has on his control slips away, and he curls in on himself, anguished sobs racking his body. "Sam is dead, again, because of me, and all I can think about every day is how I'm living the life that he deserved, and I don't."

jennifer park

It's like Mom and Dad suddenly wake up, after ten years, instincts finally kicking in as they wrap themselves around the broken remnants of a golden boy.

I thought I knew the truth of Matt, but I knew nothing.

My anger seeps away, leaving me deflated. It feels like someone else who walks to the table, someone else who kneels beside Matt and gets pulled into the circle of tears.

Dad gets to his knees in front of Matt, prying his arms down from his face. "Son, listen to me. Matt." He waits until Matt lifts his eyes. "You didn't do this, you hear me? None of this—me, your mother, even Samuel—is your fault. We all made our choices. It . . ." Dad's voice shakes. "It was an accident. I know it now, and you can't hold on to this guilt anymore, son. It will consume you, just as it has consumed us." He holds on to Matt's face, waiting until Matt finally shakes his head.

Dad reaches for Mom's hand. "The time has come for us to let this go, to start over and try to fix this family."

Next he reaches for me. "And we can't do any of this without you. I know how I've been with you. I know you've grown up in a cage without bars, and I thought that if I could keep you safe, keep you this image of the little girl I have in my mind, it would be enough to fill the hole that Sam left. But nothing we do, any of us, will ever replace him. The hole is always going to be there, but accepting that has been my greatest fear, next to losing either of you.

"Leah, I'm so sorry. Your mother and I, we still live in that day, still try to undo what was done. You two were so young then, but you've managed to live your lives and move on." He takes both my hands. "You're angry. I see it in you, because I see it in myself. But you've done the one thing we haven't been able to. You've brought us closure. If Sam is at peace, then maybe we can find our way back to one another."

"You can't just snap your fingers and fix this."

"I know that. And I know there's a lot that we may never be able to fix, but isn't it at least worth trying?"

I haven't seen my father cry since that day long ago. And seeing it now, it's a reminder that he's human, broken and lost like the rest of us. "No more lies."

"No more lies," Mom whispers, holding my gaze. Dad nods in agreement, pulling Matt to his chest.

"Okay." Somewhere inside, a dam breaks, and it's like I'm a child again, and the only thing in the world that can make the pain go away is my parents' arms. The wounds are long from healed, but as I sit there, wrapped in love, hope seeps in, and for the first time a light waits at the end of this dark tunnel.

The phone rings for a while before I pull away to answer it, hoping whoever is on the other line doesn't hear the crying in the kitchen behind me.

"Hello?"

Silence.

"Hello?"

"Leah?" The voice is gruff, but I know it's Ashley.

"Ashley . . . Hi." I wonder if she expects me to be excited to hear from her or if she suspects I know the truth.

"Leah, I'm sorry."

jennifer park

"For what?" I ask, but I probably can guess.

"I shouldn't have done it. I shouldn't have kept you away from him, and now it's too late."

"Ashley, what are you talking about?" It's an effort not to scream at her to explain.

"He's gone. He left last night and no one saw him. The sheriff had two deputies around the house and he got by them."

I can't help the hint of a smile. Of course he got by them. He's the wild boy from the woods.

"What time did he leave?"

"We don't know, sometime after midnight."

"What do you want me to do?"

"I don't know. Just stay there? I think if he goes anywhere, it will be to you." She pauses. "Leah, I'm so sorry. I was angry."

"I know, Ash. It's okay."

"No, it's not, but we can do this later. We have to find him."

"Okay."

"Thank you. Sheriff Hanson's here now to pick us up, so I'll be there soon."

She hangs up with a click. I slowly put the phone back on the receiver. Mom and Dad are talking quietly to Matt, who has yet to lift his head. I head upstairs without a word.

My mind is already ten steps ahead of me when I open the door, trying to decide how long it's going to take me to get dressed with a cast and wondering if my jacket will fit over it.

I almost walk right by him, my T-shirt already pulled halfway up my stomach.

I've really got to get curtains.

He's crouched on the roof, as casual as if he's done it a hundred times. I slide my shirt down, feeling my face flame as his lips quirk into a knowing smile. My eyes drop from his in embarrassment, only to become even wider when I see what he's wearing. I know he's shirtless, but my eyes can't get that far because they're stuck on the waistband of jeans that fit him perfectly.

He's grinning and it takes all my effort to look anywhere but at him. I lift the window, catching my breath as a burst of frigid air makes its way into the room. "Ashley called and said you left. What are you doing here?"

He looks up through his lashes. "Where else would I be?"

I have no answer for that because my heart just dropped into my stomach.

"It's cold outside." Such a lame thing to say when he just said the most perfect thing I've ever heard. "That's all you have on?" I nod to the jeans.

"Yes."

His smile is melting my caution and reason. As I begin to calculate the odds of one or all of my family members walking in that door, I suddenly realize I don't care. What I want more than anything has suddenly appeared before me, and I might not get another chance like this again.

I step to the side. "Then I guess you should come in."

jennifer park

Reed vaults into the room, landing softly on the bare pads of his feet. For some reason I notice the fact that he's half-clothed now more than I did when he was mostly naked. Maybe it's because he's sparkling clean. His hair is still long, but it's been washed thoroughly, and the thought that some nurse in scrubs likely had her hands in his hair makes me beyond jealous.

"No shoes, either?"

"Nope."

"Well, then." I catch myself before my eyes drift down again. "You shouldn't be here."

"I know. The sheriff said it wasn't a good idea for me to be around other people, including you."

"And what do you think?"

He takes a step forward, putting him well within my circle of personal space he's ignored from the first moment we met. "I think I'm right where I want to be." He runs a finger down my cheek, his eyes sparkling.

"What about your mom?" I'm scrambling for straws, anything to keep my thoughts from scattering at his touch.

His finger pauses. "It's hard. I remember her in bits and pieces. She's barely left me for more than a moment."

"But she's your mother."

"I know. But this is a lot. I miss . . ." He glances out the window toward the forest. "I miss it. I can barely breathe in that house. It's like a cage. My room is the same as when I left, which is . . . strange." His hand drifts down to my loose hair. "I feel like they're just waiting for me to do something, like I'm a wild animal."

"Well, you did run away," I say, watching as his lips curl into a mischievous smile. Now both hands trail through my hair, sending a never-ending river of chills down my spine. I sway, and he uses it to pull me closer.

"I might go back."

"You mean you might not?" I start in surprise.

His vivid green eyes are growing darker by the second. Even the flecks of gold have turned to burnished brown. His lashes drop as his fingers tangle in my hair and tighten against my scalp. A tiny gasp escapes my lips and his eyes flicker downward. I can feel him holding off, hesitant to go beyond this moment. He presses his forehead to mine, uttering my name in the softest whisper. I feel his longing as if it were my own, and then I feel something else, something he's trying to hide.

"Oh my God, you *are* leaving. Reed, you can't—"

And then his mouth is on mine, pressing my lips into silence. For a moment I want to fight, to make him explain, but my control slips and then none of it matters, because I want to remember this without anger, fear, or heartbreak.

They will come soon enough.

Time slips into a fog, and my mind along with it. Every touch of his hand feels like the last, like he's trying to memorize my face for the moments when I'm no longer in front of him. Air leaves my lungs and enters his, until I'm aware of nothing but the smell of skin, the sound of breath, and the taste of lips. He is a drug of the most exquisite kind, something I would sell my soul for again and again.

"I'll stay if you ask me to," Reed says against my lips, tightening his grip around me.

"Your family is here." *I'm here.*

"Not all of them."

Understanding dawns.

"My father is shot. My sister is scared and alone. My mother is helpless and hungry. I can't stay here when they need my help. I can't just change lives. I know everyone wants me to, but it's not that easy," Reed says bitterly. "I've got to find him. He needs help."

"He probably needs a doctor."

"They're strong. Much stronger than us."

"Withstand-a-bullet-wound strong?"

"Maybe. I won't know until I find him." I don't know if the door even made a sound when it opened or if we were too wrapped up to notice, but someone clears a throat.

Matt is standing there with red-rimmed eyes, looking like a shadow of himself. "The sheriff is coming. He just called, said he thought you might be here, and I thought he might be right."

"Where're Mom and Dad?"

"Waiting."

"For what?"

"Whatever you decide to do." He glances back and forth between me and Reed. "Here." He presses a white box with a red cross on the top into Reed's hands. "It's a first aid kit. I don't know if it will help him, but take it."

Reed stares down at the box. "Thank you, Matt."

From the open window the sound of sirens comes drifting out of the silence. Reed stares at me, chest heaving. He pulls me close, wraps his arms around me and presses his lips to my forehead. "If I don't go now, I may not have the chance again," he mumbles against my skin.

"I know," I whisper, pressing my face into his neck. "When will you come back?"

"I don't know. I don't know how hard he'll be to find. Will you do something for me?"

I wait, wanting him to ask me to come, knowing I can't say yes. I'm not foolish enough to think I can.

"Can you take care of Bee?"

"What?" That's not what I was expecting. "You want me to take care of her? How?"

"Just check on her."

"Me? Check on your six-foot, three-hundred-fifty-pound sister? Why can't she go with you?"

"They'll track her. It's too risky." Reed squeezes my hands and attempts a smile. "You can do this. It's easy; she goes where the food is. And she likes chicken."

He sobers when the sirens grow closer. "I've got to go."

I don't think I could have let him go if I didn't see how bad he wants to stay. He starts to speak but changes his mind and turns for the open window. "Wait." He halts at my words. I don't even think he's breathing. For a moment I wonder at the power I have. If I told him to stay, I believe he would. But then I would be the monster. "Come downstairs. We'll go together."

Reed nods without hesitation, reaching through the window for his old pack he pulled from the grotto and the wolf pelt.

"You don't want more clothes than that?" Matt asks, eyeing his jeans, pelt, and bare feet.

Reed smiles. "They itch."

"You were always a little off." Matt grins and walks through the door, acting like it was yesterday, and not ten years ago, when they last talked like this.

Reed takes my hand and we follow Matt down the stairs. Mom and Dad rush to their feet when we enter the kitchen, tears in their eyes. "Reed, I'm so sorry. Please, please forgive me." Mom wrings her hands, her fragileness at complete odds with the woman I saw in the woods. Reed takes the hands she offers, and to her complete surprise, he hugs her.

The sirens grow louder until suddenly they stop. A few moments later several car doors slam.

"Go. Hurry, Reed." Dad moves out of the path to the back door, and we rush by.

Reed swings the door open and Ashley is standing there.

"I knew you were here."

"Ashley, it's not what you think."

"Really? Because it looks like you're going back to the woods."

"Ashley," Reed says. "I'm not running away."

"Then what are you doing? Why did you leave us?" Her voice breaks.

"I'm going to find my father."

She couldn't look more shocked than if he'd slapped her. "Our father is dead."

Reed glances away, toward the forest. "I have to find him."

"So this is it, then? I get you back only to lose you again? How is this fair?"

"One of my sisters has already lost her father. I'm trying to keep the other one from losing hers."

Ashley hugs herself, nodding slowly, and then moves out of the way. Matt puts his arm around her. "Go. Dad just opened the front door."

Reed and I run for the fence, and he vaults over while I climb through. "This was easier when I couldn't remember anything."

"I'm sorry, it's my fault that—"

"No." Reed stops in front of me. "This is not your fault. From the moment I saw you that morning with the apples, this was inevitable." He presses his hands to my cheeks and kisses me, pouring every word he doesn't have time to say into that action, until I've memorized every one by heart, and it shatters all over again. "And it was my choice."

We run, and I'm breathless by the time we sprint across the pasture. Someone, probably the sheriff, calls Reed's name, followed by the clacking of boots climbing the distant fence. We stop inside the protection of the forest, sunlight painting

jennifer park

a circle of light around us, the place where it all began only weeks ago. Now, instead of feeling torn in half, as I should be in the midst of all this pain, knowing what's to come, I feel like the two halves of myself have finally found each other. It's heartbreaking, that this is what it took to break my walls.

Nothing I say will make this easier, so I speak the only words I can. "Be careful."

"I will, promise."

"Don't make me have to come looking for you." My attempt at humor falls terribly short, but he smiles anyway.

"You found me once." His eyes soften as he pulls me close. "I know where home is now. I won't get lost again."

My fingers curl against his chest as I breathe him in one last time. "Just come back to me."

"Always." His fingers wrap tightly in my hair. It feels like he'll never let go, and then suddenly he does, leaving me in cold silence.

I fall to my knees, the torture of watching him walk away already overwhelming. The shouts are growing closer, and I wish he would just run, no matter that his every step pulls my heart farther from my body. As the tears fall, the forest wraps itself around me, easing the pain as it always has, reminding me that, for the first time, there is hope ahead instead of darkness, that this is no longer the only place I can find myself. I have nothing left to hide now. The boy from the woods has given me that.

Wherever I go in this world, whatever path I choose to take, I know he will find me, whether it's here in the forest or on the other side of the earth. The ties of grief and guilt that have bound me to this place have fallen, leaving me free to find my place in a world that now goes beyond the limits of the forest and this town.

His future is mine now, no matter what lies ahead.

Ten feet away, Reed stops. I think his hands are shaking. Or maybe it's just me. "It's always been you, Leah." His warm voice drifts back on the wind. "Even when I forgot your name and lost your face, your memory stayed with me, tucked away in the places that don't ever forget."

Once again he walks away, his steps silent on the dark ground. His head turns until I can just see his distant smile, but he doesn't stop, and he doesn't look back.

By the time his words register, imprinted on every cell in my body, he's gone, lost in the forest of shadows as if he were never there at all.

jennifer park

acknowledgments

I have so many people to thank for getting me to a place I never thought I would be. Five years ago, the idea of writing a book was the equivalent of climbing a mountain, something I would never consider and impossible anyway. My mom likes to remind me that I only chose college applications based on how short the required essay had to be. If it was over a page, it was a no, because I didn't have the words. Now, somehow, I've found the words, and most of the time I'm still not sure what to do with them. Luckily, I've had the privilege of meeting countless individuals who do.

To my agent, Mandy Hubbard, I'm certain a more perfect offer letter has never been written. It's framed right next to pictures of my kids. Thank you for your unshakable faith in this book and for loving it so fiercely. It wouldn't have had a future without you.

Special thanks goes to my editor, Jennifer Ung. I'm eternally grateful you took this book on and turned it into something more beautiful than I could have ever accomplished on my own. Your undying enthusiasm kept me going when I thought I wasn't enough, and you likely saved my computer from a fiery death more than a few times. I can never thank you—and the entire team at Simon Pulse—enough for your support.

Unending gratitude to Russell Gordon and Neil Swaab for a luminous, haunting cover that never ceases to amaze me. And to Sara Sargent, thank you for saying yes.

To my critique partners and beta readers, who read all or part of those frightening early drafts, helped with queries, loglines, and the dreaded synopsis, you shaped this book into what it is. So endless thanks to Julie Artz (for feeding your kids cereal!), Jessica Bloczynski, Gabrielle Byrne, Laurel Decher, Halli Gomez, Sussu Leclerc, Michelle Leonard, Richelle Morgan, Elizabeth Staple, Heather Truett (for the kindest words), Jessica Vitalis, and Kate Watson. And thanks to Shane Stover, my favorite brother-in-law, for reading and being impressed.

To the amazing members of The Clubhouse, it will always be a privilege to be among you. To The Winged Pen, I am so lucky to be a part of such a spectacular group of writers. And to my first writing group—Elizabeth Staple, Lora Palmer, Kate Watson, and Rebecca Santelli—look how far we have come on this roller coaster ride!

Thanks to Naomi Hughes for a spectacular query that finally nailed it. I am forever grateful for your help. To Jenn Davis for brainstorming titles on short notice and for The Train Ride We Will Never Forget. You are an amazing friend. And to Dawn Ius for listening. I wish we lived closer so the beer doesn't always have to be virtual.

To Sybilla Irwin—and the members of the Texas BFRO— thank you for welcoming me with open arms and sharing your stories. If only the world could see what you have experienced. Until that day . . .

acknowledgments

Thank you to my family, though those words will never be enough for everything you've done. To Dad, for your never-ending supply of ideas, and Mom, for being the world's best cheerleader; I'm glad you finally convinced me a Bigfoot love story could be a good thing. Your endless patience, support, love, and encouragement for me to follow my dreams has gotten me here.

To the Davis clan, who introduced me to the world of YA during a hurricane evacuation with a little book called *Twilight*; to Aunt Jan, for the never-ending supply of romance books; and to June Wood, grandmother extraordinaire.

To my naughty minions, Sarah and Chloe, Mommy loves you more than anything, especially when I'm hiding from you so I can write.

To Adam, your understanding and support has meant everything. I couldn't write fairy-tale princes without having met one first.

Father God, your blessings and mercies are infinite. You see my heart, and you love me anyway.